FRIENDSHIP
AND CONFLICT IN
VAN DIEMEN'S LAND

Umarrah & George

ANGELA
BAKER

ISBNs
Paperback 978-1-7635965-1-1
eBook 978-0-6455675-5-7

Publisher:
Forty South Publishing Pty Ltd, Hobart, Tasmania
www.fortysouth.com.au

Printer: IngramSpark

Front cover
Steve Roden, Settler's Cottage, Coal River Valley, Tasmania
steveroden.net

Rear cover
Robert Dowling, Group of natives of Tasmania, 1860
Wikimedia Commons

Table of Contents

List of Characters from the Historical Record in Order of Appearance

Umarrah Also known as Kanneherlargenna and Moulteherlargenna; warrior of the Leterremairrener clan in the north of Trouwerner

George Collins Son of convicts, born on Norfolk Island

Elizabeth Hayward George's mother; former convict

Elizabeth (Eliza) Nicholls George's eldest half-sister

Joseph Lowe George's stepfather; former convict

Kennedy Murray Friend of George

Margaret (Meg) Nicholls George's older half-sister

Norfolk Piper Eliza's child, born on Norfolk Island

Planobeena Also known as Plorenernoopperner, Umarrah's younger sister

Parwareter Clansman of Umarrah

Trepanner Clansman of Umarrah

David Gibson Scottish-born convict, early settler in Van Diemen's Land

Lachlan Macquarie Governor of New South Wales, with authority over Van Diemen's Land

Mary Ann Sydes Daughter of convicts, born on Norfolk Island
Anthony Cottrell Settler, living south of Launceston

John Batman Settler, living south of Launceston, pursuing bushrangers and Aborigines

Laoninneloonner Woman from a northern clan, Umarrah's first wife

Lacklay Also known as Probelatter and Jimmy, of the Punnilerpanner clan from the Port Sorell area; an ally of Umarrah

Kickerterpoller Leading Poredareme warrior from the Oyster Bay nation of the east coast, raised by whites, and who worked on Robinson's 'conciliation missions'

Gilbert Robertson Chief Constable of the Richmond area near Hobart Town

George Arthur Lieutenant Governor of Van Diemen's Land between 1824 and 1836

Thomas Hayes Young settler in Bagdad, southern Van Diemen's
Land

John Hayes Thomas' brother and neighbour; married to Louisa

George Augustus Robinson Government employee, engaged to
'conciliate' the Aborigines

Captain Donaldson Officer of the 40th Regiment

Kubmanner Clanswoman of Umarrah

Mannalargenna Chief of the Trawlwoolway/Pairrebeenne clan from
the Cape Portland area; an enemy of Umarrah

Woolaytopinneyer Larmairremener woman from the central
plateau

Truganini Nuenonne woman from Bruny Island, who accompanied
Robinson on many 'conciliation' journeys; partner of Woorrady

Tanleboneyer Wife of Mannalargenna

Pevay Also known as Peevay and Tunnerminnerwait, a man from
the Parperloihener clan of the Robbins Island area

Beth Hayes George's niece

Montpelliater Chief of the Larmairremener or Big River people of the
central plateau

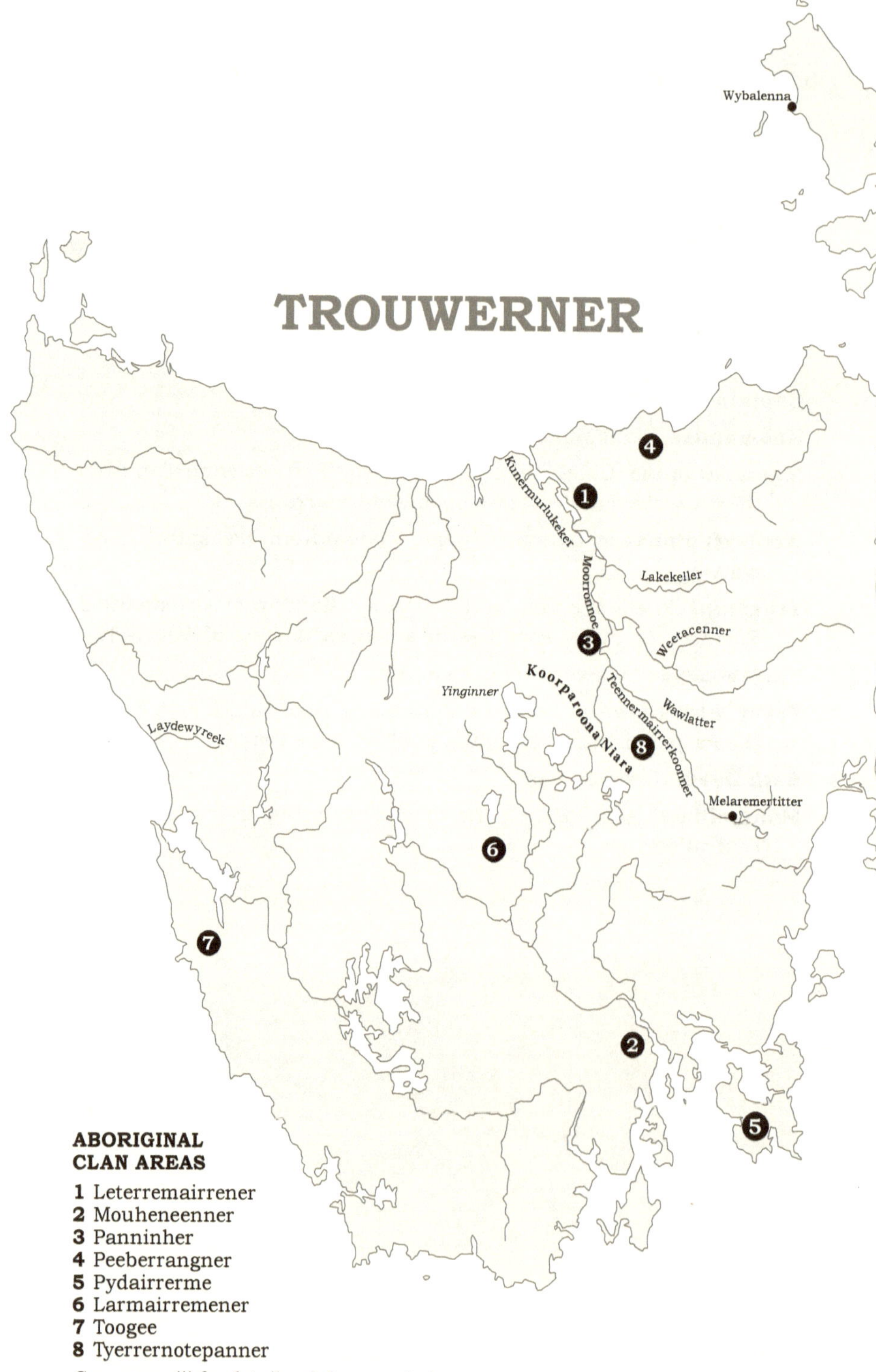

ABORIGINAL CLAN AREAS

1 Leterremairrener
2 Mouheneenner
3 Panninher
4 Peeberrangner
5 Pydairrerme
6 Larmairremener
7 Toogee
8 Tyerrernotepanner

See page viii for details of clans and place names

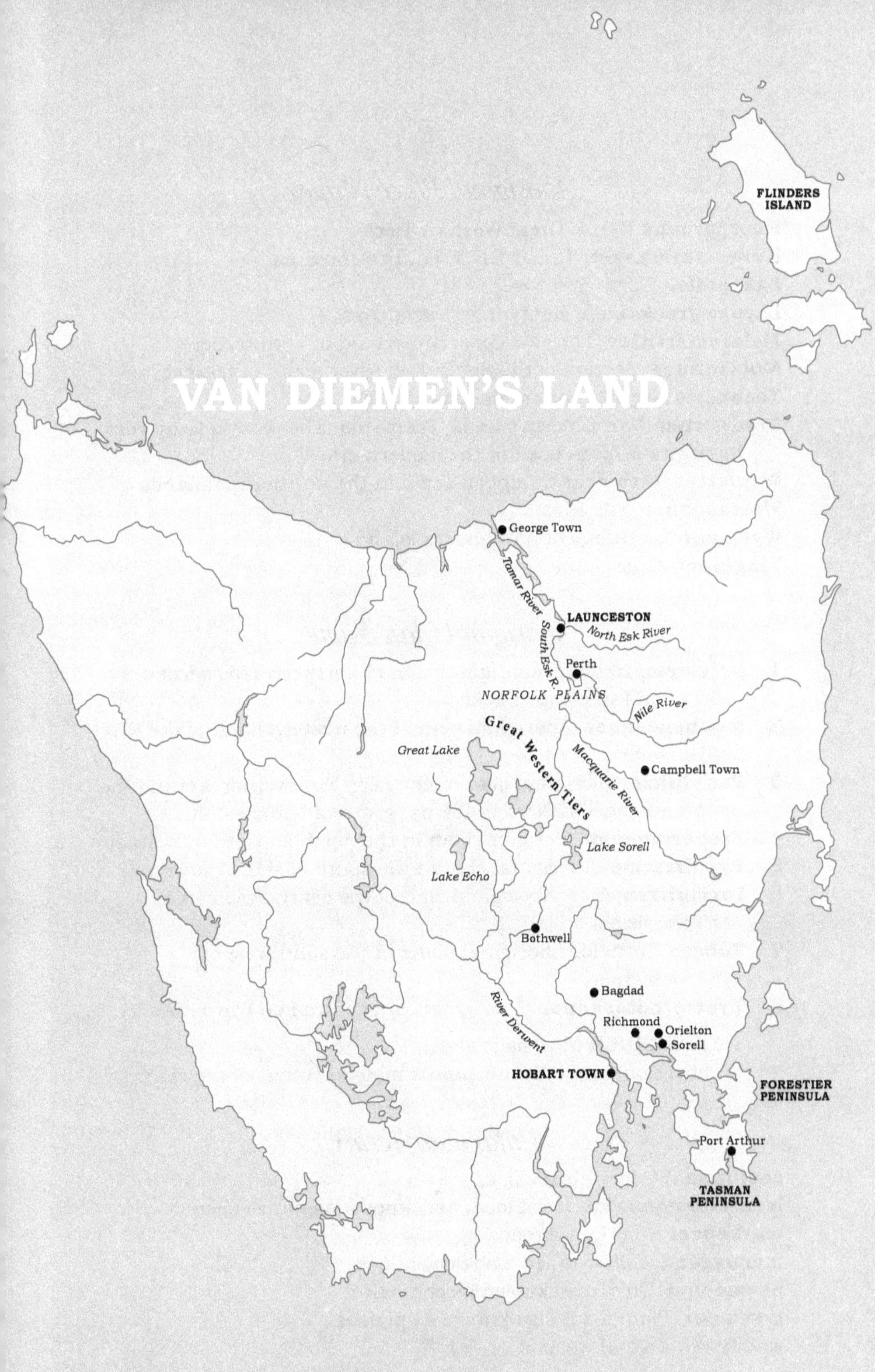

VAN DIEMEN'S LAND
FLINDERS ISLAND
George Town
Tamar River
LAUNCESTON
North Esk River
South Esk R.
Perth
NORFOLK PLAINS
Nile River
Great Lake
Great Western Tiers
Macquarie River
Campbell Town
Lake Sorell
Lake Echo
Bothwell
Bagdad
River Derwent
Richmond
Orielton
Sorell
HOBART TOWN
FORESTIER PENINSULA
Port Arthur
TASMAN PENINSULA

Aboriginal Place Names

Koorparoona Niara Great Western Tiers
Kunermurlukeker Tamar River, Launceston area
Lakekeller North Esk River
Laydewyreek Little Henty River, west coast
Melaremertitter The east coast hinterland of Trouwerner
Moorronnoe Section of the South Esk River south of Launceston
Teennermairrerkoonner Macquarie River
Trouwerner Van Diemen's Land/Tasmania. The palawa kani word
  lutruwita is often used in the modern era
Wawlatter Area near Campbell Town in the northern midlands
Weetacenner Nile River
Wybalenna Settlement on Flinders Island
Yinginner Great Lake

Aboriginal Clan Names

1 **Leterremairrener** Aboriginal clan of northern Trouwerner,
centred on Kunermurlukeker
2 **Mouheneenner** Aboriginal clan of the western bank of the River
  Derwent
3 **Panninher** Aboriginal clan of northern Trouwerner, around the
  area known as Norfolk Plains, south of Launceston
4 **Peeberrangner** Aboriginal clan in the north east of Trouwerner
5 **Pydairrerme** Aboriginal clan in the south east of Trouwerner
6 **Larmairremener** Aboriginal clan of the central plateau of
  Trouwerner
7 **Toogee** Term for Aboriginal clans in the southwest of
  Trouwerner
8 **Tyerrernotepanner** Aboriginal clan centred on Wawlatter

  TROUWERNER MAP page vi:
  Numbers on map indicate approximate locations of the clans.

Unfamiliar Terms

cockinna Wedge-tailed eagle
leenterloommerler Plant food, also known as native cherry
markenner Aboriginal roads
menuggana Yellow-tailed black cockatoos
neemooner Tree, also known as she-oak
trynueler Plant food, also known as pigface
waddy Aboriginal weapon

Umarrah & George

CHAPTER ONE

February 1807 – Yinginner

Despite his best attempts at denial, the sun dropped to the western horizon earlier each day. The cobalt blue sky would sprinkle with faint stars, brightening infuriatingly while he was still having fun. Then the call would come and he would have to wave goodbye and trudge back to the campfire. Mother and Father gave him plenty of warning, his friends pleaded with their parents, and one or two of them won a couple more days of summer. Umarrah was not one of them.

So he strung out his goodbyes, disappearing with friends for a few more hours on the last day until the wrath of his aunties, and his mother's exhausted eyes, fell upon him. The next morning he got up and grasped the extra water carriers without complaint. As he fell in line behind his mother, his guilt grew. Luwanna had been getting bigger by the day and the growing baby would make travel more difficult. The way was steep – east to the head of the pass, down the Koorparoona Niara mountains and back through the plains of Wawlatter. His mother wanted to get home before the baby came. He'd tried so hard to delay them.

Umarrah turned back and scanned the plateau's flatness one last time. It was his ninth summer here at Yinginner, full of games, feasting and adventures. Long, warm days, short starry nights and the jaw-dropping spectacle of so many people, travelling from distant parts of Trouwerner to meet every year on the high plateau at the island's heart.

His mother's growing belly was not the only thing that was different this year. Sometimes raised voices had woken him, debating late into the night.

Always about the strangers.

They'd arrived two summers ago, disgorged onto the riverbank of Kunermurlukeker from enormous, tall-winged canoes.

They were not the first strangers here, but alarmingly, unlike their predecessors, had not gone away again. Now the white-skinned people clung to the coast in two places on the island.

Last night, around the fire, the voices from his clan were particularly angry. But he couldn't remember who had said what.

"Umarrah, don't forget the water before we leave Yinginner."

He turned and glanced up at his father's frowning face, spears standing tall beside him.

"I won't," he replied. Beyond Largenna's massive bulk he could see the others were well ahead. His father nodded, turned and strode on while Umarrah hurried beside him. They caught up but soon after, the group's pace slowed. Luwanna's lithe, brown limbs were tiring in the summer's heat. Eventually they reached Yinginner's southern shore, with miles of sky-reflected blue glistening to the north. The aunties helped ease Luwanna beneath some wind-blasted shrubs while Umarrah delivered a water basket. She put her lips to the smooth interwoven kelp, drank eagerly and rewarded him with a tired smile. He looked at her dark brown closely cropped curls soaked with sweat and ran back to the lake shore for more. His return delivery was met with closed eyes and heavy breathing. They walked no more that day.

The next day hot winds from the north sapped everyone's energy. There was relief all round when they staggered to the start of the pass at dusk. No one bothered to build a fire. Leftovers were shared and then it was time to settle in for the night. Umarrah heard his mother gently snoring before his own fatigue overcame him.

A deep rumbling woke him in the darkness. He navigated his way through the trees until he reached a vantage point from where he could watch the light show displayed in a tempestuous night sky.

"It's beautiful, isn't it?" came a voice, and a kiss on his head.

"I didn't think the thunder would wake you. You were so tired, you didn't even say goodnight!" Umarrah replied.

"Well, when you have a baby inside, you have to pee a lot. Even at night. That's what woke me, not the thunder."

A large, jagged fork crackled to the earth. Their wait for the subsequent boom was only brief. "It's not far away, is it?" he asked as the rumbling rolled away.

"Not a long way away, but not too close," she replied. He wriggled over as she eased herself next to him on the rock. They watched the storm together for a little while, heading back to shelter as a scattering of large raindrops began to fall.

The next morning they could smell smoke. The passing storm had brought little rain to quench the summer dryness. Largenna went out scouting to assess the situation. There was a fire to the north of their route, he reported on his return. Lightning strikes probably. Not too close and not a problem as long as the winds didn't strengthen. Umarrah saw his father's forehead crease. "We need to get going," he urged, looking at Luwanna warily.

She smiled. "It's a cooler day. I'll be fine."

Their descent began but was soon hazardous. The track was very dry and Luwanna was not the only one who slid on loose stones. His father walked ahead of her, with one of the aunties behind. She concentrated hard on where each foot went, arms grasping tangled eucalypts as the sky above narrowed.

The steep incline started to level out. Frustrated by the slow pace, Umarrah accelerated downhill ahead of the adults. He hadn't gone far when his father's voice stopped him in his tracks. He trudged back, head down. "Don't go too far ahead," came the parental caution.

Framed by a full head of reddish-brown ringlets, Largenna's molten eyes twinkled at his son. Umarrah nodded.

"Umarrah?" called Luwanna. He turned to his mother. "Come back and tell me how far we are from the stream," she asked wearily. "And take the water basket."

"I will," he replied, grabbed it and was off.

The path meandered, in a few places becoming almost flat. He ran then, heedless of his father's words. Occasionally dappled sun pierced through the tree cover and shone down on his strong limbs, as he joyfully revelled in his own freedom.

After some minutes he slowed down, straining his ears for the first burbles of the stream.

Faintly at first, but then louder, came different sounds. Voices, with heaving breaths and incomprehensible words. He shrank back from the path till the bush hid him, his heart pounding. Then came splashing and laughter. After a few minutes of strained listening, curiosity overrode fear, and he inched his way downward. Finding a shady spot overlooking the stream, one eye and then the other peered slowly at the figures below.

A single glimpse was enough. He shot back behind the tree. White men! Five of them. Blocking their way.

Retracing his steps, he crept upwards through the trees, then emerging on the track some yards later, sprinted back to the others.

"Slow down, what is it?" his father cried as he barrelled into him.

"Down there," Umarrah pointed. "Five white men. At the stream."

One of the aunties laughed. "You are telling stories again, Umarrah," she said.

Largenna's eyes narrowed. "No. He's seen something," he argued, exchanging glances with Luwanna.

She spoke softly. "It can't be whitefellas. They've never been this far inland from Kunermurlukeker."

"I'll go and see," Largenna replied, grabbing a waddy in his left hand and a spear in his right. Four pairs of eyes followed him down the track until he disappeared.

Another auntie nudged Umarrah with the water carrier and he gulped greedily before handing it to his mother. He waited for her to wipe her lips then raised his head and sniffed the smoke. "What about the bushfire?" he asked.

Luwanna saw her son's wide eyes staring at her. "I'm sure it's no closer," she reassured him.

Suddenly his father was running towards them. Luwanna, leaning against a rock, saw him and pushed herself upright but overbalanced. Umarrah grabbed her arms, then heard the clatter of spears falling to the ground as his father's arms replaced his. "Hide!" he hissed. Umarrah threw himself into the bush and crouched low. Largenna wheeled Luwanna around and pushed her towards the arms of her sisters, who had already leapt off the track. As they pulled her in, he grabbed his spears and leapt behind a large boulder, his face tense.

The waiting silence was filled with anxious breathing. He saw his father turn to check on their positions and frown at where Umarrah crouched. I'm too close to the path, he realised. His father shook his head – there was no time now to move. The strange voices became louder and one by one were made flesh. The whitefellas climbed the track towards them in single file, panting and wiping their crimson faces. Closer, and then almost touchable. Umarrah looked back at his mother and aunties, invisible to all but the keenest eyes.

A large group of menuggana meandered overhead. The whitefellas, panting, paused their uphill climb to watch the yellow-tailed cockatoos screeching their laconic cry. Umarrah peered at the bulky coverings over their skin. No wonder they are panting, he thought. The last man retrieved from his coverings a round shiny object. He lay it on his palm, stretched out his arm, moved it around in several directions before inspecting it carefully. Umarrah watched it glisten in the filtered sunlight. The man said something to the others, they each replied, then the shiny object disappeared back into his coverings. They resumed their trudge upward. Umarrah's nostrils flared at the dank smell of sweat trailing in their wake.

No one moved for several minutes after the footsteps faded. Finally his father emerged, followed by his mother with the help of her sisters. Umarrah stopped in front of his father's worried face. "We cannot know if more whitefellas may come," Largenna noted, his voice grim. "I will go ahead and keep watch." He looked at Umarrah. "Can you watch our back?" Umarrah nodded. Largenna turned to Luwanna. "Can you walk faster?" His mother slid her hand under her swollen belly, bit her lip, then nodded.

Largenna led them down the pass, spears in hand. The group moved in complete silence and with barely restrained haste. Umarrah anxiously watched his mother's every step, her face a picture of concentration. He had so many questions about the whitefellas, but knew that now was not the time to ask.

The track followed the stream down the pass; the refreshing waters supported their progress, but by late afternoon Luwanna needed more and longer breaks. They paused at a lookout where the grassy plains of Wawlatter fanned out before them. Umarrah walked ahead with his father to scan the view. They turned to each other and smiled. The rest of the way looked safe. Relieved, he turned to tell his mother the good news just as she cried out, grabbing her belly with one arm and a tree branch with the other. Water splashed to the ground between her legs. Her sisters rushed to her aid and guided her to sit down. Umarrah wheeled round and saw the smile fade from his father's face.

CHAPTER TWO

January 1813 – Norfolk Island

George sat and watched his last sunset. Tomorrow they would be leaving, sailing away from the only home he had ever known. To another island, a much bigger one, they said. And they would never return.

He'd listened to the adults complaining about the Norfolk Island settlement closing down. He knew this was not their choice. People also had different reasons why they didn't want to go to Van Diemen's Land. His mother and Joseph said they were too old to become farmers. It would be too cold there. But there was no going back. They all knew it – even those who'd resisted, and dug in their heels for as long as possible. But who said convicts ever achieved anything from digging in their heels, George remembered his mother saying. She'd laughed when she said it, but she wasn't smiling.

Sometimes he felt like no-one was excited but him. After eleven years, there was no part of Norfolk Island that he didn't know. The prospect of a larger island for a new playground, with everyone he knew joining him, was the perfect adventure, and it started tomorrow morning.

The sunset faded to a dull pink. With a warm breeze at his back, George trotted home, anticipating the day to come. Suddenly, he ground to a halt, his ears pricking. He heard voices, raised, angry, jarring with his excitement.

"I just don't understand why they won't let you come with us, Eliza."

His heart sank as he listened outside the door to his mother's familiar argument.

"Mother, I told you, they won't change the passenger lists. Please can we not go over this again?"

"We should be together as a family! A few weeks on the open seas ..." her voice trailed off.

There was a strained silence, broken eventually by his sister's voice. "We're all heading to the same place. That's what matters."

"We are being transported again, you mean. And what awaits us there? Have they told us the truth?"

"Well, I think saying you are being transported again is going a bit far. You're not a convict anymore."

"But after twenty-three years here, I am being sent, against my will, to an unknown destination. Sounds familiar enough to me."

His sister sighed.

"I'll only be a few weeks behind you, Mother. And the weather looks fair for sea travel, so that's something."

There was no answer. He peeked into the doorway and saw his mother frowning.

"A smooth and safe journey is the most I can hope for," she said. "Go home and put Norfolk to bed, Eliza. My complaints will achieve nothing. Perhaps some of George's enthusiasm, and your determination, will rub off on me."

George saw his sister's eyes blaze. "As long as I get what I've been promised, I'll have no complaints, and no regrets," she replied.

Elizabeth squeezed her daughter's hand. "I do understand, you know I do. You're young, the only woman with stock on this island, and have a son who bears the governor's name. With two grants of land coming your way, Van Diemen's Land is a real opportunity."

Judging it a good time, George stepped inside.

"Finally back then, little brother?" Eliza scolded, turning around. "Make sure you help Mother with any last chores. It's a big day for you all tomorrow." She gave her mother a kiss, ruffled George's wavy hair, and walked out the door.

George looked warily at his mother. She tried to smile. He smiled cautiously back at her.

The moment of quiet was interrupted by Joseph's return.

"Well, everything seems ready," he announced, shutting the door and taking off his shoes.

"That's good," Elizabeth replied vaguely. "Eliza's just gone home so Margaret should be back soon."

Joseph shrugged. "I'm off to bed. Early start tomorrow."

"I'm going for a final walk," Elizabeth declared. "George, you can come if you like. We'll leave your father to his rest." George scowled, then smiled, pleased to be going out again. Elizabeth turned to Joseph. "Can you let Margaret know where we've gone when she gets back?" He nodded, George opened the door and they headed out into the warm night, following the path one more time down to the beach.

"Do you think people will ever come back here?" he asked.

"Possibly," she replied cautiously, "who knows what the people in charge will decide, George. They thought this would be a good place to settle, with timber and flax for the ships, but clearly, they were wrong."

"But a bigger place will be good for us, won't it?"

Elizabeth's mouth hardened into a thin line. "We'll do our best to make it work, especially for your sake. I'm sure the other parents feel the same. We made our mistakes and were punished for them alright, but if closing this island down and packing us all off to Van Diemen's Land brings you children opportunities, then it might just be worth it."

As they neared the beach, they spotted torches bobbing along its length. "Look," Elizabeth pointed. "We're not the only ones saying goodbye to the island." George glanced at the scene, committing it to memory.

The day of departure dawned bright and clear. Joseph was out early with the rest of the boat crew, loading final cargo onto the *Lady Nelson*. The sturdy little ship was moored in the bay, its sails billowing in the warm breeze. The gleaming turquoise of the island's shores turned a deeper hue as the Pacific Ocean's vastness stretched out to the horizon. George and his friend Kennedy sat on the hillside and watched the spectacle.

"When we're all on board, she won't sink will she?" asked Kennedy nervously.

"No. Joseph says she's a great little ship. He says it will be an adventure," George declared.

"I hope so," replied his friend, biting his lip.

George remembered their recent conversations.

"I thought you were happy to go, Kennedy!"

"Neither of us have ever been on a ship, George. We've only been on boats, and never that far out. Won't you be nervous out on that huge ocean?"

"I hadn't thought about it," George conceded. "The ship looks big enough to me – and we can swim."

"Mmmm ..." replied Kennedy, unconvinced. "But I'm not as good a swimmer as you, and I wouldn't want to have to."

George was trying to think of a response when he heard Margaret calling him. He jumped up. "Gotta go," he said then started to race down the hill. "It'll be okay!" he shouted behind him.

Two hours later, they were lined up with everyone else in an orderly beachside queue. George glanced at Mary Ann Sydes, who stood patiently with her parents. "Why do they get to go on board before us?" he grumbled. "They're in first class," replied Margaret.

"What does that mean?" he persisted.

"George, it doesn't matter!" snapped his mother. "The ship won't be leaving without us." Margaret frowned at her little brother and shook her head slightly. He followed her gaze beyond the queue to see Eliza and little Norfolk walking towards them.

"Time for that big adventure, George!" said Eliza, smiling and giving his arm a squeeze. She and Margaret exchanged knowing glances. Margaret grabbed Norfolk's hand and Eliza threaded her arm through her mother's. "How are you, Mother? Did you get some sleep?" she asked gently.

Elizabeth swallowed. "A bit, here and there. But I couldn't bring myself to eat anything this morning. You were right about the weather though – it looks good."

Eliza and Norfolk walked alongside them as the queue inched forward. After what seemed an eternity, it was finally their turn to be ferried over to the *Lady Nelson*. Before they stepped into the rowboat, Margaret bent down and picked up her nephew. "Oh, I shouldn't do that" she groaned. "You're far too big a boy, and you'll be bigger still when I see you next," she added, giving him a kiss. He giggled and entwined his fingers in her long, wavy hair.

Elizabeth hugged her eldest daughter tightly, unable to speak. "We'll see you soon," whispered Eliza. She gently pulled away from her mother and turned to grasp her brother's shoulders. "Look after Mother, George."

"I will," he answered seriously. In the dread of separation, no one spoke further. Then it was time. Margaret put Norfolk down, kissed her sister, lifted her skirts and climbed into the rowboat. Elizabeth took George's hand and they followed.

As they were rowed over to the ship, George looked at the people still waiting – some looking back at their island home one last time, others gazing fixedly ahead into an unknown future. His mother was very quiet. George slipped his hand in hers and squeezed it gently. "It's just another adventure," he whispered.

She looked down at the freckles scattered across his pale face. "My boy," she said quietly, her eyes glistening with tears. The rowboat met the ship's side, she let go of his hand, and grasped the ladder.

Thirty-nine mornings later, George was up on deck early. Today they might have the first glimpse of their final destination. He squinted at the crewman aloft in the *Lady Nelson*'s crow's nest, watching him scan the horizon. No cry of recognition. Frustrated, George plonked himself down on the main deck and tried to ignore his growling stomach. There would be no breakfast for a while.

He cast his mind back to Sydney, their last port of call. Nearly everyone on board – adult or child – was glued to the ship's rails as they passed between the jaw-dropping Heads and entered the huge harbour. After docking beside the town, they were told that they had to stay on board, but luckily there was much to observe around them, and the time passed quickly. Once the ship navigated back through the Heads and turned south, life on board returned to predictable routines, and for George, boredom. His mother had said that their new home would be nothing like Norfolk Island. He wondered what she meant. One of the crew told him there would be beaches rolling away to left and right, cliffs jutting out to sea, towering mountains in the distance and rivers full of fish. Sometimes he wondered if they were making fun of his enthusiasm.

One still, becalmed day, his mother talked to him about the *Sirius*. He'd asked her before about it. You could see the shipwreck from the beach in Kingston. She'd always brushed him off before so he was surprised when she started talking about it. "I nearly drowned in those awful waves," she said, her face haunted as the memories resurfaced.

"How old were you?" he asked.

"Sixteen," she replied. "But I was only thirteen when we left London."

"Thirteen!" he exclaimed.

"I was the youngest female on that first fleet of ships," she replied. "Wrenched from everything I'd known and sent half way around the world."

Now he understood why she didn't want another sea journey. He pondered this as he waited for breakfast, then decided to go below decks and see who else was awake. As he creaked his way down the wooden stairs, he heard a sudden shout.

"Land ho!"

George swivelled around at speed and raced up to the deck.

"What can you see?" he shouted.

"Van Diemen's Land!" called the crewman. "Young George, you can tell Cap'n Johns I see the coast. We are to the east of the river mouth."

George ran towards the captain's cabin, nearly knocking over a member of the crew who was about to knock on the door. He breathlessly passed on the news before heading back to the deck. The crewman above shouted reassurance. They wouldn't see anything from the deck just yet. But it would not be long.

The news quickly spread and competition amongst the older children for first sight of land became fierce. Hungry eyes, bored after weeks of unremitting ocean, constantly scanned the southern horizon. Margaret cuffed George's ear when he tried to stop some younger children squeezing their way among the bodies lining the deck side. "Margaret!" he complained.

"George," she reprimanded, "you're not the only one who wants to see Van Diemen's Land."

Less than an hour later, the northern coastline appeared, illuminated by the sun breaking through the morning's clouds. Cheers erupted on deck. "It's nearly over," sighed Elizabeth, standing beside Margaret. "If I never have to do this again in my life, I will be well pleased."

Margaret put her arm around her mother's shoulder.

The coastline drew nearer. Two narrow promontories extended towards them and drew the little ship into a river mouth between. The murmurs of the passengers were replaced by loud commentary back and forth amongst the crew about the incoming tide. George could feel the river sucking them in. He swung around to see the wide ocean reduced to a rapidly receding patch of blue.

Joseph brought water over and they drank absentmindedly as the *Lady Nelson* headed inland, passing a small scattering of buildings on the eastern bank. "George Town," announced Joseph. Not much there, thought George. Margaret gave the settlement a cursory glance then mopped her reddening face with her handkerchief and rolled up the sleeves of her dress. A short while later, heads swivelled from left to right as the river channel narrowed and sandy shores or rocky outcrops approached, alarmingly close. "I'm glad we're not doing this in a gale," said Elizabeth.

"No, that'd be tricky" agreed Joseph. "I think it could take a long time moving down this river if wind and tide were against us."

The afternoon wore on. Soon they appeared to be in the middle of a large lake with the river extending out in three directions. The wind dropped and the ship appeared undecided as to which way to head. Some passengers moved below out of the sun. "Which way now?" asked George.

Margaret shrugged and waved her hankie in front of her face. "I think I'll go below too," she said to their mother. Elizabeth and Joseph nodded and moved away from the deck.

"Are you hungry, George?" asked his mother. There was no answer.

"He must be riveted," chuckled Margaret. George scanned each arm of the river, including downstream. But the ocean had long gone. Then he slowly turned in a circle and gazed in awe at the most land he had ever seen. The world he had known had inverted – land surrounded by water now replaced by water surrounded by land. Hills in the distance were not the green he knew but were tinged with a bluey grey. And the land went on as far as he could see.

"Don't you want it?" asked Kennedy, nodding at the bread topped with beef in his outstretched hand.

"Thanks," mumbled George, grabbing it hungrily. They stood there chewing in silence. Kennedy trotted off and came back with water. He handed a cup to George just as a crack rang out. The ship's sails filled with wind and she lurched to port, spilling water down George's front. They laughed and grabbed the rails. George looked up at the sails and saw cloud banking up to the north as they headed towards the eastern arm of the river.

The gathering wind sped their journey. The river widened and narrowed, meandered east and west but headed inexorably southward towards the small town of Launceston. The sun dropped towards rising hills to the west. Gradually, more buildings dotted the riverbank and then a small but sturdy wharf appeared on its eastern side. By this time everyone was back on deck, nostrils wincing as they filled with the smell of mud, eyes witnessing the slowing approach to their final destination.

The little ship creaked and groaned as she was tied to the wharf and her anchor dropped. Suddenly there was a flurry of activity. Everyone seemed desperate to disembark.

George remembered how much they had to pack and groaned inwardly. "I bet I know what you're thinking," teased Margaret. "Don't worry, we've brought almost everything up. There's just a handful of things that you need to get. Off you go." His eyes brightened and he headed below.

Joseph assisted the ship's crew then double checked their family's belongings when he returned. "The sum total of what we own," he sighed. "Well, we've made it. Here's goes nothing."

Elizabeth's smile widened with the headiness of relief. "I'm going to look at it as a new adventure," she declared.

"I'm wondering what my first bout of sea legs is going to feel like," Margaret laughed.

"Me too," exclaimed George.

"You won't be the only ones," Joseph replied.

Once disembarked, in the gathering dark, they had to move swiftly. Everyone pitched in to erect tents not far from the wharf. As the final streaks of orange dimmed in the evening sky, George's gaze took in small points of light dotted atop the distant hills. "What are they?" he asked a passing crew member. "Native campfires," came the reply. George watched the lights brighten against the dark before he ducked his head inside the tent.

The next morning, after a swaying sleep-interrupted night, arrangements were still to be made for the land journey ahead. They took the opportunity to walk off their sea legs and wandered around the settlement. Launceston clung to not one but three rivers, the Tamar River formed by the merging of two others, the North Esk and South Esk. It was also a town clinging to importance, they heard. Governor Macquarie in Sydney had imposed his authority, said the locals, and was insisting that the principal northern settlement should be George Town, the even smaller cluster of buildings they had passed near the mouth of the river. They noted much disgruntlement at this decision.

A few days later, the trek to their land grant on the South Esk River began. Norfolk Plains was to be the name of the new settlement, in honour of their former home. The tents were packed up and loaded with their belongings onto carts attached to oxen, who stood stoically in readiness.

As they headed out of town, George raced ahead to see the view, then bolted back to his mother.

"I can't see much," he said. "How far do we have to go?" he asked her.

"They told us yesterday, George," she answered. "Nine miles."

"We'll get there tonight, won't we?" he pestered.

"Yes, yes, I'm sure we will," she replied dismissively. "You can keep walking with the other boys. Just don't go too far." He raced off with a fleeting glance at Joseph, who was walking up to Elizabeth.

"His enthusiasm is wearying sometimes," she sighed. They watched as George ran towards Kennedy.

"There'll be precious little time for idleness and play from now on," Joseph warned. "I know he thinks it's a big adventure, but the fun is over. Your son is going to discover what hard work is." Elizabeth's face paled as he continued. "We all are."

CHAPTER THREE

April 1814 – Panninher country

He slowed to a stop, and grimacing, tried to shift the wallaby's dead weight to ease his aching shoulders. Largenna turned around and Umarrah saw the knowing smile flit across his father's face. "I'm alright," he protested. His father nodded and resumed his purposeful stride. Umarrah forced himself to keep pace and focus on the success of the morning's efforts – a good-sized wallaby brought down by *his* spear. He remembered his father's pride at his efforts, and it sharpened his appetite for the meal to come.

A shout jolted him. "Umarrah!" cried Planobeena, racing up to him. She stopped, panting and looked at the wallaby. "You catch it?" she asked.

"Yes," he confirmed. "Good, I'm hungry," she said and turning back, ran ahead to the campfire.

"You've done well, Umarrah," smiled his mother. He slung the carcass gratefully from his shoulder and it thudded heavily on the ground. He squatted by the fire and his father joined him.

As he stretched his tired muscles, Planobeena sidled up to him. "Rub my back, will you?" he groaned. She pressed her small fingers into his skin and moved them around haphazardly. After a few minutes the rubbing was replaced by slaps. "Ouch!" he shouted. She giggled, and continued. "Stop," he growled, and stood up.

"You can't catch me," she laughed, and raced off. He launched after her, his long legs eating up the space between them, till she squealed as he cuffed the top of her head and kept going. Then it came – the inevitable howls of protest. He looked back to see her rooted to the spot, wailing, her dry eyes watching for his return.

"Stop it!" he thundered. "You're just angry that I'm faster." He marched back and grabbed her hand. "If you want me to let go, be quiet, and we might go to Teennermairrerkoonner for a quick paddle."

He knew that the promise of a walk to the river would work. She pretended to rub her eyes and looked up at him. "Carry me!" she ordered.

"Only if you don't pull my hair."

"I promise," came the reply.

She turned and stood in front with her back to him. He knelt down and lifted her up over his head. She landed with legs in practised perfection onto each shoulder. He could feel her enmeshing her fingers through his ringlets.

"No pulling!" he reiterated. "I'll drop you!"

She disentangled her fingers immediately and wrapped her hands around his neck.

"And no choking either," he added.

They set off through the wide sweep of grassland towards the river. He glanced back towards the camp, conscious of his parents' warnings. A large group of whitefellas had been trespassing downstream on the banks of both Teennermairrerkoonner and Moorronnoe. Not only trespassing on the rivers, but staying. Trees were being chopped down, and shelters were being built. There were men, women and children. He'd seen them himself, and was curious but wary. Their presence had meant his family had to camp further south than normal, to keep a safe distance away until they knew more. Were other invaders coming? Would they pay for their trespass? They had many questions, but so far, no answers.

But today was too glorious a day to be ignored. The grassy plains, fired to attract all the kangaroo and wallaby they would ever need, swayed in the autumn breeze. He stopped, lifted his head towards the sun and shut his eyes. He could feel the warmth on his face, spreading to his neck and chest. He shook his head and his ringlets swished around him. Suddenly there were howls of protest.

"You're hitting my legs!" she accused.

"Sorry," he replied. Planobeena wriggled.

"Keep going," she said. "I'm thirsty."

In silence they meandered on, passing generously spaced eucalypts. A few kangaroos grazing in the distance registered their presence and hopped away at a leisurely pace.

"I want to get down," complained Planobeena a few minutes later.

He was only too happy to oblige. She was down in an instant, and trotted off ahead of him.

"Don't go too far," he ordered.

Sudden movement near his feet caught his eye. Just ahead, a tiger snake slithered through the grass. He froze and waited, alternating between watching the snake's progress and Planobeena's head getting smaller. Then she disappeared, though he could hear her singing. The snake finally moved on, and he broke into a trot.

Her singing became fainter, then undetectable. He stopped to listen, turning his head in each direction as he tried to pick up the sound. Nothing. He scanned ahead towards the eucalypts marking the bend of the river.

Perhaps she'd already reached the riverbank, and gone in? He knew she could swim, but he had no idea what the river levels were like. How much rain had there been lately? Will I have to go in after her? he panicked. His youthful legs ate up the space and then he was dodging the trees on the riverbank before he came to a sudden halt. There she was, looking with wonder at a shiny object in her hand. His back to Umarrah, a white man squatted on one knee a few feet from her, watching her intently. Two other men, fishing rods in hand, stood a short way off. They looked up and saw Umarrah. One of them called out to the kneeling man, who stood up and carefully turned around. Planobeena followed the man's gaze. Umarrah saw her expression move from curiosity to guilt, then fear.

"Run!" he shouted, with arms outstretched towards her. She hesitated for a second then dropped the object and leapt towards him. But the whitefella was fast. In two quick strides he caught her, picking her up and retrieving his watch while one of the anglers grabbed a musket from the grass, pointed it at Umarrah and fired. He dropped to the ground, his hands reflexively covering his ears as the sound whizzed overhead. Then her screams pierced the air. He crawled to a tree, stood up slowly behind it and peered out. The men were running away, with their musket and fishing rods and Planobeena's head and limbs bobbing up and down, tucked under a pair of white arms. He set off after them, trailing carefully at a distance. Her cries guided him, but then he heard a slap, a scream, a cruel laugh, then silence.

The whitefellas reached a cart and lifted Planobeena up, tied her with rope, and climbed up beside her. The cart horse, whose contented grazing was suddenly over, was whipped into action. The man who'd grabbed her turned around as they lurched away. Umarrah felt a chill run down his back as he saw the twisted smile. Planobeena turned her head too, and Umarrah watched her face, wide eyed and tearful, receding.

Immobilised in disbelief, he stood there, until reality intruded and he raced back to his parents.

They listened to his blundering outburst, horror spreading across their faces.

Now it was Luwanna's screams that pierced the air before she rushed towards the river.

CHAPTER FOUR

October 1814 – Norfolk Plains

It was the warm breeze in the end. It felt like home. George stood there as the memories flooded in. He ached for the subtropical ocean, its warmth and turquoise blueness surrounding him, soothing his body. I've had enough, he decided. It's time for a swim. There's no one here to ask, I'll probably get into trouble, but I don't care.

He threw the axe down, wiped his face with his shirt, checked that Elizabeth and Joseph hadn't come back from visiting neighbours, and started walking, slowly. Everything seemed to ache, his arms, his legs, though his back was the worst, so running to the river was not going to happen. He distracted himself from his aches and pains by indulging his grievances as he walked.

One, the chores were never ending. Constantly chopping down trees. They had spent so long trying to clear the land. He had no idea that forty acres would be so big. And they were lucky, with frontage to the South Esk River on almost two sides of their land, they had less fencing to do than some of the other families. And building a hut, and from that, a cottage.

Two, he hardly saw his friends. The families were scattered on either side of the river. The ford was not so close that they could cross to the other side easily. All the children were working hard with their families, so even if they could cross, there was precious little time to roam free.

Three, he felt like an only child. His sisters he hardly ever saw. Margaret had married Thomas at the beginning of the year and Eliza was busy in town with her new baby girl, and her Lieutenant Holmes. I feel like an orphan, George grumbled, especially when Mother goes into town and I'm left here with Joseph.

A flock of yellow-tailed black cockatoos approached, calling languidly to each other as they passed overhead and then landed in some large gum trees ahead of him on the track. He squinted up at them as they chewed and dropped bark to the ground. Approaching the ford, he looked across the sky towards a curtain of dark clouds to the south. Still the same, he thought. They must have had rain down that way for four days now.

The sun warmed his muscles and after an initial grimace, he began to jog. Working up a sweat and a thirst would make that jump off the bank even sweeter. The track wound past some of the other settler huts and he returned a few waves. A few times he slowed down to walk, his breath heavy and his lungs filling with cooler air from a rising, southerly wind.

And then he could see it ahead. His favourite spot, a clearing with wide flat river banks and plenty of space, all to himself. But then voices, clear in the sun-filled air, arrested his anticipation. He scanned and saw a large group of Aborigines at the ford, some standing on the far bank and some crossing towards him. He hesitated. They're at the same spot as last time, he thought, remembering the day last autumn when he first saw them. He salivated as the smell of their dinner cooking wafted across the air and wondered if he should turn around, but the desire for a swim won out. Keeping his distance, he walked through the clearing. Some of the Aborigines turned and regarded him cautiously. Self consciously he lowered his head and walked to a spot upstream where the trees would grant him privacy.

As he stood by the bank, George noted the river height, a bit higher than normal, and the current, a bit faster than usual. He removed his trousers, dipped his toe in, grimaced, walked back a few paces, then ran forward and jumped in. Contrasting perceptions of pleasure and surprise came with the coolness of the water and the stronger current. He surfaced, took another breath and then dived under for as long as he could. The water gradually warmed against his skin. For a few moments he shut his eyes and felt surrounded by the ocean.

Opening them again, the pleasurable thought dispersed as he realised how close he was getting to the Aborigines. Most of them had crossed, though a few men remained on the far back. One of them, despite his tall athletic build, hesitated. Another swimmer shouted and waved encouragement, then gave up as he worked harder than anticipated to make the opposing bank. The young man tentatively moved forward. George watched his hesitant steps into the water and followed his glance upstream as the water churned its way towards them.

Although familiar now with this winding river on their doorstep, George had never seen its levels rise like this. Kicking his legs hard, his sore muscles forgotten, he decided to play it safe and headed for the river bank. Then a cry rang out and he saw the young man being swept into the current, the churning water breaking over his head. In only a few moments he was in trouble, and without thinking, George swivelled his arms and kicked hard in his direction. In no time, he tumbled into the stranger, who looked astonished as well as alarmed.

The rush of water roared around them both. George kept his head up, but the man's head was more often below the surface than above. Some large rocks on the eastern bank loomed towards them as they were swept downstream. Alarmed, George reached out, grabbed an arm, and kicked hard, pulling them both away from danger. The rocks slipped by. Relieved, George looked around to find the closest riverbank, but the young man seemed not to share George's relief and started to panic instead. He pushed George down as he tried to hold on to him. George's head plunged under the surface. I'm smaller than him, he realised. Panic will drown us both.

The river straightened. George kicked his legs hard, resurfaced and gasped for air. The desperate man was frantically trying to see, wiping a mass of curly red-brown hair from his face. George manoeuvred behind him, hooked an arm around his neck and regained control. Downstream, they were approaching a tree, its overhanging branches dangling in the water.

This was their lifeline. They had to grab those branches.

The young man stopped struggling, and George wondered how much water he'd swallowed.

His lungs and muscles burning, George kicked hard and with his free arm lunged desperately. His hand grabbed a small but sturdy branch and clung on. Against the pull of the current, he slowly drew them both into the safety of the tangle of branches. His feet found the muddy river bed and he released his grip from around the stranger's neck. Then his adrenalin was spent and his legs started to give way.

Suddenly voices and arms were all around them. The two of them were pulled from the tree branches and hauled up the riverbank. They were laid side by side on the grass, their chests heaving before their breathing gradually slowed.

The young man turned and vomited onto the grass.

George lay there, his eyes closed, as unrecognisable words floated above his head. The man beside him sat up and coughed over and over, his breathing still laboured. In the silence after the coughing, George felt the young man's gaze upon him. He opened his eyes, struggled to sit up, before cautiously turning his head towards him, observing his reddish-brown skin and ringleted hair, contrasting with the pattern of scars across his upper chest and arms. Their eyes met. George's breath froze as he registered surprise, anger and then a softening pass across the dark face. Finally there was a hint of a smile, but so brief as to be almost imperceptible. George looked away as a woman gazed at the young man. The tone of her words sounded anxious and loving. Curiosity overcame him and he turned back to look at them both. Her hair was very short, like a man's, George thought. Then his eyes widened as he took in their onlookers. Some of the men held spears, tips pointing to the sky, bases in the ground.

"George, thank God!" shrieked a familiar voice as his mother nearly collapsed beside him. His face was covered with kisses, and his body patted all over, as if checking he was intact. Mortified, George squirmed under this attention, and cast a sidelong glance at his companion, who had stood up and looked away.

"Mum, I'm alright," George coughed, and stood up too. Embarrassed but intrigued, he called out to the young man. "I'm George," he blurted. There was a hesitation then a turning back. George felt his face being studied once more. Then the stranger's gaze shifted and his body suddenly stiffened.

George wheeled round to see Joseph plunge into the group. "He's here Joseph – he's alright!" Elizabeth shouted as Joseph's strides came to a stop and he bristled at the proximity of the Aborigines. The air congealed around them all in a tense silence.

"Let's go," said Joseph with deadly calm, returning the young man's gaze with narrowed eyes.

"Now."

George turned.

"Goodbye," he said and waited for a reply. He was granted a brief blank gaze, then Joseph grabbed George's arm. It was over. He looked back to see his mother nodding and smiling awkwardly to the Aboriginal people around her as she retreated.

They walked off in strained silence. After they were out of earshot, Elizabeth rounded on him. "Why did you do that, George? You're only eleven for heaven's sake!" she shouted. "When we saw the river start to rise and we couldn't find you, I was so frightened. "

"I'm sorry Mother – I just wanted a swim. I didn't know that the river would rise like that."

His legs felt like jelly. He looked across at Joseph, waiting for the anger to break.

"Where will the native families go if it floods badly?" he asked his mother.

"How the hell should we know?" Joseph interrupted. "What on earth were you doing with them anyway?"

George's shoulders slumped. "I got swept downstream when the river rose, and ... the young man ... he got swept up too. When I started to rescue him, he panicked, and at one stage I thought he'd drown us both."

"I don't know how on earth you managed to help him," Elizabeth replied with surprise. "He's clearly bigger than you."

"Neither do I actually," he mumbled.

"You shouldn't have been there in the first place," fumed Joseph. "Don't go down to the river by yourself – you hear me? And I don't want to see you near the natives."

George looked at his mother. She gazed back at him with a barely perceptible shake of her head, but said nothing.

The next day he woke late to a sun high in the spring sky. He leapt out of bed expecting a reprimand but Joseph only muttered about his mother insisting he sleep in. To everyone's relief, they'd lost no stock in the rising waters, though their fields closest to the river were flooded. "I'm going for a walk," said George, "to help my stiff legs."

Joseph frowned sceptically. "Don't be long," he grunted.

George ignored Joseph's instructions, and the protests from his aching body, and headed back towards the ford.

But the Aborigines had gone. Disappointed, George trudged up and down the muddy bank. The river ignored him and swirled turbulently downstream. He looked across to the far bank and replayed it all from the beginning.

He hoped that the natives would come back. And that the young man would be among them.

He wanted to know his name.

CHAPTER FIVE

October 1814 – Panninher country

With their usual campsite beside Moorronnoe now flooded, they had little choice but to move. Umarrah was recovering and insisted he could keep up. So the decision was made to head up to Yinginner, though it was earlier in the season than they preferred. As they followed the road west, the rivers they forded had not flooded, and their progress was steady. At the base of Koorparoona Niara they rested, and then threaded their way up the mountain pass. The waterfalls beside the steep path quenched and refreshed. It was always a strenuous climb, but this time Umarrah felt his lungs would burst. He could see his mother's worried glances when he coughed.

They emerged at the top of the pass and paused at the lookout, taking in the sweeping view of the plains below. A cockinna observed their arrival from contemplative circles above, the eagle soaring on impressive wedge-shaped wings before heading off in search of much more reasonably sized prey. Umarrah turned his gaze from the sky to Yinginner in the distance. A season of long summer days awaited. Time to recover.

As other clans gradually joined them over the lengthening days there was only one topic of conversation.

"They're staying close to the rivers." was one comment.

"For now," said another voice. "With rivers in front of them, and such good country behind, they may not leave at all."

"This is our Country," someone growled. "What permission have they asked from us to be on it?"

Silence.

"They may not stay where they are," argued Largenna. "They saw what happened when those spring rains fed

Teennermairrerkoonner and Moorronnoe. When those two rivers flooded, it caught them by surprise. They may decide it is not safe to stay there and move on."

"Or just move to higher ground," added Umarrah.

They all stared at him. The young man with the sister stolen by the invaders, and now saved from drowning by a whitefella boy. He stared back.

Guilt stalked his days. He was very conscious that his near-drowning only added to the heartache of his parents, who were desperate for news of Planobeena. The grief ate away at his mother. More lines appeared on her face and the muscular definition of her body slackened as her appetite waned. The other women would say "Eat Luwanna, eat, you must keep up your strength, to find Planobeena." But their pleas fell on deaf ears. His father's efforts to comfort her too were complicated by his own undimmed grief and fury.

But the worst was hearing his mother crying. She would take herself away from the others, usually at night, and surrender to it. He followed her once and stood there, listening. Planobeena's disappearing face filled his vision, and his throat tightened. His mother heard him sniffing, sighed and wiped her eyes. "I'm sorry I couldn't stop them," he sobbed.

Her hands cradled his face as she gazed at him. "Don't, Umarrah. There was nothing you could have done. I could have lost you too."

The days began to shorten and they prepared to head back down from the plateau. Now was the time, he decided. His makeshift plan had been percolating in his head for many nights, and with some trepidation he approached his parents.

"These whitefellas, the one who rescued me and his family, they might know about Planobeena," he started. "I want to pretend to make friends with the boy, and find out what I can." Largenna was silent, considering. He's not saying no immediately, thought Umarrah, and waited.

"How are you going to do that, Umarrah? You speak whitefella?" his father argued.

"No, but I can learn," he replied. His father grabbed his shoulders. "Gaining that knowledge could be a dangerous process, even if you found out something."

"I know it's risky." He shrugged. "It might sound strange but I think that boy liked me."

"It's not strange," agreed Luwanna. "I thought that you might have an idea like this Umarrah, and I didn't want to encourage it. But you have anyway. The day it happened, afterwards Parwareter and Trepanner followed the whitefella boy and his family when they left the river. They saw where their hut was and watched them move their animals away from the swollen river. Late the next afternoon they saw the boy heading back towards the river. They followed. The boy walked straight to the spot where you'd been hauled out the day before. He stood there for a while and then moved up and down the river bank. He was searching for you, they were sure of it."

"And I can use that," Umarrah argued.

His father's face was thoughtful. "Alright, but you mustn't do this on your own. You take the other two with you at all times."

"Yes, you must," agreed Luwanna.

"The three of us can watch them together," he argued, "but I have to approach the boy and his family on my own. If I'm going to have any chance of making friends with him, I must be by myself. Three of us will be too much."

"Umarrah, don't think I'm not thankful that this white boy rescued you, but we know nothing about them. Next time you might not be so lucky and those same people could turn on you," Luwanna insisted.

"If this works, the more likely I will find out something about Planobeena. I think they'd only accept one person, and that has to be me."

Hearing Planobeena's name, his mother's eyes filled with faint hope. Umarrah could see her fighting with herself – letting him do this versus the risks. Finally she nodded. Umarrah looked at his father. He paused, then did the same.

Their journey passed in a blur of anticipation, negotiation and logistics. The clan would stay by the ford on Teennermairrerkoonner, rather than Moorronnoe. Their group of three must not be away for more than one night at a time.

As they approached Panninher country, questions and doubts intruded. Who is this boy? Why did he rescue me? Would I have done the same? And unwelcome memories too – the faces of Planobeena's kidnappers.

He'd been up close to so few whitefellas, and now he was deliberately getting closer. The idea was about to become reality.

The clan set up their riverside camp, and the following morning the three of them set off. Threading their way amongst the grasses, they headed towards the whitefella settlement on Moorronnoe. A few hours later they were studying the whitefella huts, found the right one, and settled down to watch.

Little happened for a few hours. The daylight gradually gave way to dusk. As they contemplated returning to camp, a lone figure trudged along the flattened grass path towards the cottage. "That's him," said Umarrah. Parwareter and Trepanner nodded their agreement.

"George!" called out an angry voice from the cottage doorway. The boy shouted a reply and broke into a run. The same man who had come to the riverbank after the rescue appeared around the corner of the hut and strode up to him. The boy cowered as the man berated him. When he'd finished, the boy stepped warily around him. As he did so, the man swung his leg and landed a kick to the boy's legs. He pitched forward onto his hands and knees, banging his forehead on the dirt. Umarrah, Parwareter and Trepanner flinched reflexively. The man stood over the boy for several seconds. Stunned, the boy gradually hauled himself up and staggered inside.

They kept watch on the hut for a while longer. There was shouting, one voice a woman's. She and the man argued. There were no more sounds from the boy.

Eventually they decided to head back. Today had clearly not been a good day for making contact. As they walked through the fading dusk light, they discussed what they'd witnessed.

"That man, be careful," warned Parwareter.

"I will," replied Umarrah. "Don't tell Mother and Father about what we saw, please." His companions were silent. "I didn't like the look of the man that day by the river and he's just confirmed my suspicions. So now I'm prepared."

"We'll be watching closely," said Trepanner.

"Thanks," replied Umarrah. "I'm not saying I'm not scared though."

"Maybe all the whitefellas are like that," Parwareter commented as the campfire light drew them in. "Or maybe the boy is still being punished for rescuing you," added Trepanner.

"We'll soon find out," muttered Umarrah.

CHAPTER SIX

April 1815 – Norfolk Plains

"Do you think they'll come back?" asked Kennedy. The two of them sat on the riverbank, their feet idling back and forth in the cool water.

"The natives? Good question," replied George. "It's been six months and no sign."

"Maybe they won't come back this way after your contact with them," his friend suggested.

George nodded. "Could be true."

"The thing that I don't get is, no-one ever said anything to us about there being Blacks here, like before we left Norfolk Island." Kennedy looked at George. "Did you know about them?"

"No," he answered. "The first I heard, or saw, anything was the night we docked. I saw lights on the surrounding hills. One of the crew told me they were native campfires. Don't you remember that?"

"No, I think we were just so relieved to get off the ship, we didn't notice."

"I wondered then if they were watching us. I would if I was them," speculated George.

He could feel Kennedy staring at him, but didn't turn to meet his eyes. "If you were them, don't you think you'd want to keep an eye on us?" George added.

Kennedy pondered this question. "Perhaps."

"Maybe the Commandant on Norfolk Island decided to keep the information from us," suggested George.

"Or they told our parents, and they agreed to keep quiet. It still doesn't matter, George. Here we are."

George shrugged.

"Do you want them to come back, George?"

"I do," he admitted. "Aren't you curious?"

"No. There's enough about this place that's strange. Why add to it?"

Realising that Kennedy didn't share his interest, George decided to head home. "I better go," he declared, reaching down and scooping several handfuls of water from the river. His thirst quenched, he stood up. "Joseph will have a go at me if I'm late."

"Okay. See you," replied Kennedy, looking up. George turned and started to run, his legs revelling in the long grass. As he gathered speed, he scanned the view, the grass extending as far as he could see, trees occasionally punctuating the pale yellowness. The occasional kangaroo and wallaby head bobbed up at a distance as they felt his feet thudding into the earth, before they bounded away. George felt like he could run forever and smiled as the sun warmed his back and the grass brushed his legs.

Gradually he slowed down and came to a stop. As he caught his breath, he scanned the swaying grassland for the riverbank to get another drink. But he couldn't see it. Puzzled, he turned to look in the opposite direction, but rapidly realised he'd lost his bearings.

He looked to the west and saw the sun getting lower. It would soon be dusk. How could you be so stupid, running like that, he berated himself, knowing he'd promised to stay in sight of the river. He was lost, and if he managed to get back home, he would also be in trouble. He didn't want to think about Joseph's reaction.

A flock of black cockatoos meandered overhead, their familiar laconic screeches sounding like accusing laughter. He watched them descend into a nearby eucalypt and chat amiably before heading onward. Their calls began to fade. The stillness enveloped him.

Then came a voice from behind.

"George."

His eyes widened. He swivelled. It was the young man he'd rescued.

"Oh my God," blurted George.

They regarded each other for several seconds.

The young man took a few steps towards him then stopped.

"You remember my name," said George.

There was a faint smile in reply.

"How do I find out what's yours?" George murmured.

The young man seemed to understand. He placed a hand on his own chest.

"Umarrah."

George repeated the name slowly, practising the pronunciation. "Oo-mah-ruh." It felt like a secret word had been exchanged, a prelude to something. Wanting the moment to continue, he groped unsuccessfully for something to fill the silence. A few moments later, Umarrah gestured for him to follow then walked away. George hesitated at the unexpected invitation, then began to follow, caught up and traipsed alongside. He felt awkward as they strode silently through the grass, all the more uncomfortable in sensing that Umarrah was not.

Before long they reached a riverbank, but one with which George was not familiar. The water reflected the pinkish gold of the sunset. George followed Umarrah into the shallows to quench his thirst. They then followed a riverside path, and a short while later the scent of wood smoke mingling with the delicious smell of roasting meat heralded their arrival at the camp.

They rounded a small group of trees and George froze. Two Aboriginal women tended a campfire, a dead wallaby cooking in the coals. Their conversation ended with the interruption. One of the women stood up. George recognised her as the woman who had watched anxiously over Umarrah at the flooded riverbank. Perhaps she's his mother, he thought. Umarrah spoke to her as she scrutinised George. The other woman picked up a container and disappeared from the campfire. Umarrah gestured to George to sit down and the woman offered him some meat. He ate greedily while they watched, and, he suspected, discussed him.

Despite his disorientation and unfamiliar surroundings, George realised he was not afraid. There was something about

Umarrah's behaviour with regard to him that was deliberate. He suspected that Umarrah had been watching him and followed him after he left Kennedy, though exactly why, he couldn't determine. The only fear he felt was when he remembered that it was getting even later and his mother and Joseph could already be out looking for him.

The meal was brief. Umarrah and the woman did not eat. They stood soon after George had finished. Umarrah gestured again for George to follow. He was offered water from a container before departing. He mumbled his thanks to the woman before following Umarrah back along the river. The sky was darkening but his companion's steps were no less confident.

Not long after they started back Umarrah called out and two other young men appeared. George's heart pounded as he noted their spears. They separated and flanked Umarrah and George on either side. They did not acknowledge George, and none of them spoke as they moved through the grassland.

The fading colours of the sunset signalled night's arrival and the darkness prevented George from recognising the return of familiar surroundings until he was nearly home. Then he heard his mother's voice calling out his name. Elizabeth held up a lantern and gasped at the sight of George walking alongside Umarrah towards the hut, flanked by the two other young men. The four of them halted.

"It's alright Mother, I'm fine," he called out. He turned to Umarrah and gestured for him to follow. They walked together towards her while the other two stayed behind. "Mother, this is Umarrah," he smiled. "You will recognise him from six months ago. I got lost this afternoon and he found me, took me to his camp and his family fed me, and as you can see, brought me home."

Elizabeth stepped towards Umarrah. "Hello," she nodded, "thank you."

Umarrah held her gaze, then nodded in return. She smiled with brief formality then turned back to George. "Joseph is out looking for you. We thought you might have been bitten by a snake."

"No, I just lost my bearings after I left Kennedy."

"Well, you'll have a lot to tell me inside." She emphasised the last word.

"Goodbye, Umarrah," said George. "Thank you." He hesitated and gestured towards the cottage. "I hope to see you another time, maybe."

Umarrah's eyes narrowed slightly. He smiled briefly then turned and walked back to the others. George and Elizabeth watched them disappear into the darkness.

CHAPTER SEVEN

September 1816 – Panninher country

Did they have enough, pondered Umarrah, as he looked at the carcasses on the ground. One wallaby and one kangaroo so far. He looked over at George, who had brought and shared some large water bottles as they stalked their quarry in the early spring sunshine. George wiped his mouth after a large swig refreshed him, and turned to look at Umarrah with a 'what now?' expression.

"One more," said Umarrah, calculating it would boost his favour with George's family if George took meat home from the hunt. George nodded and slung his water bottle over his shoulder before grabbing a spear leaning against the eucalypt. Trepanner and Parwareter walked ahead to a copse of trees that bordered the grasslands. George followed and Umarrah brought up the rear. Let's see how he goes, thought Umarrah.

"George," he called out. The younger man turned around. "This one for your family."

George's face showed enthusiasm mixed with apprehension. "Alright," he replied.

Umarrah nodded and relayed this to the others. They kept walking. And your mother and Joseph will thank me for it, Umarrah calculated.

They hid behind the cover of trees bordering the grassland and waited. Gradually a few kangaroos edged closer. George's grip on his spear tightened. Trepanner signalled directions and Parwareter crept quietly to hide behind a different tree. A kangaroo's head bobbed up and its ears swivelled momentarily, before resuming its meal. George glanced at Umarrah for guidance but held his position. The kangaroo was within range. Parwareter glanced outward from behind the far tree and suddenly George leapt forward with his arm high. The spear flew from his arm but landed well clear of its mark. The kangaroo bounded off. George's shoulders slumped.

"I know, I know, I rushed it," he said.

"It's alright," Umarrah replied. "More are coming."

He was right and within the hour George had speared a young wallaby. They walked over to the dying animal, Umarrah handed George a waddy and he finished it off with two quick blows to the head. Umarrah noted his willingness to dispatch the animal. He'd learnt quite a lot even if his accuracy with a spear, and his patience, still needed improving.

"You carry it," Umarrah said to him, as Parwareter and Trepanner hoisted the earlier kills on their shoulders.

"Alright," George replied. Umarrah turned to the others and after a brief discussion, they called out their goodbyes before turning to head home. George waved goodbye, then grabbed the wallaby's legs and dragged the carcass around on the grass until as much blood as possible was wiped off. He then lifted it up and hoisted it around his neck.

"Come and eat with us," George invited. "You've done most of the work anyway."

Umarrah thanked him, matched his pace to George's and they headed towards the settlement. He was grateful once again to George for getting lost. Being able to rescue him enabled repayment of the debt he owed. He was building on that mutual gratitude and obligation each time they met when Umarrah's clan travelled through the plains during spring and autumn. He made sure he didn't wear out his welcome, and George and Elizabeth in particular seemed comfortable with this seasonal acquaintance.

As they approached the cottage, Umarrah scanned to see if Joseph was there. There was always a warmer reception in his absence, although it would be good for him to see George's first kill.

They turned the corner of the cottage and Joseph stood in the doorway. Umarrah and George stopped.

"Well," said Joseph, with a nod, "what's this?"

George leaned over and the carcass slid from his shoulders, landing with a satisfying thud on the ground.

Umarrah smiled, anticipating George's pride.

"A wallaby I killed myself," beamed George.

Joseph looked the carcass over as Elizabeth came through the doorway.

"The hunters are back then," she smiled.

"George tells us he's killed this himself," said Joseph sceptically.

"Well done, George," said Elizabeth. "Did you really?"

"Yes," insisted George. Joseph snorted.

"You hunt good, George," said Umarrah in support.

"Well you'd better get that carcass hung up in the shed," ordered Joseph, seeming to tire of all this praise.

"The weather's cold enough – it should be fine there for now," nodded Elizabeth.

"Okay," replied George.

"I can help tomorrow," offered Umarrah, and waited for the offer to be taken up.

"Alright, yes," Joseph grunted. "We need to move the herd to the far paddock. Just in case the river rises."

"Thank you Umarrah," said Elizabeth politely.

Umarrah nodded.

George bent down and grabbed the wallaby's tail. "I'll get this hung up," he said quietly, and started to drag it along the ground. "See you tomorrow," he said to Umarrah, before turning away.

As he strode away, Umarrah considered Joseph's behaviour. The man's attitude had not softened. He needed careful watching. But Umarrah felt an unexpected stirring of something else – sympathy for George, who had to live with him.

He brushed this aside and focussed on finding Planobeena. He, Parwareter, Trepanner and others had searched the area whenever they passed through. When Umarrah was with George, he used every opportunity, every casual contact with other whites from the settlement to sight her. But nothing yet. He pondered whether his relationship with George was ready for him to reveal what had happened to her.

If he did, could he expect their help in finding her?

As he neared the camp, he could hear his mother's cries of distress and broke into a run. One of his aunties was comforting her.

"What's happened?" he demanded.

"It's your father," his mother cried. "He didn't come back."

"From the raid?"

She nodded.

He hesitated, then turned and ran blindly along the riverbank. Where were the men who'd gone with his father on this carefully planned raid? He remembered the discussions; how they would retaliate against an earlier raid for their women from their neighbours to the north east, what route they would take, the proportional response they would pursue. He had wanted to join them, but he knew when he asked that the answer would be no. He had a sister to find.

He found the men who'd made it back. Their news was grim. A young warrior from the other side who had taken one of the Leterremairrener women refused to surrender her. He speared Largenna twice. The force of the second spear to the chest propelled him backward. He had grabbed a tree branch, but lost his grip and fell backwards over the cliff above Lakekeller, and into the river. Another of their warriors had received a wound to the leg, though they had inflicted spear wounds on two of their attackers. Both sides then retreated, their enemies to the mountain above. The Leterremairreners' homeward journey was lengthened by having to go around a small whitefella settlement on the river.

The river was swollen with spring rains and his father's body had been carried downstream. They had not been able to retrieve it.

Umarrah sat with the men during the night, time passing in a blur of shock. His only relief was knowing his mother finally slept from exhaustion.

The next morning dawned with a sky of steel grey, cold but with little wind. He checked his mother again but she hadn't stirred. He washed his face in the river, ate some cold meat by the ashes of the fire, then forced himself to head over to George's.

He refused Elizabeth's offer of food after he arrived, and waited outside. George grabbed his last mouthful of breakfast just as Joseph shouted to them both from the shed. They headed over to begin the day's work.

As the morning wore on, Umarrah could tell George was watching him. A few times his fledgling understanding of English failed him and George had to repeat instructions. But despite his exhaustion, there were moments when the hard work felt good. A day like yesterday. The waters of Moorronnoe sparkled as they moved the sheep and cattle as far away from the river as possible. There hadn't been much rain since the weather had started to warm up, but the settlers were not taking any chances.

By lunchtime it was nearly done, earlier than they had expected. Elizabeth brought out some cold meat, damper and flasks of water. She and Joseph made quiet conversation and then both got up, Elizabeth gathering the remains of lunch.

"I'll get some rope from the shed to help with the last stragglers," said Joseph.

Watching them go, Umarrah felt the crushing return of reality. He stood up to fight it off and swayed momentarily. George jumped to his feet. "Something's wrong," he said. "What is it?" Umarrah looked at him and couldn't calculate whether unburdening himself would have any consequences, and if it did, whether they would be good or bad.

"My father is dead," he confided.

"My God," George blurted. "When?

"Some days ago."

George hesitated. "What happened?" he asked cautiously.

The question hung in the air.

"He got sick," Umarrah fudged.

"Oh," said George. "I'm sorry."

They stood there awkwardly. Elizabeth called out to Joseph. A whitefella couple had appeared at the cottage. The woman began to chat animatedly with Elizabeth while the man watched Joseph walk over and hand the rope to George. The man saw Umarrah, nudged his wife and she turned to stare. The conversation froze. Elizabeth hastily bundled them all inside the hut as Umarrah watched a scowl pass across Joseph's face.

"Let's go," said George.

They walked silently towards the paddock.

"I'm really sorry about your father," repeated George a few minutes later.

Umarrah looked at him. He means it, he realised. The sincerity soothed the knot in his stomach just a little.

"Thank you," he replied.

CHAPTER EIGHT

October 1818 – Norfolk Plains

George looked down at the South Esk River, fast moving once again from spring rains. He watched as David paced, counting aloud. Several minutes after the older man, soon to be his brother-in-law, disappeared from view, George wandered slowly down to the river bank, took off his boots and gasped as his feet cooled in the river's flow. He filled his flask, drank, refilled it, then rubbed his aching legs.

In return for his labour, he hoped David would reward him with answers to some pressing questions.

He followed the course of the glinting river as it stretched away to the south. And then he saw the smoke. Several thin lines gently wound their way upward, diffusing amongst the sunshine and cloud.

"Right, I've done that," panted David, as he clambered up to George. "Paced out the whole twenty-five acres we have to set aside for cultivation. Twenty-five out of eighty isn't too bad I suppose, but that's a lot of clearing to do."

George offered him a water bottle.

David drank greedily then paused to look around. "Are they native campfires?" he pointed, after wiping his mouth. "How far away do you think they are?"

"Just a few miles," George answered. "I expect they'll be here in the next couple of days. Their arrival doesn't usually vary more than a week or so."

But I still don't have any good news, thought George. About Planobeena. After Umarrah revealed his sister's abduction, George rashly promised that he would try and find out where she might be. But he'd had no luck. His mother, appalled, but, George thought, strangely not shocked by the kidnapping, promised to ask around. She'd asked as many of the other

Norfolk Plains settler women that she knew, but that had drawn a blank. George reluctantly asked Joseph. Having promised to supply meat from their herd regularly to the government stores in Launceston, Joseph was in town occasionally and might be able to discover something. Joseph mumbled a few words about trying but had probably made no enquiries, and said "No" every time George asked. He persisted for a while then gave up. David gave him an opportunity he wanted to seize. Still George hesitated. Would asking this first question mean he forfeited help with a second?

He also wanted David's help to get land of his own.

As he watched the wisps of smoke drifting skyward, he could feel David's gaze upon him.

"Are you happy, Mr Gibson, with the size of your grant?" George asked. "Aye, George it's a start," smiled David as he turned to look back at what he'd surveyed. "I intend to do well in this spot. The river frontage is good and putting the house on this rise should hopefully avoid the flooding that your father has had to contend with."

"My stepfather, Mr Gibson," corrected George. "Yes, we've certainly had to deal with that over the last five years."

"Stepfather, duly noted," replied David. He swept his gaze over his thirty acres and the adjacent fifty granted to George's sister Eliza. "If I am going to give your sister the future she deserves George, I must make a go of this," he determined. "Shall we have a look at where to start felling?" he suggested, before striding off. George had nearly caught up with him when David stopped and turned to look at him. "And will you please call me David? I know I am quite a bit older than you but we'll soon be brothers."

George smiled hesitantly. "Alright."

They kept walking.

"May I ask you something, David?"

"Of course."

"Have you heard of anyone kidnapping a young Aboriginal girl, not recently, a few years back?"

David stopped and surveyed George with renewed interest.

"Eliza told me that you rescued a young native man from drowning a few years ago. Are these … things … connected?"

"The man I rescued – it's his sister who's missing."

David raised an eyebrow. "I see. So you know the natives then?"

"A few of them. Mainly him, Umarrah. That smoke – that's probably his clan heading this way. They pass through in the spring and autumn. They move between the high country and the rivers. I've been out hunting with him and his friends when they're here, and he and sometimes the others have helped us on the farm."

"Really! Are you not frightened?"

"No."

"How do you communicate?"

"Umarrah speaks some English now. Picked it up quite quickly".

"How old is he?"

"Not sure. A few years older than me, I'd say."

"And your mother and Joseph allow all this?"

"Yes. Mother likes Umarrah. She doesn't mind at all him being around."

"And Joseph?"

George thought for a moment.

"He's grateful for the extra pairs of hands."

David paused. "So what did Umarrah tell you about his sister?"

"That some white men took her from the banks of the Macquarie River. He's shown me the place where it happened. I asked Mother and Joseph to make enquiries but no one has heard anything. Did you ever hear about it?"

He scanned the older man's face. David began walking again.

"No, it's news to me. But I'll see what I can find out, George. I can't make any promises, mind."

"I know. But I can tell Umarrah that you are making enquiries."

"If you like."

George took a deep breath.

"I have another question, if you don't mind."

"Yes?"

"Could you put in a good word for me to get a grant of my own?"

George saw David's sharp glance his way.

"How old are you, George?"

"Sixteen."

David smile was withering. "I don't think the Governor is likely to grant you land for a few more years yet."

"How many more years?"

"I couldn't say. I don't know his mind, or that of the Colonial Secretary. Why are you in such a hurry?"

"I've worked enough for Mother and Joseph. I've seen them struggle. Their hearts aren't in it. They never wanted to come here. We have to pay rent on the land now. Our stock numbers are growing, which is good, but Joseph promises a lot of meat to the government stores then doesn't like the price he gets. He thinks the reason why is because we're associating with natives, despite the help that's given us. Now he's started talking about going back to sea."

He sighed. "I just want my own place."

"But you couldn't leave your mother to struggle on the land on her own, if Joseph did go back to sea."

"She'd rather be in town anyway. They have an allotment in Wellington Street."

David stopped. "Here's the spot. I think if we start clearing at this point, we can work our way back and get the best sun for planting."

George waited for an answer to his question.

"Why don't you do some work for me first, George? The more experience you get, the better. I can see why you would want your own land but I think you're too young to get a grant."

George's face fell.

"You're disappointed," acknowledged David. "I understand that."

So, I'm just more free labour, thought George.

"As you can see," said David, looking at the bush in front of them. "It's going to be a lot of work to clear twenty-five acres. I'll need more help than even you could give me. Perhaps Umarrah and some of his people could help me like they have you. Then if I find out something about his sister, I'll be able to tell him directly. And of course, I'd arrange some way to pay them."

George made no reply, David's refusal to help him still smarting.

"I'd be obliged to you as well, George. I'd put in a good word for you as soon as it's right."

"Alright," conceded George. "I'll help you, and I'll ask Umarrah when I see him. Thank you for being willing to ask about his sister," he mumbled.

As he headed home at the end of the day, George replayed their conversation. If I'm too young, then aren't you too old? he fumed, unwilling to acknowledge that perhaps David was right. Who would possibly give a sixteen-year-old Norfolk Islander any land of their own? His mother had commented about David being a twice sentenced-to-death ex-convict from Scotland who was clearly going to do well when he married Eliza, combining her adjacent grant with his, and in one fell swoop, doubling the size of her and Joseph's forty acres.

The truth of the matter was that instead of getting help to pursue his own grant of land, George would now have to work even harder to help other people on theirs.

The only thing salvageable from the day was that he had something slightly encouraging to tell Umarrah.

Three weeks later, George's recruitment of extra labour had made a difference. After long and backbreaking days, they had made good progress in clearing twenty-five acres of David's land. His soon-to-be-brother-in-law seemed delighted with the progress made by his one convict servant, plus George, Umarrah, Parwareter and Trepanner. George and Umarrah stayed behind late one afternoon after Parwareter and Trepanner had already departed with a carcass of mutton.

"You do not like him," observed Umarrah.

George shrugged. "No, I don't, even though he is marrying my sister."

"This is why you don't like him?" asked Umarrah.

"No," replied George, unwilling to say more.

"Because he takes more land than Joseph?"

"No. Well, yes and no. They gave this land to both my sister and him. Adjacent land," George gestured. "The grants are next to each other, and as they are getting married, it all makes sense," said George flatly.

"Who gave?" asked Umarrah.

"Governor Macquarie in Sydney, via the Colonial Secretary," sighed George. "The controller of all our fortunes."

Umarrah listened carefully, then nodded in the direction of David, who strode towards them.

"David pay us for using the land," he added.

"Yes, that's true – he does. He's better than many settlers in that way," replied George.

"He say anything about Planobeena?" asked Umarrah.

"Not yet, but why don't you ask him now?" replied George.

"Thank you again for all your help," said David formally to Umarrah. "I am very grateful."

"Thank you for the meat," Umarrah replied. "You are looking for my sister, Planobeena?"

David looked uncomfortable. "Aye, I have made a few enquiries about her. But there is no information as yet."

Umarrah scrutinized David's face for several seconds. "For my mother, it is a long time to wait," he replied.

George thought that David was going to say something then thought better of it.

Umarrah glanced at George, said goodbye to them both, then headed off towards the clan's camp by the ford. George and David watched him thread his way through the trees.

"I am grateful to you, George," said David. "I never thought we'd make this much progress. I've told Eliza how much of a help you've been."

He patted George's shoulder, and walked back to admire the day's handiwork. George bristled, feeling like a schoolboy dismissed after a day in class.

CHAPTER NINE

March 1819 – Panninher country

U marrah glanced up again to see the clouds' scalloped edges reaching ever higher in the sky. Heat from the strong northerly wind spread discomfort and unease in equal measure. Galahs and eastern rosellas had taken their birdcall with them and gone elsewhere. A few wallabies lay under some trees, trying to avoid both the effort of movement and the wind's hot gusts.

He scanned the farm. More animals than last time, he noted, as the sheep and cattle huddled under the eucalypts' meagre shade. Elizabeth and Joseph would be inside trying to escape the heat, and he could guess where George would be. He turned and headed for the river, his skin sucking in the sun's heat, thirsting for the cool water.

At the river's edge, relieved to get shade, he cooled his feet in the shallows and watched unseen as George swam towards the opposite bank. While he waited, his thoughts turned to the latest settlers. These new arrivals were taking up alarmingly large pieces of land on the banks of both Moorronnoe and Teennermairrerkoonner, and spreading out well beyond them. They dwarfed the small pieces of land occupied by George's family and the other earlier settlers.

He needed to find out what was going on.

George reached the far bank and turned around. Umarrah stood up. George saw him, waved and after a few moments started to head back.

He watched George swim confidently, managing the river's current with ease. In the nearly five years that had passed since they first met in Moorronnoe's turbulent flood waters, much had changed. A thin smile creased Umarrah's face, softening as he remembered his gratitude to the young man swimming confidently towards him. Umarrah always suspected loneliness, a desire to escape and simple curiosity had initially propelled George towards him. And Umarrah had exploited this ever since, learning much about the invaders, though with no success in finding Planobeena. He never expected to like George. The boy, now a young man, had made that easy, and unexpectedly complicated.

George hauled himself up onto the bank. He shook his head and sprayed Umarrah with water.

"Thanks," accused Umarrah.

"I've cooled you down so don't complain," smiled George, throwing on his shirt and glancing up. "That storm will be here soon," he commented.

"Don't want to be in it," replied Umarrah.

"Let's get back then!" George shouted as a hot gust of wind assailed them. They turned for the cottage, the sky continuing to darken. The trees swayed alarmingly and dislodged flying bark. George froze as a large rumble of thunder closely followed a flash of sheet lightning. Umarrah overtook him and walked ahead into a clearing. George had nearly caught up when a crack pierced the air and a sharp hiss flew between them. They both quickly dropped to the ground. "Gunshot!" George shouted.

The wind dropped in the pause before the rain. Then a voice rang out through the eery silence.

"George!"

Umarrah looked at George, who stood up. "Over here!" he called out, waving. Umarrah stood up beside him.

"There you are," said Joseph as he reached them. "Are you alright, George?"

George nodded. Umarrah's eyes widened as he saw the shotgun. Joseph flicked a glance his way before turning to his stepson.

"Why have you got that gun?" cried George.

"I took it off someone who's drunk, again," replied Joseph. "Think the heat addled his brain. I was looking for you because of the storm, and that's when I heard the gunshot. Someone must've been out hunting before the storm."

"It went right between us. We could've been killed!" he snapped, looking to Umarrah for confirmation.

But Umarrah was watching Joseph. And then he realised. Joseph's not shocked. That bullet was meant to come our way. Or my way. Joseph didn't know, when I walked into the clearing, that George was behind me.

"Well you're safe," replied Joseph. "Let's get home before the storm breaks."

George turned to Umarrah. "Come with us?"

Umarrah saw Joseph grimace momentarily but say nothing.

"No, I see you tomorrow," he replied.

"All right," George muttered before trudging after Joseph. Umarrah watched raindrops begin to plop on and around him, then moments later the clouds opened and George and Joseph disappeared behind a curtain of rain.

His ringlets dripping, Umarrah pulled the kangaroo skin tightly around him and huddled underneath some low wattles.

As he waited out the storm, his fury intensified. He forced himself to consider his options. He couldn't attack Joseph. He'd immediately be under suspicion. The whitefellas would come for him. And this one rash act would wipe out the gains he'd made.

And then he would never find Planobeena, or get any valuable information about the latest settlers.

Finally the storm passed to the east and the sun cast sidelong rays across the plains. He walked through the freshly washed, eucalyptus-scented landscape to the river, drank his fill, made a final decision and headed back to the camp.

When the soft light of sunset fell, he returned to the cottage and waited. Joseph came outside to check the stock, look at the river levels, and relieve his bladder against a tree.

"Joseph!" he called out, not too loudly. Joseph spun around as Umarrah walked towards him carrying a spear, shoulder high, aimed.

"What do you want?" Joseph stuttered.

"I know you try and shoot me," he accused.

Joseph's mouth fell open. "That's not true," he panicked.

"Shut your mouth, whitefella."

Joseph's mouth snapped shut.

"Come here," he commanded.

Joseph did not move for several seconds, then approached very slowly. Umarrah picked up his spear and levelled it at Joseph again.

"Please don't!" Joseph cried. "I'm sorry."

Umarrah's mouth twisted. He kept the spear trained on Joseph.

"Tell me about the new whitefellas. They taking big land by Teennermairrerkoonner."

"Where?" stuttered Joseph.

"The Macquarie," spat Umarrah.

"Oh, Archer and the like? They're free settlers, unlike us. They've come of their own free will, bought their way here, and the Governor can give them as much land as he feels fit to bestow," he said bitterly.

Umarrah's eyes narrowed as he watched Joseph's fear change to anger.

"Joseph?" came a voice.

They froze.

"I kill you if you tell them about this," threatened Umarrah.

Joseph's head swivelled towards the cottage. Elizabeth was peering from the doorway into the darkness.

"Let me go, please," he whispered, staring longingly at her, before daring to turn around and face his enemy.

But Umarrah had gone. He'd got what he needed, and was keen to share it with Parwareter and Trepanner who waited amongst the trees.

The next morning, Umarrah watched his mother walk slowly back from the river, sit down and begin to pick reluctantly at the recently foraged trynueler and leenterloommerler in front of her. He offered her some cold roasted wallaby leg and she took it without enthusiasm. Her appetite was even less nowadays and she was the slowest among them when they were on the move.

As they ate, he gave her an edited version of the previous day's events.

"So we have information about the new whitefellas," she confirmed.

"Yes," he replied, "though I'm not sure how that helps us."

"But still no one has information about your sister."

"No," he said reluctantly. "George and his mother, they have asked. Joseph and Gibson are like most of the whitefellas. They don't care about a young Leterremairrener girl," he added. Instantly regretting his angry words, he glanced at her face, the lines of grief etched deeper since Largenna's death.

"I will keep trying," he said.

Her lips twitched in a brief smile. "I know you will. Your father and I would expect no less." She picked a berry and rolled it round in her mouth till it split.

"This George," she began.

"Yes?" he answered.

"Be careful," she cautioned, "with an enemy who is also a friend."

He was very still, before biting off a hunk of meat, and chewing silently.

"How do these new settlers differ from the ones already here?" she asked.

"The new whitefellas, they choose to come here. The ones already here were forced to come by the leaders. Many did not want to. George's family didn't."

"So if the new ones have chosen to come, they will be more determined to stay. And if they come in greater numbers, and take larger pieces of Country, what happens then?"

His stomach clenched.

"I don't know," he conceded. "I wish Father was here. He would know what to do."

The sun filtered through the needle-like leaves of the neemooner tree and caught her eyes glittering with tears.

CHAPTER TEN

December 1820 – Norfolk Plains

George stood on the highest point and let his gaze roll down the hill towards the South Esk River. What a view! He shook his head slowly and smiled. The early summer patchwork of clouds and blue sky fell away to meet the peaks of the Western Tiers in the distance. The cold, unseasonal, westerly wind assailing him did not even register.

Sixty acres, elevated, with the river below. Unbelievably good. Twenty more than Joseph's grant. Ten more than Eliza's first grant of three years ago. Double that of David's original grant next to hers. Don't be smug, his mother told him, but she'd smiled and hugged him tightly. Joseph congratulated him, though George felt he was mostly disappointed at the loss of a pair of hands. Which was ironic since Joseph had given up on the farm, started to sell the stock and planned to go back to sea. George was enormously grateful to David for putting in a good word. It must have worked.

Think about the positives, he told himself. Because it wasn't all good. His sister tried to keep it from him, but it had to come out eventually. On the same day as he gained his sixty acres, David and Eliza had received one hundred acres, right next door. They'd also been granted a further seven *hundred* acres a few miles away. George was stunned. He couldn't comprehend it. They now owned eight hundred and eighty acres in total. How could you work that much land? How many convicts would the government give you to even attempt it? And what had David done to get it? He remembered his mother's bluntness. How many ex-convicts, with a twice-commuted death sentence, she repeated, end up with that much land? Serious theft and piracy are not exactly minor crimes. And it appears he's been richly rewarded for them, complained George.

He rubbed his arms against the cold. Concentrate on what's yours, he told himself. All that hard work with Joseph standing over you, and then working for David, has been worth it. "Sixteen acres to be cleared and cultivated," the grant declared. There was lots to do, but as his mother had said, if there's one thing you do not lack, it's motivation.

And then Mary Ann would one day, perhaps a day not too far off, marry him.

Their mothers had been plotting it. It was so obvious. At first, he wanted to run a million miles away. But in the last year or so, he could see the advantages. He liked Mary Ann. They hadn't really known each other that well on Norfolk Island, but there was a shared understanding of what it was like to be forced from one island and deposited on another. Mary Ann appeared very maternal with her younger siblings. And the reality was there were not many other young women of marriageable age around.

But it was Eliza and David's wedding last year that changed things. Mary Ann was different. Her long brown hair, tinged with golden flecks in the sunlight, was plaited and shaped into a knot, exposing a pale slender neck above a simple elegant dress. George felt a strange combination of familiarity and newness about her. Her little sister Margaret was not clinging to her legs all the time, and George had a chance to see her as herself, older, fifteen, she said. He liked what he saw.

He could see his mother and Ann Sydes smiling and exchanging looks. Mary Ann was not immune to this pressure either. She leaned in to speak to him conspiratorially.

"They can't help themselves," she said.

Her blue eyes twinkled with mischief. And she smelt wonderful. For the rest of the day his eyes followed her, and he tried to regain her attention whenever possible. He realised he was probably being quite obvious, but it wasn't as if he was doing the wrong thing.

She confided in him that she sometimes tired of being the big older sister, always on hand to help with her younger siblings. And she lingered a little, just to talk to him, more than before. Was that something? Or was he imagining it, caught up as they were in family celebrations?

When he stood on his new land for the first time a few months ago, he found himself wondering how much it would please Mary Ann to see it.

But yesterday was awful. He could still see her crying softly as they buried her mother. They did it quickly, the hot weather that preceded this cold change making it essential. The whole family, friends and neighbours, were in shock.

At the wake afterwards, he tried to offer her comfort. She had never seemed vulnerable before, and he felt a new protectiveness towards her, though frustratingly they didn't get any time alone. He knew now that he wanted to marry her. But her father needed her more than ever, so the chance that it would happen any time soon, was remote. It only intensified his desire.

Here, in the last few days before Christmas, he stood upon his land again, thinking, planning, hoping. That next year would be his year.

Some pink galahs flew overhead. They settled in a gum tree and laughed away at him as he slowly twirled around to take in all the view, stopping where he could see the riverbank below. If I build up here, he mused contentedly, I'll never get flooded. He calculated where he would clear and start planting, considering how high any flooding might reach. Out of the corner of his eye he saw Umarrah, Parwareter and Trepanner approaching from the south. Yanked from his contemplation by their sudden appearance, he did not know how to break the news that he now had land of his own. News he'd avoided sharing. As the trickle of free settlers settling on larger grants became a flood, he worried it wouldn't be a welcome topic.

"I didn't expect to see you," he blurted.

"My mother is no better," Umarrah replied. "We may not make it to Yinginner this summer."

"I'm sorry to hear she's not improving," replied George. "Will you stay by the river?"

"Yes, she's not strong enough for the climb to the mountains."

He imagined Luwanna had been overwhelmed with the shock of Largenna's death, on top of Planobeena's kidnapping. Umarrah didn't really talk much about his mother. The fact that he said this much meant he was really worried.

"That's really awful, Umarrah," said George.

They looked at each other.

"How did you know where to find me?" asked George, changing the subject.

"We went to Gibson's but he told us where to find you. Why you here?" asked Umarrah, gazing at the sweeping view.

George gulped and decided to get it over with. "I've been granted this piece of land," he replied.

Umarrah's head swivelled. Something about his penetrating gaze made George suspect that he knew this was coming. Parwareter and Trepanner tensed and drew in on either side of him.

"How much land?" he asked.

Flustered, George stretched out his arm. "From the riverbank here, to there, along there and back to the river," he pointed. "It's not a lot, just sixty acres." Three pairs of eyes followed, then silence.

"It's plenty enough though, isn't it?" came the disapproving reply. "This Macquarie fella give it to you, did he?"

"Yes," George mumbled.

"Why you not tell me this before?"

"Because I haven't seen you to tell you. And because I thought you'd be angry." He sighed. "Look, I don't want much, just somewhere small of my own. God knows I've worked hard for Joseph and for David, as have you all," he said, adding the last few words hastily. "But I just want my own place. And compared to what David's now got, it's nothing."

"What has David got?" interrupted Umarrah.

"More land. That boundary on the northern side is the start of his and Eliza's one hundred acres. But he's also been given another seven hundred acres further along the river." He waited, unsure whether the numbers were sinking in.

"That's big land," replied Umarrah, his voice quiet, ominous.

George looked at him anxiously. "Yes, it is."

Parwareter prodded Umarrah for a translation. George winced as he watched his and Trepanner's reactions.

"Why has he been given so much?"

George stared into the distance, and shrugged. "Perhaps because my sister has a child by the Norfolk Island governor, or that she and David have a growing family of their own, or perhaps he's just good at knowing the right people, I don't know."

George could hear jealousy in his own words. He pushed the acknowledgement aside.

"Whitefellas taking more and more of our Country. Moorronnoe and Teennermairrerkoonner, these rivers, Country, they important to us," asserted Umarrah.

"I know. But as I said, my grant is small," George protested.

Umarrah imitated George's gesture and swept his arm in a cynical wide arc from the blue-hazed Tiers in the west down to the southern plains. "This, our Country, we belong to it," he declared. He turned to George. "Whitefellas cannot give it to themselves. What will you pay us for using it?" he asked.

"You know I'll give you what I can," George replied. "It's just I can't yet, I haven't got anything."

Umarrah appeared unmoved.

"Look, I don't want to fall out with you," argued George. "It's just a small place of my own. I've been Joseph's, then David's, slave for years."

Trepanner turned and walked away, Parwareter flicking a glance at Umarrah and then following.

Umarrah looked at George, opened his mouth to say something, but decided against it.

"I'm sorry," pleaded George. He couldn't tell what had given the most offence – that he'd not confessed his grant earlier, the size of Eliza and David's grants, or the increasing amount of land being taken up by the settlers overall.

A grim smile briefly passed over Umarrah's face.

"I am too," he replied and walked away.

George watched him go. He really needed Umarrah's help to work the land, but wondered now if he would ever get it.

CHAPTER ELEVEN

May 1821 – Panninher country

Since those angry words, their first, Umarrah stayed away, despite knowing George needed a lot of help. He couldn't bring himself to reward him for what he'd done – getting the land and keeping it secret. So he ruminated. One day he nearly went back to tell George that Joseph had admitted he'd tried to shoot him. But at the last minute he changed his mind.

He used the time to watch over his mother. Gradually Luwanna seemed to improve. Resting on the plains beneath the watchful towering gaze of Koorparoona Niara was the right decision, the local Panninher clan having readily given permission for their small group to stay, and not make the summertime climb to the plateau.

It was Luwanna who suggested he go back. He knew she could see his conflict, exactly as she'd predicted. So he did. He realised he was always going to. There was too much to lose if he didn't. George was relieved to see him again and grateful for any help. He was struggling on his own. Joseph appeared occasionally. George's friend Kennedy, in awe of George having his own land at eighteen, worked a few days. David appeared a few times, but with all his own new land to manage, it appeared he had little time. Umarrah was aghast as he saw how much David was accruing.

Parwareter, Trepanner and Umarrah began helping George to clear some land and build a small stable and hut.

And they were soon rewarded, though not by George. Elizabeth visited one day, and came with news. The Governor would be visiting from Sydney. The whitefella Macquarie, their leader who gave away land that was not his to give, was going to be travelling through the island, and staying with the Gibsons.

Since then, there had been much discussion amongst the clan about what to do. George had revealed that in fact Macquarie would be staying with David and Eliza twice, firstly when heading north to the Launceston settlement at Kunermurlukeker and again on the return trip south. So there were two opportunities, but no decision had been made as to how to exploit them.

While working on George's stable roof, Umarrah's thinking was interrupted as David came hurtling towards them on his horse, leapt off, and without any greeting, asked for George. Deciding to overlook David's rudeness, but not acknowledging him either, Umarrah peered down to the stable floor just as George emerged into the daylight.

"George," David panted, "A big surprise for you. Governor Macquarie will be passing by here shortly." Having delivered this unexpected news, he bent over to catch his breath. George, in contrast, gasped. Umarrah looked past both of them to see two carriages and a group of men on horseback heading towards them at a leisurely pace.

"They coming, George," he said.

David glanced quickly behind him. "We're on our way to Woolmers. With Macquarie are Sorell and Mrs Macquarie, Archer, Cox, and a few others. This is your chance to impress him, George. Be profuse in your thanks for your land."

George swallowed.

"And Umarrah, you should go," David ordered, jerking his head in the direction of the stables.

Umarrah's eyebrows shot up.

"You can't be seen!" hissed David. "Go – now!"

Umarrah glared at him, and waited for George to intervene. But George was still taking it in and all he got was an apologetic look. Determined to still view the proceedings, Umarrah withdrew, unsure who he was more angry with, George for failing to stand up to David's command, or David for making it.

He strode to the stable and watched from inside the doorway.

A carriage soon bounced and jerked towards them, coming to a stop at the half-completed cottage. A woman sat in the carriage, covered in so many layers of clothing that even her face and hands were barely seen. She gazed around, pointing out items of interest to a boy seated beside her. The boy attempted to get down but she restrained him. Umarrah turned his gaze to the thickly dressed men astride their horses as they sat, slightly apart, chatting amiably. The other men, soldiers he guessed from their sameness of coverings, looked bored, their horses also appearing restless to continue.

David marched a nervous George up to one of the riders, who looked away as they approached and spoke firmly to the boy in the carriage. He turned back and looked down at David and George. David deferentially introduced George to the man, whose grey, almost white hair, contrasted with his thick dark eyebrows. He cast a small eye over George's building efforts to date and simply nodded. George stumbled a few words of appreciation, and the man replied with less. There was a slight pause. The man called out over his shoulder "Which way, Archer?" and then the group began to move on. David spoke briefly to George before running to his horse, mounting and catching up with the other riders.

Umarrah waited a few moments then walked up to George, who was still watching the departure of his unanticipated visitors. Neither spoke.

"So, that was Macquarie?" asked Umarrah.

"You saw him?"

"Yes, I not going to miss seeing the man who thinks he can give away plenty land."

George tensed. "I'm sorry," he said. "About before, I mean. It caught me unawares. I never thought they'd come this way."

He paused.

"I can't do anything about Macquarie."

But you didn't have to take his land, thought Umarrah. He ignored the apology and allowed George to feel awkward for a few moments, then let it go.

"I seen Macquarie before," he announced.

"Really? When?" exclaimed George, astonished.

"A long time ago. He came here with a few other whitefellas, and that woman. They looked around for a while and then left. We watched them head to Kunermurlukeker."

"You followed them to Launceston!" gasped George.

"Some of our men did, yes."

"Actually, that makes sense. I heard Macquarie came here ten years ago, two years before we arrived."

"So, we thank him for you come here," replied Umarrah.

"I think so," said George, feeling rattled.

"Will he go now?"

"Head back south? No, my understanding is they will stay one more night at David and Eliza's."

That was what Umarrah hoped to hear. A plan was forming. Later that night they finalised it, though he insisted on doing it alone so as to present the least threat and risk of overreaction.

He headed off early, and was outside the Gibsons' as the sun rose. A clear late autumn day sparkled. Umarrah watched the house closely. He would insist on an introduction with their leader. It was just a matter of timing.

The sun rose higher and slanted its long angled rays on the crisp ground. His stomach grumbled. They emerged from the house, a smaller group than yesterday. No carriage, no women. They mounted their horses, David included. Umarrah melted further into the trees and watched as the group headed north at a leisurely walk.

Their slow pace made them easy to follow. After a while it was clear that they were heading for Moorronnoe. He swung around the group, and hidden by bush on the eastern bank, overtook them.

The group paused on the river's edge. Macquarie spoke to the foreman. Another man seemed to be writing furiously. Then Macquarie made a speech. "I name this village Perth!" he exclaimed ceremoniously at the end of a short speech. Three cheers rang out. After a few minutes of jovial discussion, they turned the horses and started to retrace their steps.

Some of the soldiers were given permission to canter back towards the Gibsons'. David did not join them, preferring to remain at the Governor's side as they headed back at a gentle pace. Umarrah flitted through the trees, keeping slightly ahead of their progress.

The moment came. He let them get as close as possible, then emerged from behind the closest tree and approached David's horse. "I want to speak with Macquarie," he demanded. Macquarie, on David's other side, leaned forward to see Umarrah's face. David's head swivelled from Umarrah to the Governor. A soldier, who had been following at a short distance, kicked his horse to a gallop and raced towards Umarrah with his whip raised.

"No!" cried David. "There is no need for that, sir. I know this man. Let me talk to him." Macquarie issued a swift order and the soldier diverted his horse to the Governor's other side, but kept his whip at the ready.

David turned to Macquarie. "Please go ahead, your Excellency, and I will catch you up."

Umarrah and Macquarie's eyes met, and measured the other.

Macquarie turned to David. "Thank you, Gibson," he said, and broke into a trot. The soldier followed.

Umarrah watched them go, furious at being thwarted.

David glared down at him. "How dare you approach the Governor!" he hissed. "What could you possibly hope to gain from such an action?"

"He is your leader. He is giving whitefellas, like you, much land," Umarrah retorted. "But it is not his land to give! We saw him last time he come here. He must speak with us this time, and pay for using the land."

Shock and disbelief rendered David speechless. He glanced ahead to see that Macquarie had stopped and was watching them.

"You fool, Umarrah," he growled. "You will never get an audience with the Governor this way." He paused. "I've paid you, and generously."

"You pay us for our work. Not for taking the land. Macquarie must understand this."

"You have no right to dictate terms to the Governor," lashed David.

He lifted his head, drew the reins tightly, and turned his horse. "Go home" he ordered, "and don't ever expect to work for me again."

Umarrah watched him gallop away to join Macquarie, who was still observing them intently. His only chance of forcing a conversation with the invasion's leader had gone.

Hovering around him was the power and utter disdain wielded by Macquarie. Umarrah shook himself in an attempt to fling it away. He considered David's words, his tone. He was not now surprised at George's lack of courage.

It was a chilling thought.

He looked ahead. David turned and glanced back at him. At least we know now what we are facing, thought Umarrah. There is much for me to share.

He met David's gaze, then Macquarie urged his horse on and they rode away.

CHAPTER TWELVE

September 1822 – Norfolk Plains

George stood up from the barley planting and stretched his back. Once again he scanned the area where the South Esk and Macquarie Rivers flowed from the south, looking for campfire smoke. And this time there it was, thin wisps heading skyward on the cool September afternoon. They were back from wintering on the east coast.

He had news for Umarrah. There'd been a possible sighting of his sister.

Therein lay the angst, thought George. How will he react when I tell him? Am I giving him false hope?

He'd talked about it with Mary Ann. In terms of what to do next. It raised more questions than answers, but they had to share what they knew. The discussion had made Umarrah seem real to her, helping to smooth the apprehension she had about meeting him when George, after their wedding, revealed the acquaintance. He'd acknowledged the longevity of the relationship and had stressed how much Umarrah, Parwareter and Trepanner's labour had helped him get set up. He was not surprised when she was taken aback. Like many Norfolk Island families, hers had stayed close to the river and clung to their exiled community. Girls in particular were not encouraged to explore their surroundings, and contact with Aboriginal clans moving seasonally was ignored or avoided.

George headed down to the riverbank. There'd been dark clouds to the south in recent days and he was conscious to check the river's height. Old habits died hard. But it looked good, and reassured, he started trudging back uphill. As he passed the hut's open door he smiled as Mary Ann's singing wafted into the air. The notes enveloped him and he paused, filled with images of their two months of married life. Their wedding night, and the nights afterward. The days of melding together their few possessions as well as their hopes and shared secrets in a space of their own. Hesitancy and awkwardness in every way at the start. It had been a cold winter, but she had brought kindness and warmth. He hoped for more to come.

Turning his thoughts back to work, he reached the barley as a familiar voice shouted his name.

He turned to see Umarrah approaching.

"I saw you'd arrived," said George when Umarrah reached him.

"Taken long time. Much rain on the journey," Umarrah replied.

"What are the river levels like upstream?" asked George.

Umarrah smiled. "It's okay, George. You no need to worry." He turned his gaze to the sheep and cattle, and George watched him noting the increase in numbers and the new fencing.

"You working hard," was the comment.

"Very hard," he acknowledged.

"George?" called out Mary Ann.

"Over here," he shouted. He turned to Umarrah. "There's someone I'd like you to meet." Mary Ann rounded the side of the cottage, saw them standing together, and froze, her eyes wide. Her gaze flickered across to George, then, after a few seconds, she wiped her hands on her apron, and walked towards them.

"Mary Ann, this is Umarrah," said George. "Umarrah, this is my wife, Mary Ann." There was a pause then Mary Ann, tentatively, held out her hand.

"Hello," she said. Umarrah looked at her extended hand, took it and shook it gently.

"Hello," he replied.

George watched her take in Umarrah's thick, shoulder-length reddish brown ringlets. She searched his eyes, nearly obscured by his heavy ringleted fringe. Her gaze travelled to his wide shoulders, the shine to his brown skin, and the large fur slung over one shoulder and down his torso.

"I wondered who had called out to you, George," she mumbled.

"I can imagine," he smiled.

Mary Ann turned to Umarrah. "Would you like some water, or tea?" she asked.

"Have you eaten?" added George.

"Not much today," Umarrah replied.

"I'll go and prepare something," said Mary Ann. " Excuse me," she said to Umarrah and headed back inside.

They watched her go.

"You been *very* busy George," Umarrah chuckled. George stared down at his feet.

"When you meet her?" he asked.

"Oh I've known her a long time. Our families came out from Norfolk Island together. Her mother died a while back and her father has moved to George Town. He's a blacksmith."

Realising he was prattling on, George stopped. Umarrah said nothing and George noticed that his eyes were distant.

Inside, they found Mary Ann busy making tea and warming up leftover stew. George threw a couple of logs on the fire. Umarrah noticed a large bed had been added to one corner, partly obscured by a curtain. They sat at the table that was now covered by a white cloth and surrounded by more chairs than at his last visit. Mary Ann poured tea. George noticed Umarrah watching her hand shaking slightly.

As they ate, mostly in silence, George decided to raise the subject.

"We have something to tell you," he announced. Umarrah looked up. George hesitated. "There's been a possible sighting of Planobeena."

"What you mean?" Umarrah replied.

"Mary Ann has heard something," continued George. "I'll let her explain."

"That's right, I heard something," she stumbled, "but I didn't see anything myself."

Umarrah's eyes narrowed.

"It might be nothing, of course, but it's about that Mr Hardwicke, the one they're saying is going to be made Chief Constable."

"What about Hardwicke?" asked Umarrah.

"I heard gossip that he's had a native girl in his household. For a while, apparently. They say there's even been a painting done of her."

"Did they say her name?" blurted Umarrah.

"They said her name is Fanny. Fanny Hardwicke."

"They give her a whitefella name," argued Umarrah.

"Possibly," said George, unsure.

"How long you know this?" asked Umarrah.

Mary Ann took a sip of her tea. "I heard about it around the time of our wedding," she recalled. "Later George told me about your sister and I wondered if it was the same person."

"So, two months," George added.

"It could be her," said Umarrah.

"Possibly," said George.

"Where this Hardwicke live?"

"Let me talk to David," George replied, sidestepping the question. "He's coming over in the next day or so."

"David! He won't help," thundered Umarrah.

"I know you probably don't want him involved. But he's becoming friendly with the big landholders and he could try and find out more about how this girl came to live with them." George paused. "I wouldn't find out anything just turning up there and asking. They don't know me and they'd get suspicious."

"You asked David about Planobeena long time ago. He didn't help then, so why now?"

"True," George conceded. "But David's got influence as well as land. Having people like Macquarie to stay, will give you that. If he asked questions, carefully and tactfully, he'll likely get the information you want."

Umarrah scowled.

"I'll see what else I can find out," offered Mary Ann. "People love to gossip."

"I think we go over there, to this Hardwicke place," demanded Umarrah.

"I've told you – we can't just do that," argued George.

Umarrah stood up.

"Tell me where they live, George."

There was an awkward silence. George looked at Mary Ann, whose face had turned pale.

George stiffened. "No, we need to think this through. If it is her, it's even more important that we tread carefully. If she's been with this family all this time, they're not just going to give her up."

Umarrah's thunderous expression suggested immediate action was the only option.

"And I'm sorry to say this, but are you sure she would recognise you, or even want to come back?"

"She knows me, I'm her brother."

"Think what this could mean for your mother," pressed George. "If there's any chance it's Planobeena, for her sake as well we must think very carefully about what to do."

Umarrah's anger suddenly evaporated.

"She is dead," he finally said.

"Oh my God, I'm so sorry," George whispered.

"She never hear about Planobeena. And she miss my, our, father. She been sick longtime."

Umarrah walked over to the door, opened it and stood looking out at the fading light. George hesitated. He turned to see Mary's Ann's cheeks wet with tears. This is close to the bone after her own mother's death, he thought. But that was not a death cruelled by years of waiting, of concurrent grief, hope and longing. Of giving out in the end, just before this news came through.

Things might be tantalisingly close. But there was also doubt, and danger.

Umarrah wiped his eyes and came back to the table. His eyebrows lifted slightly as Mary Ann sniffed and blotted her face with a handkerchief.

"I'm sorry," she whispered.

He nodded. "I go now," he said.

"Umarrah?" called George.

Umarrah stopped at the doorway but did not turn around.

"We are very sorry about your mother. I will do everything I can about Planobeena, but we must be careful," he said.

Umarrah walked out into the night.

"The timing of all this is so cruel," said George, as they stared blankly into the fire afterwards.

"Do you think you should have told him where the Hardwickes are?" Mary Ann asked.

"No. Even though he'd probably, and quite safely, stake the place out first to see if he saw her, it's what would happen after that if she *is* there that's the worry. If he, alone or with others, confronted the Hardwickes, I've no idea what could happen."

"Would he start searching all the local properties by himself?"

"Possibly, but even with Parwareter and Trepanner's help, and maybe others, and even discounting the settler farms where he already knows who lives where, there's still too many places. He knows that."

George sighed. "I'll talk to David and see if he'd be prepared to help."

"Umarrah may come back again tomorrow and demand again that you tell him. I would if I was him," said Mary Ann.

"I know."

"George, why did he react so angrily when you first suggested asking David?"

"I don't know. I think something happened when Macquarie was here. Neither of them will tell me, but Umarrah has not worked for David since. He was mainly helping me by then anyway, but after that time, the look on his face if David's name was mentioned or how he'd react when David came over, it was a definite change."

"So if the Hardwickes do have his sister, what then?" asked Mary Ann.

"I have no idea," replied George. "I've heard of a few settlers who've adopted Aboriginal children. No one really talks about how they came to be supposedly orphaned. What's the possibility of a family member appearing and wanting to take them back?"

He shrugged.

"What a mess," said Mary Ann.

CHAPTER THIRTEEN

January 1825 – Panninher country

Koorparoona Niara's mountains, covered in their eucalyptus-infused grey-blue, beckoned Umarrah to make the summer pilgrimage. His gaze lingered at the slope where the familiar stream they always followed would be tinkling its way to the plains below. He could almost taste the chilled water that had always refreshed many a dry mouth, and smell the leafy grove where tired legs rested during the climb.

But they would not be going this summer. Travelling now meant frequent detours around whitefella buildings, fences and hedges that blocked their usual routes, and crucially, access to water and food sources. It seemed like new routes had to be found almost every time a journey began. After a short debate, the decision was made. Instead of heading to Yinginner, the local clans would join up and go to Kunermurlukeker, where beside the river their large group hoped they would find food in Launceston.

And blankets, he thought, as he walked amongst them. Thin skins were draped over people's shoulders, insufficient for the cold of the next winter.

His eyes met several others as he automatically scanned for any sign of her. After the failure of the potential sighting two years earlier, he clung to the only certainty – that they didn't know for sure that it *wasn't* Planobeena at the Hardwickes'. Although George had consistently refused to reveal the Hardwicke farm's location, he had fulfilled his promise and talked to David. David, in turn, had uncovered that the Hardwickes did have an Aboriginal girl in their household. He'd confirmed her given name was Fanny Hardwicke, but the family would not say when or how she came to be there. Then they had moved away to other land they'd been given on the north coast. David was of the opinion that if Charles Hardwicke was made Chief Constable, he would be back, closer to Launceston. Despite the appointment being announced, and Hardwicke often now being in town, his family and household rarely accompanied him.

So stop thinking you might see her here, Umarrah rebuked himself, though his eyes and ears disobeyed him.

Once ready, they set off, a two-hundred-strong group of Tyerrernotepanner, Panninher and his own clan, the Leterremairrener. After walking for several hours, they reached Launceston, and soon after, it was clear the visit was a mistake. Heading for fresh water at Kunermurlukeker's riverbank, Umarrah saw the faces of the townspeople, and read shock and fear on the vast majority of them. "They're frightened by our numbers," he cautioned. "It's not safe." They dispersed along the river bank to make camp, hoping that smaller family groups would appear less threatening. But it was an uneasy night. A few townspeople provided meat and potatoes, and a small number of blankets. But other whitefellas huddled by torchlight in muttering groups, the occasional abusive shout piercing the warm night air.

The sun had barely risen when news spread that one of the women had been raped. It was unclear whether she had strayed from the main group, or been abducted from her sleeping place. But her distress, and that of her family, reverberated through them all. The threat of more violence was evident. With hasty agreement, they packed up and headed out of town, the sense of urgency palpable. Then at a slower place, they began to traverse the riverplains between Moorronnoe and Lakekeller. Suddenly loud cracking sounds rang out. The group began to disperse in panic, people falling, others screaming or paralysed in fear. Umarrah searched frantically for the source of the gunfire, but it was over in seconds as their invisible attackers melted away.

His heart pounded as he heard cries of pain, and he raced to join the search for casualties. But relief and astonishment washed over him as they discovered no-one had been shot.

A few people, including Trepanner's mother, had been injured in the fleeing crush of people, and would need help to keep moving. They needed a safe place to rest and recover before heading up to the plateau, detours or not. It was the only place reliably without the invaders.

As the group edged southwest, moving to the pace of the slowest person, Umarrah and Parwareter discussed their attackers' goal. It was clear it was to terrorise. And they'd achieved it. After an initial burst of adrenalin-fuelled energy, fear of what might happen next was draining them. They needed a safe place to rest, and soon. Umarrah could only think of one option. They would head to George's farm.

There was debate as to whether George would provide assistance, given the large size of their group, but there was general acknowledgement that in the absence of any other plan, it was worth trying. They would head for the ford and wait there, while Umarrah went ahead to speak with George.

Moorronnoe's level at the ford was low. The group spread out to rest, some keeping careful watch. Umarrah plunged his feet into the river and bent down to drink greedily. He tried to assess its depth, hesitated then started wading. Reaching the far bank sooner than he'd hoped, he hauled himself out and then started running.

Arriving at the farm gate a short while later, he stopped to catch his breath. George saw him as he was walking across the yard and came straight over.

"You're in a rush," quipped George. Umarrah did not reply.

"What's happened?" he asked, looking worried.

"Whitefellas shooting at us."

"What?" blurted George. "When was this?"

"Today, after we left town. We went there yesterday but they attack one of our women. Then whitefellas shoot at us after we leave."

"Is anyone hurt?"

"Four people. George, we need somewhere to stay tonight. We are down by the ford, but that maybe not safe. Can we come here? Tomorrow we will go to Yinginner."

George swallowed. Umarrah noticed the briefest of hesitations. "Yes, of course come here," replied George. "We'll do whatever we can to help."

"Thank you – I go back and bring them," replied Umarrah.

"How many people are with you?"

"Many."

George opened his mouth to reply but Umarrah had already turned around.

He signalled from the riverbank and the crossing began. The injured, frail or young were carried. As they headed towards the farm, Parwareter reported that some people were not convinced of the wisdom of the decision. Asking for help from a whitefella, even one that could apparently be trusted, was a bad idea.

Umarrah moved to the front as they neared the farm. The group came to a halt and watched as Umarrah walked ahead to George and Mary Ann, who stood at their gate in shock at the large number of people before them. Then Elizabeth appeared in the doorway with her new granddaughter in her arms. Also stunned at the scene before her, she stood transfixed.

"There must be well over a hundred people!" gasped Mary Ann. "George, if these people have been attacked, how do we know they won't exact retribution on us?" When he failed to respond, she ran to her mother-in-law, grabbed baby Annie, and disappeared inside the cottage, slamming the door behind her.

Elizabeth walked up to Umarrah and George. "You're a very large group," she said. "I think it's overwhelmed her."

Umarrah nodded.

"We don't have much food," George protested. "I have some mutton to hand out but we'll need to slaughter a few more. We can certainly make rounds of damper to start, and of course tea."

"Thank you – we will hunt also," Umarrah replied.

"Are you sure that's wise?" interjected George. "I think you should stay here – you don't want to be seen."

"You're right," Umarrah conceded.

"Spread out wherever you like," said George. "The injured are welcome to use the barn. There's plenty of hay in there. I'll bring out as many buckets as I can spare for you to get water for everyone. The woodpile is full too, so help yourself. Is there anything else you need?"

"No, that's plenty. Thank you, George," he replied, anxious to get everyone settled.

"Umarrah?"

"Yes?"

"Stay as long as you need."

George and Elizabeth watched as the group flowed onto the farm and began to disperse. Umarrah, Parwareter and others distributed firewood, and small campfires soon began to glow as the air cooled with the gathering dusk. The injured, including Trepanner's mother, refused the barn and lay on blankets by a larger fire in front of the cottage.

Later, as Umarrah was helping to distribute mutton, he heard raised voices and saw flaming torches beyond the farm gate. A few minutes later, George walked up to him as the lights faded into the distance.

"This is a large group of people. A few settlers were ... concerned," reported George.

"Maybe they were the ones who shoot at us, George," Umarrah replied angrily.

George's voice was tense. "They demanded to know why I was helping you, and for how long."

"I told you earlier – we will go in the morning."

"And I said you can stay as long as you need. It's just a shock for some of my neighbours."

Umarrah grimaced. "Shock for us too. We go in the morning."

"I'm sorry," said George.

"For what? You didn't do it George," Umarrah replied.

"I know but I'm sorry anyway. Where will you go?" he asked.

"To the mountains," Umarrah replied.

The next morning's dawn promised a day of warmth and summer sun as if to mock yesterday's horror. The group slowly gathered itself in readiness for the journey southwest to the mountain pass of Koorparoona Niara. It would be a slow climb up to Yinginner.

Umarrah and George walked at the rear of the group. "Maybe *you* have enemies now, George," Umarrah warned.

"You could be right," replied George.

For a moment they tried to read beyond the sleeplessness in each other's face. Then Parwareter called out and it was time to go. Perfunctory goodbyes were exchanged.

As they moved through the next, slow, stage of their journey, Umarrah was increasingly consumed by a frustrated desire for retribution. But how to go about it, eluded him.

Then an opportunity arose.

Rounding a small hill, they spied ahead two whitefellas sawing wood. The group instinctively edged away, closer to the river, but for Umarrah, it was one detour too many.

All might have been well had they not been seen. The sawyers followed them and shouted abuse at the rear of the group.

Umarrah froze.

He and Trepanner peeled away from the group, edged around to a vantage point and waited.

Having vented their spleen, the sawyers headed back to their camp and took a break.

Umarrah and Trepanner left the scene, their spears, having found their mark, still quivering, and raced to catch up with the others.

CHAPTER FOURTEEN

June 1825 – Norfolk Plains

The Great Western Tiers hurled a fierce, icy wind across the plains, battering George as he rode home. By the time he reached the point of turning for the ford, he couldn't feel his fingers. After looking up at the feeble rays cast by the sun, he made a quick decision and turned his horse towards the inn, lured by the promise of a warm fire, warm food and the chance to open the letter he carried and digest its contents.

The bleak weather matched his dread. Six months had passed since his second land application would have reached the authorities. As the weeks and months had dragged on, his confidence had leached away. At least the wait was nearly over.

After reaching the inn and hastily tying up his horse, George walked stiffly towards the entrance, above which a sign emblazoned 'The New River' rattled in the wind. Pulling open the door, he was immediately embraced by warmth. Faces inside scowled at the blast of cold air. George hurriedly shut the door and approached the bar. He ordered a drink and asked if someone could stable his horse. The barman nodded curtly, extended his hand for coin and George obliged. A reedy youth hovering nearby received instructions for the horse, and departed.

After gathering his drink George spied a seat at a table near the fire, thanked the barman and headed towards the warmth. He put his drink down and walked over to the fire to defrost his hands.

"Appalling wind out there," said a young man at the next table. Having no desire for company, George shut his eyes for a moment and sighed inwardly.

"Yes, it is," he replied. "I think my fingers have forgotten that they are attached to my body." He saw the young man smile and stretch out his hand. "Anthony Cottrell," he said. "Please join me. Gosh, you do need defrosting," he added as their hands met.

"George Collins. You must be new to the district. You have land nearby?"

"Yes, near the Nile River, not far from James Cox," said the newcomer. "I've been here less than a year, so it's early days. And you?"

"Our family's been here since 1813. I was granted my own sixty acres on the South Esk five years ago, south of the Perth punt."

"How is it going?" asked Cottrell.

"It was slow at first, but now my stock is bursting at the seams. I applied for another grant last December. Actually James Cox wrote in support of my application."

"Well that must be good, with Cox being a magistrate," replied Cottrell politely.

George grimaced. "I hope so."

"How many sheep and head of cattle do you have?" asked Cottrell.

"Five hundred sheep and eighty head of cattle, as well as oats and barley."

Cottrell whistled. "I don't know how you've fitted all that on sixty acres. That would be a problem I'd like to have, to be honest. My land is quite rocky. I might only be able to graze on it."

"How much have you got?"

"Six hundred and fifty acres."

Stunned, George's brain went into comparative calculation. That much land for a single man, and of similar age to him.

He struggled to reply as the door once again blew open, and Cottrell smiled in recognition. "John!" he called out.

The man waved, called out an order to the barman and headed towards them. He pulled a nearby chair over and sat down close to the fire. "Perishing out there," he announced. "John, this is George Collins," announced Cottrell. "George, this is John Batman. John's property is Kingston, south of here."

George leaned over and shook the newcomer's icy hand.

"George lives just south of the Perth punt," related Cottrell, "and he's doing well – bursting at the seams with his stock."

"I've applied for more land – just haven't heard anything," said George.

"James Cox has written in support though," added Cottrell.

Batman scrutinized George for a few moments before recognition dawned.

"So you're the George Collins who let the Blacks onto his land when they left Launceston."

Cottrell's head spun from Batman to George.

George's mouth was suddenly dry. "I am," he replied cautiously. "Why do you ask?"

Batman rolled his eyes. "Well for starters, I think Cox wouldn't have supported your application if he knew you'd do something like that."

George opened his mouth to defend himself but Batman continued. "I'm not surprised you haven't heard anything about your land, Collins. They probably won't even bother replying. There was widespread alarm at how many Blacks went to and from Launceston in January. Some people felt they had to send a message that no-one is to trespass on their land."

Cottrell looked at Batman. "John, you'd have to agree that as more and more land is being settled, that's problematic for the natives."

"And how will it help settlers if there is revenge violence by the Blacks?" said George, encouraged by Cottrell. "Don't you think there is a case to be made for helping them where we can, as some form of payment or compensation for the land we've taken? Even if it's just as an insurance policy against attacks?"

"So you've not heard about the murders of Booth and Arnold then. They may have only been convicts but they did not deserve to die at the hands of the natives," said Batman angrily.

Cottrell saw the colour drain from George's face, but Batman seemed not to notice.

"Cox and Barclay are furious that they've lost two valuable men, and Cox told me that the investigations are taking a heavy toll on him as a Justice of the Peace. I can only assume it is a revenge killing."

"I didn't know about this," admitted George, aghast. "But if the Aborigines hadn't been fired upon, this retribution might not have happened."

Batman looked thunderous. "If the Blacks hadn't been moving about in such a large group, no one would have felt threatened!"

"So you don't think they should move around as they please, even though we're the newcomers here?" retorted George.

"Was there any violence when you were first here, George?" asked Cottrell, trying to defuse things. "On the odd occasion, but there were far fewer of us then," replied George. "The amount of land being settled on is exploding. That's the problem, in my opinion."

"Look, we're all here to make the best of what we're given," Batman argued. "You've just said you want more yourself, Collins. There's obviously still plenty of land to go around."

George knew what Umarrah would make of that statement.

"How much have you asked for?" said Cottrell.

"One hundred acres."

"Well, in that case, you might just get it," smirked Batman. "It will hardly break the bank, as it were."

George wondered about the size of Batman's grant. He had a sinking feeling that it was sizeable.

Draining his glass, Batman suddenly got up. "Well, I must be off. I am sufficiently warmed up for the homeward stretch. Shall I see you next week Anthony?"

"Yes, John, thanks," he replied politely. "Collins," Batman nodded with reluctant acknowledgment, before striding towards the door.

Cottrell turned to George. "I should go too. I hope your ... assistance to the Aborigines ... doesn't impact on your application, George." He put his empty glass on the table. "John obviously wants to know who murdered Arnold and Booth."

"I understand that," George replied. "We should also be looking for those responsible for attacking the Aborigines."

Cottrell stood up. "Good luck, George."

George shook his hand, noting how Cottrell had avoided his last comment. He waited till Cottrell closed the pub door behind him then retrieved his letter.

Hastily opening it, he read quickly to the bottom, finding amongst the curved handwriting the good news he had barely dared to hope for.

He dropped the letter on the table as his face broke into a broad smile. It's time to savour the moment, he decided, and indulge in the changing of problems into possibilities.

Some time later, he glanced out the window and jumped when he saw the twilight sky. Hastily leaving the inn, he put his shoulder to the wind, urged his horse on and galloped for home. But guilt started to creep in with the cold. At some point he would have to tell Umarrah his news. The modesty of his request, in comparison to others' grants, would hopefully mollify Umarrah to some degree. Perhaps the grant's decision makers did not hear of his help to Umarrah and the Aborigines in January after all, or were not concerned if they had. As he replayed the conversation with Batman and Cottrell, more of Batman's words reverberated. Did he know who had shot at the Aborigines when they had left town? Was he one of them? And what about the two dead convicts? Could Umarrah have been involved in their murders, or have known who was?

The last few miles flew by as he tried to untangle his thoughts and prepare to deliver good news. He knew how much it would mean to Mary Ann, who had fretted as much as him. After arriving home, he ran across to the house from the stable just as stinging rain began to pelt down. Bursting through the door, he saw Mary Ann look up in relief that he was home.

"Good news!" he cried. "We're getting that one hundred acres!"

CHAPTER FIFTEEN

October 1825 – Panninher country

U marrah pulled the kangaroo skin tightly about him. Striding through a southerly spring gale, he hoped George would have some information about the new settlers arriving in alarming numbers and occupying huge tracts of land. He'd seen it first hand, having charmed his way last summer into working for one of them, Hugh Murray, who'd arrived with his brother David and their families. Umarrah had watched them from a distance and could tell they needed more pairs of hands. Hugh Murray was surprised when he turned up, but his reliable English and experience working with George and his family got him a job. He proved himself a reliable worker, did what was asked of him, kept his mouth shut, but his eyes open. The Murrays he found to be reasonable to work for. But there was no denying the fact that his home, the Country of his ancestors, was now being occupied without any apology, consideration, compensation or discussion, and on an unprecedented scale.

He turned his thoughts to Laoninneloonner, and gradually anger's heat softened into a golden warmth. He remembered the hasty rush to and up the mountains last summer, and his first sight of her as she stood among the clans who offered assistance after their traumatized group's arrival. The two of them gradually spent more and more time together, and as their feelings grew, so did their worry for an uncertain future. The only certainty they could acknowledge was that the whitefellas were not going away.

By the time the days began to draw in, they'd made their decision to be together. Laoninneloonner walked beside him down the pass to the plains below. In the months since, his gratitude for her had only deepened.

He was reluctant to be parted from her, but Parwareter and Trepanner had agreed to stay behind, protect their small group and keep watch over the settlers in the plains below. Before he left, Laoninneloonner knelt behind him by the campfire coals. Rubbing her hands together with a blend of wallaby fat and ochre, she expertly massaged the grainy mix into his skin and hair, mixing it with his ringlets. He breathed deeply and dropped his shoulders as she eased the tension from his upper back with circles of tenderness. Her hands glided from his back over to the broad expanse of his chest then temptingly down his abdomen. Her breath whispered tantalisingly in his ear and for a moment he was keen to be distracted. She read his mind and they laughed.

The wind now at his back dropped momentarily and the clouds moved on, uncovering the sun. He lifted his head to its pale rays and was grateful for the extra warming layer she'd expertly applied. He scanned the peaks of Koorparoona Niara which were shrugging off their snowy coverings, then watched the silver ribbon of Weetacenner as the river flowed towards its junction with Moorronnoe. They'd killed the two whitefellas just near there. Watched them for a while, thrown a firestick at the hut, waited till they'd run out on fire and screaming, then threw well-aimed spears to bring them down.

Four whitefellas killed. The first attack, a spontaneous act of revenge on the two sawyers, was different to this one. Outraged by the spreading invasion, Umarrah wanted the whitefellas to understand that their actions could not go unopposed.

Attacks would now be planned on the basis of knowledge gathered, and he hoped that here George would prove useful.

Arriving at the edge of the farm, he was pulled back into the memory of so many of them on that summer night, frightened, hungry and thirsty, huddling in a swathe of small groups. He remembered how he'd scanned the group for Planobeena before they'd departed for their fateful trip into the town. Now he was glad that she wasn't with them. Perhaps her life with the Hardwickes was better than what many of them were enduring.

He tried to imagine what she looked like now.

Then George was walking up to him.

They looked at each other, familiarity brushed with a little wariness.

"How are you?" asked George. "It's been a while."

"Yes," he replied. "How are you?"

George wiped his forehead with his sleeve. "Good. Have to fill the water troughs, then I'm done. Come with me?"

Umarrah nodded.

As they walked around, Umarrah noticed, in comparison to Hugh Murray, how small George's holding was, how tightly the sheep and cattle were packed together. With the remainder of the acreage taken up with crops, things were tight. He felt momentary regret for his anger when George announced his sixty-acre grant five years earlier. It was nothing compared to the Murrays'. He pushed the unexpected thought aside.

The troughs full, they headed inside. George built up the fire just as another spring downpour began to thud heavily on the roof.

Mary Ann looked shocked to see him. She said a brief hello in response to his greeting, before a few moments later bringing them steaming hot mugs of tea and a plate of damper. The memory of her frightened retreat into the house when their group sought shelter hung in the air.

"What have you been doing since I saw you last?" George asked.

"Working for a new whitefella," Umarrah replied.

"Really? Who?" replied George, surprised.

"Hugh Murray."

George shook his head. "I don't know the name."

Umarrah pointed southwards. "He come here with his brother and families. They take big land on Teennermairrerkoonner."

"The Macquarie River," said George to Mary Ann, who appeared reluctant to be drawn into the conversation.

"How did you get to work for him?" asked George.

"I watch them. They look hungry. I offer them two wallaby. Say I bring more. Say I want to work."

"So, are you here because you don't want to work for him anymore?"

"I do want to keep working for him, but I tell him I want to come to see you, since I know you longtime."

George hesitated. "We wondered how things had been after you left."

Umarrah chose his words with care.

"It look longtime to reach the mountains. We were near the river, the one you call Lake River. There were whitefellas there, chopping wood. They started shouting angry words at us."

"We heard about an attack on two sawyers in the paper," said George. "They were speared, but not killed."

Umarrah said nothing.

"Did you attack them?" asked George.

"We think they have guns and shoot us."

"So it was you."

"Yes."

Mary Ann gasped.

"Afterwards, I stayed away from here," Umarrah added, " to not bring you more trouble."

"Thank you for that at least," said Mary Ann in a flat voice.

Umarrah looked at her then returned his gaze to George. "You have any trouble since I was here?"

"No" replied George.

Umarrah nodded, then plunged on.

"This Murray, he has much land, much more than you, George."

George did not seem surprised.

"They are not the only ones. Many new whitefellas are taking big, big land. Do you know anything about this?"

George sighed. "I don't know much. I've only heard that Arthur is giving large grants to free settlers who are coming here with a lot of money. Not like it was with us Norfolk Islanders."

"So more will come?"

George hesitated. "I think it's possible, yes."

Umarrah clenched his fists. "This is getting bad, George.

After you came, you pay us, some of you, for using the land, and you make sure we can still pass through when we must."

"The new landholders aren't doing that?"

"No."

"I'm sorry to hear that," replied George. "I don't think there's anything I can do to help."

He looked up. "The rain's stopped. Could you help me do a few last things before dark?" he asked Umarrah.

Umarrah nodded and stood up. He had the sense that George wanted to get him out of the house.

Turning to Mary Ann, he asked. "Planobeena – have you heard anything?"

Mary Ann could barely look at him. "No, nothing," she whispered before gathering the cups.

In the lengthening twilight, they silently fed the animals. A child began to cry, softly at first, then in distress.

"Annie isn't well," George explained. "I need to help Mary Ann."

"I will go when this is done," Umarrah replied.

"You won't stay?"

Umarrah thought that would be the last thing Mary Ann would want. And George would know that.

"Just for supper, thanks."

"Fair enough."

He finished the chores before darkness fell, and sat on the fence for a few moments, gazing into the west. Deciding he would stay as briefly as possible, he walked towards the cottage. As his hand reached out to the door handle, the raised voices inside made him pause.

"We've no proof that Umarrah had anything to do with the murder of those two other men," argued George.

"They had names, George – Arnold and Booth!" Mary Ann flared. "Umarrah's admitted they speared those sawyers after they left here. It's quite possible he was involved in the murders as well!" she accused.

"The Aborigines had just been attacked and were just trying to get to safety," George argued. "And we don't know the sawyers didn't have guns."

Mary Ann did not seem convinced.

"And even then, it doesn't mean Umarrah has any link to the murders."

He changed tack. "The pace, and size of the land grants, especially along the Macquarie River, sounds worrying. Umarrah has confirmed what the papers have been saying. These new settlers are even bringing their own servants. They must be investing a lot in this."

"Do you think that's what holding up the surveyor?" Mary Ann asked.

"I don't know. But it's been four months and we're no closer to hearing where our new land will be. It would hardly take a surveyor that long to find a spot for a mere one hundred acres. Perhaps these rich settlers and their large grants have jumped the queue for the surveyor's attention."

"Well if you're right, it can only mean more waiting for us," she complained.

"I do hope not," George replied.

Umarrah's hand dropped from the door handle. They've been given more land! Considering everything they'd just discussed, he couldn't believe it. And yet, he admitted begrudgingly, George did need it. Compared to other settlers, it would still be small. He even understood George not telling him, given his reaction to the first grant. He'll have to tell me eventually though, he concluded.

But the deception still angered him. Yet unlike the clean rage he felt earlier in the day, this was different, murky. Why are you worrying about this whitefella's land problems? he berated himself. They only care because of the delay it means for them.

Think carefully, he told himself. Don't risk your welcome. I think George still trusts me, even if Mary Ann might not.

It appears that we each have our secrets, he concluded, as his anger subsided. But his appetite had also gone, for food or their company. Instead he craved Laoninneloonner's warmth, sharing with her, planning together.

Go in before it's too late to leave, he urged himself.

He pushed open the door. George looked up and smiled but his eyes were cautious. Mary Ann was by the stove. She did not look around but he saw her tense. The fire was blazing but Umarrah felt only the chill.

CHAPTER SIXTEEN

December 1826 – Norfolk Plains

"Have you decided whether you're going to raise it with David?" asked Mary Ann, as they sat out on the verandah. George's stomach clenched. We're both tired, he thought, reluctant to discuss things further after another long day of work plus Christmas preparations. He'd been dreading Christmas ever since Eliza had told them about David's overseer. How he'd shot four, possibly, five Aborigines, out at the Western Marshes. A long way west from Launceston. Apparently after they attacked him first.

"I'd like to see if he brings it up. Otherwise it will feel like I'm just out to accuse him."

"But when you spoke to Eliza, you did accuse him of not taking responsibility for it."

He frowned. "I know I did."

"I just don't want there to be a scene on Christmas Day," she continued. "I think that's understandable, don't you?"

"Eliza's bound to have told David what I said. I think a discussion will be unavoidable."

"Then have it between the two of you. I don't want to get involved," replied Mary Ann.

She looked over at their seven-month-old, little Libby, finally settled in her cradle after a feed. A brief smile flickered across her face.

"Let's just see how things go," he replied.

Christmas Day dawned with a piercingly blue sky. Mary Ann fed Libby during a particularly raucous dawn chorus from the wattlebirds, then put her back down to sleep just as the birds had concluded. She fell into a deep sleep beside George until they were woken by Annie chattering in her cot.

"It's going to be a hot one," announced George a little later, picking up their firstborn and heading for the door. "C'mon Annie. Let's check the ewes."

Mary Ann stole a few moments dozing before Libby woke again.

Three hours later, they were all packed and ready. "Here we go with the last of our precious cargo," he smiled as he lifted Annie up onto the seat and settled her beside her mother and Libby. He checked that the tray of food and homemade gifts were well stored then leapt up onto the seat, took the reins and flicked them to start the bullocks moving.

They settled into a rhythmic pace as they headed along the track for the short journey to the Gibsons'. Occasionally the carriage lurched and George clutched Annie. A screech of pink galahs flew overhead, settled in a tree and laughed at them. Annie pointed and laughed back.

"I imagine David's going to ask me about the grant," fretted George. "What will I say to him?"

Mary Ann sighed. "Since we've not heard anything ourselves, there's nothing to tell."

They rounded a bend and Pleasant Banks, the Gibson property, came into view. Soon they were pulling up in front of the house, and were swept up in the joy of Christmas greetings.

And there was no denying it, thought George, a little later. It felt good. Family, plenty of food, and summer sunshine. David and Eliza's hospitality was generous. And my mother, George observed, seems especially pleased to be surrounded by a growing number of grandchildren.

Later that afternoon, replete from Christmas lunch, George and David sat alone on the verandah.

David refilled his glass and with a nod from George, his as well. "Still no news about your grant?" he asked.

George grimaced at David's directness. "No," he reluctantly replied. "I can't understand why. It's eighteen months since Burnett approved the one hundred acres. I definitely should have heard from the surveyor by now."

David looked at George obliquely. "Are there any reasons you can think of for the delay?"

"No. But now I'm thinking I should have asked for more than a hundred acres. I've got so many animals that they're in danger of starving. I understated how tight things have become."

"Perhaps you should write again," suggested David.

"I'll have to. I don't know what else to do," George replied.

David nodded. "There's something else I'd like to discuss with you," he declared.

George braced himself for David's admission about his overseer and the murders of the Aborigines.

"Norfolk's land grant has come through," he announced.

"What grant?" George asked, having not been privy to any discussions about a land application for Eliza's son by a former Norfolk Island Commandant.

"Oh, I thought Eliza had told you we'd applied," said David.

"No, she hadn't," George replied, his stomach sinking. "How many acres did he get?"

"Five hundred, just across the creek from here."

Five hundred. The Gibson family's landholdings were getting bigger and bigger, while his own wait for a mere extra one hundred acres felt out of reach. Envy constricted his throat and he struggled to swallow his whisky.

"You must be very pleased," he croaked.

"We are, thank you. He is a lucky young man, my stepson," replied David. "And only eighteen years old."

As if sensing that a change of topic might be tactful, he picked up his newspaper.

"Did you see this?" he asked, offering it to George.

George took it and saw the blazing text written in capitals.

SELF DEFENCE IS THE FIRST LAW OF NATURE.
THE GOVERNMENT MUST REMOVE THE NATIVES –
IF NOT, THEY WILL BE HUNTED DOWN LIKE WILD
BEASTS, AND DESTROYED!

George threw the paper on the floor. "Yes, I'd read it. They'll have sold a lot of papers with these words, but it just inflames things," he argued. "How can they say, '*They look upon the white men, as robbing them of their land, depriving them of their subsistence, and in too many instances, violating their persons?*' Isn't that exactly what we've done?"

"I think the paper is only reflecting Arthur's proclamation and the fears of some settlers."

"David, some people will think these words give them permission to attack the Blacks whenever they want," countered George.

"Aborigines are attacking settlers and their property right across the island George! The proclamation just states that Aborigines who do that are 'open enemies' of the state."

"Is that what your overseer Baker thinks they are?" George shouted.

"Keep your voice down, George," David hissed.

"I will if you're honest about what happened."

David's shoulders dropped. "It's not really clear," he began. "I'm not the only landholder in the area. Simpson and Stocker also have men grazing their stock out there. Simpson has a man by the name of Knight, who Baker previously said has quite a lot of contact with the Blacks. We thought this meant he was friendly with them, but in fact Knight seemed to have no problem in killing them. It may be that the Aborigines decided that it was time for retribution and that Baker was a legitimate target as well. It's all very mixed up. Baker must have fired in self-defence and was probably quite outnumbered. He said he thought he shot four, maybe five of them, but there were no bodies."

"The Aborigines probably took their dead with them, if they could."

"That's possible," David conceded.

They sat in a strained silence, while the shrieks of children's laughter drifted across from the garden.

"Who else knows about this?" George asked.

"A surveyor called Henry Hellyer passed through a few days later, and he was told what happened."

"Has anything been done about it? Any investigation?"

"I've passed on Baker's evidence. Stocker's man also gave a statement to the magistrate. I know it's only their side of the story, but how can anyone get statements from the Blacks involved?"

"How soon after was it reported?"

"A while after," replied David vaguely.

"So too late to properly investigate." George couldn't hide his cynicism.

David made no comment.

"So our extended family is now implicated in the murder of innocent people," pressed George.

David glared at him. George watched him struggling to compose himself. The lines on his face were etched deeply and his eyes blazed with anger.

"It would be the Gibson name at risk, not yours," retorted David. "And talking of risk, have you not wondered whether the delay in your second grant might be because word has got around that you're ..." he paused, "sympathetic to the Blacks? Your behaviour has potentially compromised our families just as much as mine may have."

George leapt to his feet in fury. "How can you say such a thing David! I introduced you to Umarrah when you were desperate for labourers to build this house! You were happy enough to know him and his friends then."

"There is more at stake now," replied David coolly.

George forced himself to take a few deep breaths. Their conversation had turned out far worse than he had dreaded.

"Look David, no-one was ever punished for firing on the Aborigines when they passed through Norfolk Plains, if you remember. No-one. And if an investigation is not going to happen for an 'incident' close to Launceston, I don't think it will happen out at the Western Marshes." He pointed at the newspaper. "But it's comments like these that bode very poorly for the future."

"I can agree with you on that score," David replied stiffly.

CHAPTER SEVENTEEN

February 1827 – Panninher country

They crouched behind the whitefella hedge, listening to the cries of alarm. The second body had been found. Waiting for Umarrah's signal to move, their ears strained for any sign that the voices might be heading their way.

Whitefellas on their own looking after sheep and cattle were easy targets. The discovery of the first man had drawn neighbours away, and exposed the second as even more vulnerable. Umarrah allowed himself a grim smile, remembering the sounds he made as his breath left him and his blood watered the dry ground.

Refocussing his attention on the voices beyond the hedge, he waited a few moments longer, then signalled. They began to move. Trepanner and Parwareter crept to the creek and drank thirstily, still maintaining cover. Umarrah waited till last.

The whitefella fences and hedges had been tricky to negotiate, but he'd made allowances for the rerouting required in planning their exit. It would be dark soon, and then they could travel swiftly under its benevolent cover. They'd need to keep moving to be well clear of any reprisal parties. But by daybreak they should make it to their destination.

To George's. They needed somewhere to hide for the daylight hours, and with guaranteed food and water.

He wasn't entirely sure about the reception he'd get. The group had argued about it during the days spent observing the shepherds' movements. Lacklay had been particularly vocal in his opposition. But not for the reasons Umarrah expected.

"This man George. You fear us going there could bring trouble for him."

Umarrah raised his eyebrows at his young companion, standing before him tall and with growing still to come.

"We're attacking whitefellas, Lacklay. Do you think I care about the feelings of this one?"

"I think you like him. You said you know him longtime," he replied.

"He won't betray us, and he won't tell," Umarrah insisted.

He could tell Lacklay was not completely convinced. And he's right, Umarrah acknowledged. If my calculation is incorrect, the risk of dire consequences is great, for us, and for George.

Once they'd all quenched their thirst, they crept in single file behind the hawthorn hedge, the red glow of the sunset above them. The irony of a whitefella-made barrier assisting their escape was not lost on them.

In the middle of the night they rested briefly, having picked their way through another creek bed, nearly dry from the summer's heat. Umarrah couldn't sleep. He could still hear the shots and screams when they passed through this area on that fateful trip into Launceston two summers ago. Where were they all now? he despaired. Felled by disease, bullets, and grief. His mother included. Their faces had nearly disappeared from his memory.

He looked at his small group, drawn together in their fury against the increasing attacks on their people. These young men had bloody stories of their own, some shared, some not. If the whitefellas had not invaded, this group wouldn't even be here. They'd be with their clans and reaching manhood in the right time. They were too young really to be seasoned warriors. But he did not doubt their commitment.

The late summer dawn broke to reveal a cloudless pale blue sky, a blue that would deepen with the promise of another hot day. They'd made good progress but their pace was slowing. They reached Moorronnoe and forded it at the usual place, avoiding the Gibson farm and threading their way carefully towards George's. Umarrah motioned the others to wait behind some trees at the border of the farm, then he climbed the fence and headed warily towards the farmhouse.

Outside the barn, he saw George talking to a whitefella he'd not seen before. The man looked over George's shoulder, and froze. George turned around. "Umarrah!" he blurted.

"Hello George," said Umarrah quietly. The other man's eyes widened.

George turned around. "Thomas, it's alright. Remember what I told you. This is Umarrah. He and I have known each other a long time."

The other man nodded but said nothing, and did not take his eyes off Umarrah.

"George, we need help."

"Okay," replied George cautiously. "How many of you are there? Is anyone injured?"

Umarrah noted his expectation that they would be.

"No one hurt. Five of us – very tired, and hungry."

George's tone softened. "Come up to the barn," he offered. "I'll get some food." He gave instructions to Thomas, who disappeared into the cottage.

"Thank you," replied Umarrah. He shouted instructions of his own towards the trees, and waited for the others to emerge. As they did, George glimpsed one of them carrying a spear and waddy.

"What's going on?" he demanded.

"Nothing. We been hunting all night," Umarrah fudged. "I am sorry. They not bring spear or waddy here."

He barked an angry command. There was a short flurry of activity amongst the trees before the four of them re-emerged empty handed.

Umarrah smiled reassuringly at George, whose expression was now less welcoming.

Mary Ann emerged from the house, but stopped a few paces from the doorway. "It's alright," reassured George. "They're going to rest in the barn for a while." Thomas walked past her carrying a tray of food. Once they were all inside, he set it down and retreated to the barn door.

George watched them eating, noted the young faces amongst them, and tried not to imagine the circumstances that might have brought them to Umarrah's acquaintance.

"Find out who that is," said George to Thomas, at the sound of galloping hooves approaching, followed by a hasty stop. Thomas opened the barn door and stepped out into the yard.

"Get the master. It's urgent," barked a familiar voice.

George gave Umarrah a penetrating look then walked out. As the barn door slammed shut in front of them, Umarrah heard the words he dreaded.

"Bad news, George," David announced. "Two more murders."

They all stopped eating and were still, listening intently. They heard George shepherding David into the house. Umarrah began calculating. How quickly might George realise what had happened? If so, would he tell David they were here? Should they leave now?

"They know what's happened," said Umarrah, watching the others drop their food in panic. But they were trapped. They'd be seen if they tried to leave. With a sinking heart, Umarrah knew this news could be the deal breaker, and the years he and George had known each other might not be enough.

He could only hope that George would not betray them.

They waited in strained silence for the sound of human voices, and a short while later, heard George and David emerging from the house, and then the receding sounds of a horse's canter.

Footsteps marched over to the barn.

The door swung open and George stepped inside.

"Tell me what's going on," he hissed.

"Was that David?" asked Umarrah innocently.

George smirked. "You know it was. He came to tell me that two men were murdered near here late yesterday."

Umarrah said nothing. George looked at the others but they were also silent. He turned back to Umarrah.

"Do you know anything about it?"

There it is, thought Umarrah. The assumption.

"The dead men – are they blackfellas or whitefellas?" he retorted.

George looked stunned.

"It must be whitefellas. Would you ask me if it were black-fellas, George?"

"Did you kill them?" George insisted.

There was a long pause.

"Yes," answered Umarrah evenly.

George gasped.

"One of those men is a stock-keeper to James Hill, a friend of mine!"

"What about the whitefellas who shoot our people? Remember what happened near here two years ago?" he retorted.

"I haven't forgotten about that. But you don't know if these men – and their names were Spence and Fairley – were responsible for that attack."

"No, but does it matter? Too many of you whitefellas come here, take our land, and not only that, you kill us."

George was stung at his implied inclusion. Umarrah could see it, and almost regretted the words.

But he kept going.

"You are greedy too, George. I know about your new land. I hear you talk about it."

George reeled from the second shock, but then rebounded.

"I haven't got it, actually. The authorities have stalled. Looks like they might've found out I've helped you."

Umarrah wondered who would have told them.

"I don't have much here, compared to others, as you well know," retorted George, "and I could lose everything if it gets out that I've harboured murderers. I doubt I'll get any more land. Be lucky to not get arrested."

Umarrah regretted his decision to come, but reminded himself that, in their eyes, they had little choice.

Umarrah watched George's eyes upon him, studying him, then saw another truth dawn on his face. "You killed those other men, Arnold and Booth, didn't you?" accused George. "On the Nile, two years back."

There was no reason to deny any of it now.

"Yes," he admitted.

"My God," George muttered.

"Did you tell David we are here?" Umarrah asked.

"No."

"Thank you," he replied, relieved. "Will you tell anyone?"

"I haven't decided yet."

Silence stretched between them.

"Were they involved?" George demanded, pointing at the others.

"Yes, we all were," came the reply. "All their family dead."

Umarrah watched George cringe, wrestle with himself, and come to a decision.

"You can stay till nightfall," he decided. "I'm not going to say anything. It's not going to help either of us. And don't worry about Thomas. He's loyal."

Umarrah turned, translated this last sentence and watched cautious relief spread across his companions' faces.

George walked to the barn door. He hesitated, and turned around.

"Mary Ann heard some news of Planobeena."

"What news?" replied Umarrah, shocked.

"The Hardwickes said she was taken away from the coast by a sealer, a man called John Baker."

"Another whitefella has abducted my sister?" Umarrah interrupted.

"Well no. Apparently this Baker is a black man from America."

Umarrah opened his mouth with more questions when Thomas' voice called "Master! Mrs Collins is anxious for you to come in."

George looked at Umarrah.

"That's all I know."

"You must know more!"

"No, I don't" said George angrily.

They held each other's gaze for a moment. Umarrah knew George wanted something from him, thanks, an apology, but he could give neither.

"By nightfall," George repeated, "There'll be search parties out."

He slipped out the door.

Umarrah watched him go. He turned back around to find five pairs of eyes fixed expectantly upon him.

Planobeena! How could she have been abducted again, and by a blackfella. It was bad enough that she was taken by a whitefella family, but at least she was somewhere on the island. A straitsman could take her anywhere, even beyond the island's shores.

As for George, it will never be the same, he thought. I may never be able to return here. If his servant Thomas talks, both George's future and our lives could be in doubt.

The cover of nightfall couldn't come fast enough.

CHAPTER EIGHTEEN

June 1827 – Norfolk Plains

"How is Eliza doing?" enquired George, as he and David sat nursing their drinks. David's invitation that they meet at the New River had worried him. He'd spent four long months hoping no-one would find out he'd sheltered Umarrah and his fellow murderers, and was anxious that David would raise it now. But he knew that David had other news as well.

"She seems a bit better, but she misses Norfolk very much. It will be a long road, I suspect," David replied.

"Poor Eliza – to lose her first child," George shuddered. "Mother told me when I was in town that she'd heard of a few cases of influenza. I don't think anyone thought people would catch it out here."

"We certainly didn't," replied David.

"How many in your household ended up being infected?"

"A few of the other children got it too, and one of the servants was very sick, but they've all recovered, although for some it was slow."

"I'm sorry that we've not been much help. It's just with Mary Ann being pregnant again, we couldn't risk it."

"It's alright, I understand," David replied.

He changed the subject.

"Have you heard anything at all about your grant?"

"No, nothing," replied George curtly.

"You provided all the extra information as I suggested?" persisted David.

"Yes, I did. I listed all the improvements I've made over the last six years, including the seven hundred ewes, all the wethers, the cattle, and all the building work. I stressed how the stock are suffering and virtually begged for what they'd already granted. They'd be under no illusions that I'm desperate for more space. It's two years this month since I was promised that land."

George downed his glass in frustration, and called for another.

"Pace yourself, George," said David, somewhat condescendingly, thought George. "I may have a solution."

George looked at his brother-in-law with mingled hope and suspicion.

"I'll be honest with you George. I'm in an interesting position at the moment. I've totalled up my land, and I have over seven thousand acres."

George tried not to wince at the huge number.

"I never expected to be in such a position relatively soon after getting started here. I've done very well, given my history, which I know you know."

George made no reply.

David went on. "However, I get a sense now that I'm out of favour with Arthur, and with the land commissioners too. It's almost as though they think I have achieved too much, way beyond my ... humble beginnings. It's unlikely that I'll get further grants."

"The evidence would suggest that you've been in favour for a long time" countered George. "I'm the one who's been out of favour for two years now."

"You may be right George. What it's made me realise is that I'm comfortable with my lot, and I'd like to offer you a way of getting more land."

George looked at him in astonishment. Was his brother-in-law going to gift him some acreage? "David, I don't know what to say," he stumbled.

"Well this is what I'm proposing. I'd like to rent you two hundred acres."

Rent, thought George, instantly deflated. From a man with over seven thousand acres. Are those two hundred acres part of the five hundred granted to Norfolk? he thought cynically.

"What sort of payment were you thinking about, brother?" he asked.

David gave him a penetrating look, then sat back quietly in his seat.

"A fair rate for a member of my family. Let's work out the details later, but I can assure you that I do want to help."

"I'd rather know now what rent you were thinking of," insisted George.

"Alright, shall we say the same rent as for your original sixty acres?"

George's jaw hit the floor.

"That's very generous," he conceded. "Very generous indeed. I would happily accept those terms."

"Then that's settled, George. Drink that second glass at your leisure. I have another matter to discuss with you."

David requested a second glass for himself, and his face darkened.

"I've had more trouble out at the Western Marshes."

Not again, groaned George inwardly.

"It's Baker again, my overseer. Apparently two hundred of the Blacks attacked the stock hut the other day. I don't know why exactly, but something about Baker either killing or abducting a woman."

"He killed a woman?" asked George.

"I'm not sure," replied David, irritated at the interruption. "Baker managed to get away from the Blacks and reach Stocker's overseer, Cubit, as well as Williams, the field constable."

He took a large mouthful of whisky.

"Reports are that the next day they crept near to the Blacks' campfire, waited overnight, and shot up to nine of them the next morning."

George's audible gasp turned heads in the room. David said nothing until the other drinkers looked away.

"Now Baker is saying that perhaps only one Black was shot while running away," continued David in a low voice.

"Oh my God," whispered George.

He looked up at his brother-in-law. "Why are you telling me this?"

"I don't know George. I had to tell someone, and you know what happened last time."

"Dismiss him, and quickly, David. And tell the police, or James Cox."

"But Baker's a good overseer," protested David.

"And a violent one!" hissed George. "He's also at risk of being killed by the tribes in retaliation."

David drained his glass. "You're right, I'll have to remove him. It's just so hard to manage things from here."

"I can only imagine," George replied.

"There's something else," continued David, "but not at the Western Marshes this time. It's near Campbell Town. Have you heard what happened near Hugh Murray's farm?"

"No," replied George, but hearing the Murray name, and its connection to Umarrah, he tensed.

"I heard it from Hugh himself. We've got to know each other more recently. Good to have acquaintances from home. Anyway, Walter Davidson, who has land not far from Hugh's, had two shepherds murdered. It triggered a backlash. A group of police, soldiers, some settlers, not including Hugh, and their servants, went after them. They told him afterwards what happened. Hugh says it could have been as many as forty Aborigines dead, including women and children."

The words hung in the air between them as the seconds ticked by.

"Umarrah," he whispered. Could he be among the dead? Despite everything that had happened, he couldn't bear to contemplate the possibility.

David's eyes narrowed.

"What has Umarrah got to do with this?"

"He's worked for Hugh Murray. It's his Country. It's got to be possible that he's among the dead."

"How do you know he's worked for Hugh?"

"He told me himself a few years ago. I got the impression that he felt Hugh was a reasonable man, for a whitefella."

"He is," insisted David. "Sunk his life savings in, as has his brother David, come halfway across the world with their families, and did not expect an event like this to happen."

"I'm sure the Aborigines didn't either, David. Not any of this," said George, remembering the faces of Umarrah and his compatriots, tired and hungry from killing, sitting in his barn.

"I'll see what else I can find out," offered David.

"Thank you, David," replied George. "Anything you can discover I'd like to know."

"I'm glad we're in agreement about the two hundred acres," said David, changing topics.

"What? Oh yes," replied George with a latent half-hearted smile.

Back to business then, he thought.

"Don't forget to do something about Baker," added George.

"I will."

George looked across the table at his brother-in-law. They had nothing in common. It wasn't just the age difference. David preferred someone like Hugh, two big landowning Scotsmen together. George was just someone to whom he was related by marriage, and that he felt he could bestow benevolence upon.

Or to whom he could reveal his secrets.

They finished their drinks, walked outside, shook hands and parted. George swung onto his horse, and set off for home.

He rode at a thinking pace, considering the implications of their conversation.

David doesn't know I've sheltered Umarrah. He wouldn't rent me one acre if he did – having a brother-in-law who harbours murderers wouldn't get him back in favour with anyone.

I've got more land, even if it's rented.

He's not going to report Baker to the authorities. That wouldn't work in his favour either. He hopes it will all just go away. Out there in the wilds of the Western Marshes. Maybe he'll sack him, but that's all.

I don't know if Umarrah is dead or alive.

Pictures began to swirl in front of his eyes – children screaming, parents shielding, spears flung too late, gunshots, a pile of bodies. He thought of Mary Ann, little Annie, and fair-haired baby Libby, who'd just had her first birthday the month before.

He pulled his horse to a stop as the nausea rose.

Leaning over its flank, he vomited.

CHAPTER NINETEEN

November 1828 – Melaremertitter

The light was fading as, tired and hungry, they made it back to camp. It had been a long day, the culmination of reconnaissance, planning, then action. Like the other raids before it. By the time this one was unleashed, they knew how many whitefellas lived at the stock hut, who – if any – visited, and what supplies might be ripe for stealing. Today's attack was quick – there was only one man there. He hardly saw them before he was felled by a fast and accurate spear, and hit the ground face down. In a sweep of the hut's interior, they grabbed blankets, food, tea, and guns, then departed, only slowing down as the distance from the hut increased.

Umarrah silently reviewed the raid as they trekked through riverside gullies before finally climbing the hill to their camp. He had no qualms about the ongoing wounding or killing. The days of talking to whitefellas, the ones who invaded first, and negotiating compensation for their presence on the land, were long gone. That was another world. If people they found on these raids had made some attempt, some offer of payment for their presence on blackfella land, he might've listened, and been inclined to make an arrangement, or show some mercy. But since the massacre last year of the families near Wawlatter, his resolve had hardened. A killing of so many, including women and children, people he knew, on his Country, was a devastation. In its aftermath, a group drew itself together around him and began to raid far and wide, for survival, for intelligence gathering, and for retribution.

As they entered the clearing, he watched their well practised routine, guns stacked together in a hollow log for safe keeping, blankets piled together away from the firepit and food stacked close by. He glanced over at Lacklay, who had been particularly quiet during the long walk back, and watched as the younger man shoved his spear near the base of a tree and stood there, staring blankly into space. Umarrah saw on Lacklay's gaunt face the toll that the constant moving, and the raids, were taking. They'd argued about it before. Umarrah felt they couldn't have witnesses remaining to sound the alarm. "And then we'll sleep at night," he said.

"Maybe you can, but I can't," Lacklay had protested.

Laoninneloonner appeared by Umarrah's side and followed his gaze. "Maybe he shouldn't come next time," she suggested.

He frowned.

As the evening wore on, the fire's warmth and light, and the smell of roasting meat, rewarded their labours. They ate mostly in silence, tired from the long walk, the strain of ensuring the raid went to plan, the fear of having to deal with anything unexpected, and the effort of carrying back what they'd stolen, plus water from the last stream they'd passed. Umarrah watched Lacklay pick at his wallaby, and sip distractedly at his tea.

As the firelight dimmed, they each drifted away to sleep.

Laoninneloonner stepped around the embers and walked toward their sleeping area, laying down on the patchwork of skins. He sat before the fire's glow for a few minutes longer before joining her. Laying down, he curved his body around hers and pulled the fur over them both. They lay there quietly for a few moments.

"I don't know what to say to Lacklay," he said. "What can any of us say?" she replied. "No-one thought this would be our life."

She turned towards him, kissed him, then rolled over. Gradually her breathing slowed. He turned to lay on his back and looked up at the blazing night sky. Things had seemed bad when his mother was still alive. It was far worse now. He was glad she wasn't here to see it. For all he knew, Planobeena wasn't either.

And yet he had found comfort amongst the decimation. New alliances from clan remnants that brought more than protection in numbers. And Laoninneloonner. She did not flinch at the raiding, wounding, killing. That surprised him most of all.

He turned over and eventually sleep overcame him.

The earliest hint of dawn light appeared on the horizon as they slept. Suddenly the dogs began barking. He felt Laoninneloonner stir and then heard shouts. Adrenalin coursed through his veins as it dawned on him. Whitefella voices. He shook Laoninneloonner. "Get under the fur," he hissed before creeping to hide behind the nearest tree. A gunshot blasted the air and a piercing scream answered. Panicked shouts now betrayed people's terror and their location, though smothered the sounds of hasty dispersal into the bush. He peered in the direction of the gunshot, and as his eyes adjusted to the dim light, he saw someone standing near the firepit. He started to crawl towards the spears then gunshot rang out again and he collapsed, stunned, as pain streaked the left side of his face, and a deafening noise roared in his ear. Kicks began to pummel him all over until a shout stopped them.

There was quiet. He forced himself to stand up, but was nearly knocked over again as Laoninneloonner was shoved against him. He grabbed her. "Are you hurt?" he asked. "No," she whimpered, but she was shaking violently.

Someone held up a torch and Umarrah could see two men – both blackfellas.

"The Chief Umarrah!" said one of them. "We are both lucky men it seems. You, because it appears I have only grazed your face. And myself, because if I had known it was you, I wouldn't have fired at all. Well, unless you were attacking me, of course."

"Why you blackfellas shoot us?" spat Umarrah.

"Some of you were trying to get away," replied the second man. Umarrah's eyes narrowed as he took in his face.

"You do speak English," said the first man. "Good. I am Gilbert Robertson, Chief Constable at Richmond. This is Kickerterpoller, our guide. Governor Arthur has asked me to conduct roving parties to capture Aborigines. We are now under martial law you see."

"Martial law?" asked Umarrah.

"Whitefellas can kill blackfellas, plenty of blackfellas, and there will be no trouble for them," informed Kickerterpoller.

"They been doing that for longtime. You helping them?" he retorted. Kickerterpoller looked like he was going to lunge at him, but Robertson put his arm out in prevention.

"What Kickerterpoller is saying is that there are now legal protections for settlers if they kill Aborigines."

Umarrah stared at him.

"We kill whitefellas – that is what protect us."

He watched the effect of his words on Robertson. A voice in the background called out "Hang him now, I say," and there were mutterings of agreement amongst other whitefellas who had now gathered around Robertson. Unexpectedly, Umarrah saw a faint smile appear on Robertson's face as they locked gaze and took in each other's measure.

"I have orders to take you to Hobart," Robertson announced. "Clearly some of your party have managed to get away, but there are enough of you to please the Governor, yourself especially."

"Did you find anyone else?" he asked those around him.

"No-one, sir," came the reply.

"Let's get going," Robertson said.

There were only five of them left. Surrounded by their captors, they were shoved from the camp, Laoninneloonner bursting into tears as they passed the body of a young man who had been shot whilst trying to flee. He tried to comfort her but was elbowed away.

Days of trekking south followed. Laoninneloonner tried to distract herself by keeping a close eye on Cowertenninna, the youngest of their group. She and Umarrah could only hope his parents were still alive, but in the violence and confusion of the attack they didn't know what had happened to them. Umarrah tried unsuccessfully to create opportunities to talk to Lacklay and Parwareter, grateful that they were with him still. But they were watched closely to prevent any opportunity for collusion. From close observation Umarrah did notice one thing: Lacklay's reawakening. The shock of the whitefella raid seemed to have galvanised the young warrior. His eyes were clear, and cold.

Every day embedded rage into Umarrah's brain. There was the blackfella traitor Kickerterpoller for one. And the impossibility of escape, at least for now. Acknowledging they had little choice, he decided to pretend to cooperate and see what information they could gain.

As their journey continued, Robertson engaged Umarrah in conversation. He walked beside him most days and was not affronted by his fury. Umarrah eventually had to admit he was intrigued. He'd never seen or spoken to anyone like him.

One morning, as they paused on the crest of a hill, Laoninneloonner gasped at the view.

Laying before them to the south was the largest whitefella settlement either of them had seen. Below the foothills of an impressive mountain, buildings ran up and down the western bank of a wide river that disappeared in the distance into a large bay. The sight of it galvanised their captors and the pace of their forced march quickened. Umarrah, by contrast, felt only dread and a diminishing hope that an opportunity to escape would present itself.

After a week of bored, restless captivity, he was taken, along with Laoninneloonner, Lacklay and Parwareter to the largest building they had so far seen in this town. They were bundled into a room and left standing before a group of whitefellas, who were seated before them. Kickerterpoller was present, and Umarrah muttered under his breath as he announced them. Then the barrage of questions began. Umarrah answered those he understood, Kickerterpoller, with better English, translating when required. The whitefellas' faces revealed little, but power emanated from them. They seemed to be interested in his answers but it was likely a pretence, he thought. He used the opportunity to tell their interrogators he wanted to kill as many whites as possible, although admitted no specifics. At that, they looked suitably outraged, which also answered his question as to whether Kickerterpoller was translating faithfully. Their leader, the man Umarrah now knew was the Lieutenant

Governor, was tall with pale yellow hair. He asked the most questions, sighed once or twice, and glanced occasionally at Robertson, whose own face was inscrutable.

Eventually the questions ended, and Umarrah and the others were removed. He heard their interrogators debating as the door closed behind them. What they were going to do with the answers provided, Umarrah could only guess, but it wouldn't be in their favour.

As he pondered the day's events later that night, the desire to share what they'd seen and learnt intensified. But how could they escape from this town, with its foul clutter and noise, and get back home?

A possibility presented itself the very next day. As they headed north-east out of the town, closely watched by soldiers, and led once again by Robertson, his spirits rose as the land unfolded around them. Space, Country, opportunity.

But plummeted again after they entered the small town of Richmond and were thrown inside the gaol.

CHAPTER TWENTY

November 1829 – Norfolk Plains

"Nearly Christmas already," sighed Elizabeth.

"You say that every year," replied Mary Ann, waiting for George to emerge from the house.

"I do, don't I?" her mother-in-law smiled. "Must be a sign of age."

"Well, let's hope it's going to be a good one this year," fretted Mary Ann. She stroked her swelling belly.

Elizabeth reached over and squeezed her hand. "Try not to worry. Nothing will ever replace Libby, but you have Annie, little Harriet and another baby coming. Maybe a boy this time. And George won't be away for long."

Mary Ann nodded.

Elizabeth tried distraction. "Look at this beautiful sky, my dear. One thing I have always appreciated, whether on Norfolk Island or here, is the sky, such a contrast to the leaden grey of my London childhood. That I do not miss. This blue sky that starts pale at the horizon and become striking blue overhead – it's a wonderful thing."

"I appreciate you trying to cheer me up," replied Mary Ann.

"Well you and George have more land, and soon, maybe a boy."

Mary Ann nodded.

George, having finished his final instructions to the servants, came over.

He observed his mother's outward calm, but knew how anxious she had been since the arrival of Margaret's letter. The farmhouse of Margaret's brother-in-law John, next door to Margaret and Thomas, had been robbed by a group of Aborigines ("ten of them" reported Margaret). On the same day, a girl from a nearby family had been wounded in an attack. On top of all that, a hut of John's had been plundered the previous month.

"You must go to Margaret," insisted his mother, "and help her however you can. The journey's too much for me."

And Elizabeth had gone ahead and arranged everything. She, Mary Ann and the children would move to Pleasant Banks. Thomas would keep the farm ticking over and seek David's advice for any problems.

George merely had to acquiesce.

Which he did.

Nonetheless, the trip was bad timing. Libby's death the year before from influenza had left Mary Ann reeling. Desperate for the disease not to infect Annie and Harriet as well, they had been sent to their grandmother's. When Libby's tiny body succumbed all too quickly, the aftermath was filled with silence. George hated it. For her part, Mary Ann shed a tear or two when Annie and Harriet returned, and then got on with things.

Despite welcoming the new pregnancy, George felt an ache in his belly, which only eased when the dam of Mary Ann's unresolved grief finally burst. She wept most days, though tried to shield the children and hold it in till after their bedtime. George found her down by the river one evening, her body heaving with sobs, one hand on her growing belly. Sitting down beside her, he drew her to him, and gazed blankly into the distance while she wept.

Since then, he thought she seemed better. He was further reassured when, though not wanting him to go, she admitted that with family around her, and the Gibson's servants on tap, she would get a good rest.

He tied the last strap onto his satchel and patted his horse's flank.

"You have all the letters packed?" asked Elizabeth.

"Yes, Mother," he nodded. He gave her a brief kiss and then a longer, tender one to Mary Ann. "Don't fret," he whispered. She squeezed his arm. He sniffed Harriet's hair, kissed Annie, climbed onto his horse, and gave a final wave, Thomas following behind to bring back his horse once he'd boarded the coach.

By the third day, George thought his back would never recover. But as the coach lurched and rattled closer and closer to Bagdad, the excitement of seeing his sister increased. He pushed to the back of his mind anxiety about his other objective – to hand-deliver a letter to Colonial Secretary Burnett in Hobart, and request an interview. To plead his case for his land.

There'd been no time to write in advance and ask for an appointment. He wondered whether he would have received a reply even if he had. Instead he focussed on the advantages of making a personal approach.

Finally the coach pulled up at his destination, and he was delighted to see Margaret recognise him and wave excitedly.

"Welcome to Bagdad!" she shouted over the chaos of a spring gale, snorting horses and barking dogs. Clutching her bonnet, she greeted George with a kiss on both cheeks.

Thomas came up and stood beside her. "Thomas, you remember my little brother," she said proudly.

"It's been a long time, George," said Thomas, shaking his hand.

"It certainly has, Thomas," replied George. Margaret took his arm, steering him towards their cart while Thomas collected the luggage.

"Look at you, all grown up," she murmured. "You've doubled in age since I last saw you."

"More than doubled, Meg. I was twelve then, and I'm twenty-seven now."

She shook her head in disbelief. "How was the trip?"

"Never ending! My whole body aches."

She laughed. "That last downhill section from Constitution Hill – it's bone jarring, isn't it? Let's get you home and have a cup of tea. Then perhaps a warm bath to wash away the journey."

"I won't say no to either."

Thomas strode past them and lifted George's bag onto the cart. Once they'd climbed up, the horse set off, threading its familiar way along a grassy track. George asked Thomas about his work and noted the pride on his face as he described his role as constable of Bagdad and the surrounding areas, extending right up to the River Derwent.

"How do you manage your work and the farm?" asked George.

"It's not easy," he admitted, "but having John next door is a big help."

George's nieces and nephews were lined up in single file for their arrival. Margaret introduced him. The youngest, John, was held by his oldest sister, Beth. Margaret then ushered everyone inside and issued instructions. The older children began to run a bath for their uncle, put the kettle on to boil and take the youngest outside for some fresh air before bedtime. Margaret checked on the dinner before sitting down with George.

"I was sorry to hear from Mother of Libby's death," she said quietly, handing him a teacup.

"Thank you, Meg. You know it could happen – Norfolk's death was a shock to us all. But happening to one of your very own? It was awful. But we have Annie and Harriet, and are grateful they are well."

"How is Mary Ann?"

"Better. It affected her quite badly, not initially, but when she got pregnant again."

"That's understandable. But another pregnancy – wonderful news. Perhaps a boy this time?"

George smiled. "That would be nice."

He changed the subject.

"How are you, Meg? These attacks – tell me about them."

Her face turned grave. "I think the attack on the Hare's daughter upset me the most. They're only up at Constitution Hill. And it being the same day as John's house was robbed." Her voice turned to a whisper. "No-one was hurt over at John and Louisa's but ..." Her voice trailed off.

"But you're worried about a next time?"

"I'm worried about being stuck out here. You'd have to live in town to feel safe from the Aborigines."

"Doesn't it help, Thomas being a constable?"

"No. These attacks have been so sudden. He hasn't had any warning, and being constable means he often gets called away."

"You were living in town a few years back, weren't you? Would you be able to move back if you wanted?" asked George.

"And give up what we've built here? Thomas wouldn't want to do that."

Margaret's current mood was a disturbing contrast to her cheerfulness on his arrival. George watched as she smoothed the folds on her dress with slow deliberation.

"How is Mother?" she asked. "Do you have any letters?"

"Yes, I'll get them," he replied, relieved that he had some comfort to provide.

The next day he spent recovering from his journey, and that night John and Louisa joined them for dinner. They discussed the mill over the creek that Thomas had recently built, and inevitably, the political situation.

"Louisa's father runs an inn up at Green Ponds, so their family knows as much about what's going on around here as the constables," explained Meg.

"But it doesn't always help," commented Thomas.

"Especially when it comes to predicting what the Blacks are going to do," added Louisa.

John nodded vigorously. "It's like trying to chase ghosts."

"Was there much stolen from your house, John?" asked George.

"No, it was flour, sugar, tea – but they smashed some things."

"They were looking for guns," suggested Louisa.

"We don't know that for sure, Louisa," said John, with a hand on her arm.

"George is going to see the Governor," Margaret announced, changing the subject.

Aborigines momentarily forgotten, all eyes fell on him.

"I hope to," he corrected. "I was granted an extra one hundred acres a few years back, which was good news as we were bursting at the seams with stock. But the land, in fact, never eventuated. David's rented me two hundred acres, which helps, but I want what I was promised, before there's no good land left."

John leaned forward. "Be careful George. The larger the land, the more difficult it is to keep an eye on it. The Blacks have taken to killing sheep, in numbers far more than they could possibly eat."

"They do that more to deprive settlers of their livelihoods," replied George, remembering Umarrah's words.

They all stared at him.

"You know that for a fact, do you?" John sneered.

George scrambled for a reply.

"I'm not condoning their actions, believe me. But there were a lot of Aborigines around when the authorities, as our mother would say, forced us from Norfolk Island and dumped us here. I've learnt a bit about them in the years since."

He watched with relief that their faces suggested an acceptance of this answer.

"Do you have an appointment for your meeting with Burnett?" asked Thomas.

"No, I didn't have time to write and request one before leaving."

John chuckled. "You'll be lucky to get one then."

"I'm heading into town in two days and you're welcome to come with me," offered Thomas. "I know a good inn you could try for a room."

"Thank you, I'd appreciate that," George replied.

"We'll have our fingers crossed for you," said Margaret brightly.

Two days later, George sat beside Thomas on the cart, waiting at Austin's Ferry to cross the River Derwent. Mount Wellington towered over the river and the approaching town. A few specks of snow sat like blobs of icing on its flat topped summit.

Once off the ferry, Thomas pointed out a few landmarks then they settled into silence. George wondered if his mother and Eliza had ever shared information about him and Umarrah with Margaret. If she believed I was a sympathiser, he thought, they'd not have welcomed me here. It was clear that both couples were under strain. He could sense that Thomas was reluctant to be away from home, and wanted to conclude his business in Hobart without delay.

Gradually the signs of settlement increased until they were engulfed by the bustle of the town.

"Here we are," Thomas announced as the horse drew to a halt outside the inn. "I think you'll find it comfortable enough." He gave George directions for the Colonial Secretary's office, then George climbed down and grabbed his bag.

"Thank you, Thomas. I'll send word if I think I'll be more than a few days."

"Good luck," Thomas replied.

George perused the building's exterior, then opened the door.

By evening, he'd made himself comfortable in his room, had dinner and an ale, and planned what he would say tomorrow.

After a night of broken sleep, he made his way to Government House early. Lining up behind other petitioners outside Burnett's office, he settled in to wait. The queue gradually shortened as people disappeared inside to state their business, and then re-emerged. He watched their departing faces and reactions seemed mixed.

"Yes?" questioned a young man imperiously as George reached the desk and handed over his letter. "I have a letter for the Secretary," answered George. "It's regarding his approval for a land grant he made to me in December 1824. I've never actually got the land, and I'm requesting an interview with the Secretary to try and sort it out."

The young man looked up at George in confusion. "Five years ago?" he queried. "You must have written to us since then."

"Yes, I wrote in 1827. I was told that the surveyor was having trouble at the time in finding a location. I've heard nothing since. It's all in my letter," he explained, holding it out.

The young man took the letter reluctantly, didn't open it and put it on top of a pile of correspondence.

Your name?"

"George Collins."

"Mr Collins, if you have not received your land allocation in five years, we will have to investigate why. It will take several weeks to do this. Only then would the Colonial Secretary be in full possession of the facts and be willing to see you when his schedule permits."

"I've travelled all the way from Norfolk Plains and can't wait that long for an answer," pleaded George.

"That's not my concern. We will write to you once our investigation is complete. You can ask for an appointment in your reply," he said, looking around George to the next person.

George was dumbfounded.

"Please move on, there are other petitioners waiting."

He looked at the young man, glanced at the letter on the top of the pile, tried to think of something to say, failed, then walked out.

CHAPTER TWENTY-ONE

November 1829 – Hobart Town

After the third drink, the sting of his dismissal began to recede. At closing time, the barman watched warily as a swaying George climbed the stairs. He managed to eventually lock his door from inside before collapsing, fully clothed, onto the bed.

Dawn brought a tongue that felt like leather. Three glasses of water later, the bitterness of his disappointment began to wash over him. He couldn't come back in several weeks' time. It was equally impossible to remain in Hobart that long.

"I've achieved absolutely nothing," he ranted, knowing he had no choice but to wait for the next letter, once the authorities had deigned to complete their investigations.

He finally trudged downstairs to pick at some breakfast. Thinking that fresh air might help, he headed outside and began to thread his way gingerly through the streets. As his hangover eased, anger began to replace shock and disappointment. I never had a chance, he fumed. I'm a nobody, and I should've known this is how they'd respond.

Even assuming they do investigate, will that only expose why I think the grant was buried in the first place?

Because of Umarrah?

An idea stirred. Thomas would be heading back to Bagdad in a few days. I've got time to do something else, thought George. Compared to how far I've come, it's only a short trip. And I haven't seen Umarrah for three years.

He remembered the newspapers being full of his capture a year earlier, reporting with glee how the 'King Umarrah' had said he considered it his patriotic duty to kill as many whites as possible. George was simultaneously relieved to hear that he was alive and appalled by the words attributed to him. His punishment for saying such a thing George eventually found out from James Cox, via David. Imprisonment in Richmond Gaol he knew would be a bitter blow.

George debated whether to or not, and finally wrote at Easter time, with no expectations of a reply. The letter took a charitable tone, acknowledging their acquaintance and offering Christian prayers. He knew Umarrah wouldn't be able to read the letter's contents, but he hoped that his gaolers would show sufficient compassion to read it to him. He hoped too that Umarrah would see through the religious angle as the ruse it was.

Astonishingly, a reply came had come in early May.

Dear Mr Collins,

The Chief Umarrah thanks you for your letter. He has asked me to convey to you the following information:

He is well, though very angry at being in this gaol. His wife is with him though she is increasingly distressed at being so confined. She grieves the loss of the friend who was shot and killed when they were captured.

Umarrah says to tell you that he has been given a man to help him. I can confirm that this is a convict by the name of William Pahle. The Chief is pleased about this, and also pleased that Governor Arthur has decided that the Chief will be going out into the bush with Mr Robertson soon to search for more of his countrymen. Mr Robertson has had Umarrah and his countryman Parwareter to his home many times. He lives not far from the gaol. Umarrah says to tell you he has also spoken to His Excellency Governor Arthur many times as well.

He hopes you and your family are well.

William Pahle will ensure you receive this letter.

Yours faithfully,

Messr Speed

Gaoler

George slowed his walking pace and stopped as he acknowledged that given everything that had happened, in particular the massacre near Campbell Town, to say the future was uncertain was an understatement. What if he never had another chance to see him?

Back at the inn, he made enquiries about services to Richmond, and found that the journey involved a ferry trip followed by a carriage. The next service was tomorrow. Pleased that he had something to else to focus on, he spent the rest of the day doing as little as possible.

His river crossing the next morning was completely unlike the one at Austin's Ferry. The River Derwent, having opened out into an enormous harbour, was being buffeted by a southerly gale, and the little ferry bobbed and bounced on a slow journey from the western to the eastern shore. Once docked, they transferred to a carriage and headed north east.

Deposited in the town of Richmond that afternoon, he found an inn with a vacant room, rested after the journey, wrote two notes, then headed to the bar. The young barmaid, in response to his tentative question, gave him directions and asked him who was he hoping to see at the gaol. His answer made her whistle.

"He's a handsome man, that one," she laughed. "I know he's a native, but all the same ..."

George listened to her gossip, bought some food and two bottles of whisky, excused himself and set off for the short walk to the gaol. It was easily found from the young lady's instructions – a single-storey rectangular stone building atop a small rise, with a steep slope down to the Coal River on one side. There was a clear view of the countryside in all directions.

He climbed the three stone steps and knocked on the wooden door. A soldier appeared and asked his business. George handed over the whisky and the notes, one addressed to Speed and the other to Pahle. The soldier gave instructions to wait inside the doorway, then several minutes later George was ushered into the first door on the left.

After being out in the late spring sunshine, George strained to see who was inside the damp smelling room, which was lit only by a south window facing the grim prison courtyard. As his eyes adjusted, he could make out sparse furnishings and then recognised Lacklay and another man sitting against the far wall. A woman sat on a blanket in a corner. Then his gaze fell on Umarrah, whose eyes were wide with astonishment.

"Umarrah?" said George, cautiously. He took a few steps forward.

Umarrah stepped towards him, holding out his hand. George took it without hesitation.

Lacklay stood up and joined them. George nodded to him, before turning his gaze again to the woman, who appearing to have recognised his name. She rose and came over to stand by Umarrah. The third man looked at George with curiosity, coughed frequently, and remained sitting in the shadows.

In the silence that followed, George glimpsed the soldier's coat out in the doorway. No chance of having a private conversation then, he thought.

"This is Laoninneloonner," said Umarrah.

"Pleased to meet you," George said awkwardly.

She replied with a slight nod.

More silence.

"I brought some food," announced George, retrieving the parcels from beneath his jacket. "I heard you get less than you should."

"Yes, we hungry, but Speed, he get bigger," protested Umarrah. He handed the parcels to Lacklay, who shared out the food.

Umarrah gestured for them to sit on the floor while they ate.

"I read about your capture in the newspaper," explained George.

"Robertson shoot me then, and the whitefellas with him kill some of us."

"You were shot?" gasped George. "They never said anything about that in the papers."

Umarrah shrugged. "This," he gestured round the room, "is worse than being shot."

"Did Robertson put you here?"

"No, Arthur put me here. But I go to Robertson's house many times. He is interesting man. Not a whitefella, not a blackfella either. Arthur wanted, I think, to kill me, but Mr Robertson, he stop him."

"I don't know much about Robertson," admitted George.

"I say to Arthur, we must kill you people. You not pay for taking our land. You take our women, our food, our land. Long time now, long time, and you must pay. "

"Then I'm not surprised Arthur wanted you dead," replied George. "And I'm amazed that this Mr Robertson convinced him to act otherwise."

"But we are dead like this, George," countered Umarrah. "This is like being dead. We cannot live like this – no space, and long way from our Country."

George had no reply to this.

"I escape one time."

George looked astonished.

"It is not hard. They don't know Country like us. I laugh at them, in here," he tapped his head. "Robertson is not very careful with watching. But I am weak from being in this place and not enough food, so they found me."

"What else did you say to Arthur?" asked George but Umarrah did not reply. He took a portion of his food and handed it to the sentry outside. George watched him bestow his most charming smile on the man, whose eyes widened in gratitude. Umarrah winked at him, and slowly closed the door.

"Arthur and I talk about many things," he said, sitting down again. "About peace, a treaty. I learn about him. But he does not understand us."

"Peace is surely something we all want," replied George.

"I think this peace of Arthur's is something good for him, for the whitefellas, not for us."

"Maybe Arthur wants to learn from you what Aborigines want. And then maybe they'll let you leave here."

Umarrah shrugged. The question of what needed to be said or done for the authorities to release them, or for them to escape, was one that Umarrah must have turned over in his mind interminably, thought George, realising he'd made no useful contribution at all.

Umarrah changed the subject. "Mr Robertson I like. I think he understand us, more than Arthur."

"Even though he shot you," said George.

"Yes, even though he shot me."

They exchanged wry smiles.

"Why did you come such a long way to see me, George?" asked Umarrah, his smile gone. "You have news of Plano-beena?"

"No news of her, I'm sorry. I came, because," he stumbled, "it's been a long time." That was a lame answer, he thought, and not a completely truthful one. "A lot was said the last time we met, but much has happened since ... like those killings near Campbell Town."

Umarrah's face darkened.

"I'm so sorry."

"You didn't kill them, George."

"I know, but still." George glanced at the door, suspecting that their time to talk would soon be over. "The truth is, I came to Hobart to plead for that extra land I never got. And the authorities won't help me. I don't know why I thought they would. Now," he checked the door was definitely shut, "I hate them too." That was an oversimplification.

He wanted to explain himself more, but the door suddenly opened and the soldier announced, "That's it. Time's up."

Umarrah leaned in close to George. "But they not killing your people, George. You not getting what was not theirs to give you."

George stepped back. "I'm sorry. Perhaps I shouldn't have come. I hope you'll get out of here – somehow."

They held each other's gaze for a moment.

"No, thank you for coming, for writing too," replied Umarrah. "You did not have to."

George quickly nodded his goodbye to the others, stepped around the soldier and walked out blinking into the sunshine.

He walked slowly back to the inn, trying to understand what had happened. Was it a mistake to have gone to the gaol? Why did he feel the need to confess the real reason for coming south? Up to then he felt like the visit was going well. At least Umarrah got some time away from there to go to Robertson's. Did the others have similar opportunities or were they confined to that place? Robertson himself sounds intriguing. Interesting that Umarrah doesn't know what to make of him. He's certainly formed a clear opinion of Arthur.

At least he had a break before going back to Bagdad and listening to John's sardonic laugh at the failure of his visit.

The next morning he headed back to Hobart Town, where a message from Thomas awaited him at the inn, offering a lift back to Bagdad the following day. George felt a pang of guilt about his visit to Richmond, thinking now of the ongoing fear facing Margaret and her family. Do you regret it? he asked himself. The answer was No. Why, was not so clear.

CHAPTER TWENTY-TWO

December 1829 – Hobart Town

Laoninneloonner stood straight and still, looking at him with a fierceness which betrayed her effort not to cry. Umarrah felt impossibly torn, despite knowing he had no choice. He put his arms around her. "I will find you," he whispered. "Hurry up!" barked the gaoler's voice behind him, "it's time to go." Umarrah's face clouded, an image forming of his waddy striking the man in the face. He looked mutely in her eyes, hard with anger and grief, then stepped through the doorway into the sunshine.

The horses at the front of the cart trotted happily towards Hobart Town through warm air freshened from the previous night's rain. The soldiers at the front had no wish to talk to him or Parwareter. Sitting behind, only loosely restrained, his spirits rose under a piercing blue sky. I am out of that place, he smiled, pushing aside his guilt at leaving Laoninneloonner and Lacklay behind.

He remembered Gilbert Robertson's anger when the order came that he was to be taken away to a man called Robinson. He was momentarily confused – weren't they the same person? Then came a dawning realisation that he was a piece of property that was being fought over. Though insulted, it confirmed his value in the eyes of the invaders.

He would not waste any opportunity to exploit it.

The river crossing was a different matter. While the humiliation of the soldiers' laughter at his unconcealed fear rang in his ears, the little ferry made mercifully fast work of the crossing in an obliging easterly wind. Back on the western shore, horses and carts jostled for space on dusty Hobart roads. He watched the whitefella men and women, a few in elaborate and colourful clothing, walking on the roadside or sitting in carriages drawn by teams of horses. The number and size of the houses reinforced his original impression – this was a place of power, and permanence. As they passed one of the houses, its front door opened and a whitefella woman and two children came out. The woman saw him and Parwareter and shrank back inside, pulling the children with her and disappearing behind a slamming door.

A few minutes later, they pulled up outside another house. One of the soldiers jumped down, checked their restraints, then went up and knocked on the door. It opened and a round, short man came out. Yet another whitefella who wore fussy, complicated clothing.

The man held out his hand. "Where is the note from Mr Robertson?" he asked. The soldier blanched. "Er, I'm sorry Mr Robinson, sir," he stammered. "I have no note for you."

The man glowered at this answer. "An impertinence," he muttered, before turning to Umarrah. As their eyes met, he watched Robinson's frank assessment of him, the man's gaze moving over his whole body, frowning at the restraints.

"The Chief Umarrah, I believe," he said. "I am Mr George Robinson."

Umarrah nodded in reply.

"And Parwareter is here as well. Good. I understand your English is reasonable?" he asked.

"I speak some," Umarrah confirmed. He might learn more if these white men thought he couldn't understand.

"Excellent. You are to accompany me now to meet Governor Arthur. I have been told you understand that we will be undertaking a journey to the west coast of this island, and the Governor wishes to meet you before we depart."

He paused. Umarrah made no reply.

"Do you understand me?"

Umarrah nodded. "Yes, I understand." But he didn't, not fully. Robertson had told him very little. Now he suspected that was out of malice at having him removed. The words 'west coast' meant nothing. He had the feeling he was going somewhere, and most likely with this man.

"Then let us depart."

Robinson issued orders and Parwareter was taken inside the house. Umarrah climbed down from the cart and into Robinson's carriage. "Government House," Robinson instructed the driver.

"It is a great honour to be in the presence of the Governor," he announced as they rattled through the streets. Umarrah looked at him but did not reply. This man was obviously ignorant of his previous meetings with Arthur.

Robinson made no further attempt at conversation.

The carriage drew to a halt as they reached Government House. On seeing Robinson emerge, two soldiers approached the carriage and formed a ring around Umarrah as his feet landed on the ground. One soldier waited outside the entrance, as the other led Robinson and Umarrah through the door, inside of which was a small reception room, with a young man seated at a desk. Robinson stated their business and a moment later they were ushered into a larger room. The second soldier remained outside as they entered.

The three whitefellas inside looked up as they entered. Arthur walked up to Robinson, shaking his hand as they exchanged greetings. Umarrah noted a change come over Robinson, not just deference but an obsequiousness. He hastily readjusted a grimace of distaste as the Governor turned his gaze towards him.

"Chief Umarrah, it is good to know that you and your companions will be joining Mr Robinson in his important work," pronounced Arthur. "We need your help so that the tribes know there is nothing to fear from us."

Umarrah looked at him blankly. "Where are we going?" he asked.

"Let us explain."

Arthur introduced him to George Frankland then drew them all to a large table strewn with drawings and blank paper. They pored over a large map of the island, discussing the proposed route for the journey. As the discussions continued, it dawned on him. They were heading north, yes, but not returning the way he had come. They were going by boat, and then on foot, up the west coast, starting from the very south of the island.

He turned away, his heart pounding as disaster, instead of opportunity, loomed. The terror of travelling over the sea and numerous rivers filled him with dread. And this was enemy territory, only complicated by them being part of this whitefella Robinson's group. Anything could happen.

He turned back to the table, concentrating on following the discussion until his head ached from the effort. Next, he was beckoned to a smaller table. It was covered with a large piece of parchment showing four rows of drawings. On the top row, a blackfella and a whitefella stood side by side in seeming friendship, a black child and a white child held hands, and a white woman held a black baby, next to a black woman holding a white baby. Curiosity piqued, Umarrah's gaze moved down to the second row, where a small group of Aborigines, headed by a chief, moved towards a group of whitefellas, fronted by their own leader. The two men shook hands. Umarrah's eyebrows rose as he lingered on this image.

On the third row, an Aborigine speared a white man, and was hung by soldiers. He remembered George describing to him what a hanging was, after the newspapers reported with glee the deaths of two pairs of warriors a few years earlier. His eyes fixated on the crooked neck and limp body.

Then, on the bottom row, a whitefella shot an Aborigine, and was hung by the same soldiers. His hands clenched as rage welled within him. This is a lie, his mind screamed. When has justice like that ever happened?

His eyes moved back to the top row, the harmony, the friendship, and he thought of George. There was a time when it was like that, he admitted. After the initial shock and violence. When George was nearly a man, and for a few years after.

"What do you think of these pictures?" said Frankland from behind him.

Be careful, he thought. "Here," he pointed to the top row, "whitefellas and blackfellas happy together."

"Indeed," replied Frankland. "I feel that we need to show that black and white can get along together, and if not, punishment is handed out to all who transgress." What is 'transgress'? thought Umarrah.

"I think the Chief would prefer simpler words, Mr Frankland," Robinson suggested, before turning to Umarrah. "Black and white can live good together, and all who kill are punished."

Frankland looked offended at the correction.

"*Are* whitefellas punished?" Umarrah demanded, pointing to the bottom row of the drawing. "You punish blackfellas, kill plenty of us at our campfires. I not see, I not hear, whitefellas punished. You punish them here, in this town?"

Frankland and Robinson looked embarrassed.

"These pictures," stuttered Frankland, "we are making copies and sending them out across the island. All people, black or white, will understand that we want peace and," he hesitated, "justice, for everyone, black and white."

Robinson nodded in enthusiastic agreement.

"Do you think your people would like these pictures?" Frankland asked.

Neither of you answered my question, noted Umarrah.

"Yes," he replied, "if they are true."

A smiling Arthur joined them. "I agree wholeheartedly with Mr Frankland, Umarrah," pronounced Arthur. "We hope you will help us show your people that this," he gestured to the pictures, "is truly what we all want."

A young man rushed over and was instructed by Arthur to check how many other copies of the picture boards had been made to date. He returned a few moments later with a slightly smaller version. which he handed to the Governor, who passed it to Frankland, who ceremoniously placed it in Umarrah's hands.

He cast his eyes over the sequence of pictures again. They genuinely believe this will help, he thought, looking at their faces.

Arthur and Robinson agreed a departure date and discussed membership of the travelling group. Umarrah was pleased to hear Trepanner's name amongst them.

Then the meeting was over. Arthur formally wished them a successful mission. I'd like to know what that means, Umarrah thought. Robinson responded with fulsome hopes for a successful engagement with the native tribes.

Picture board in his hands, he and Robinson were then ushered out the door and back to their carriage.

"The Governor is very pleased with your interest," Robinson proclaimed as the carriage headed back along the same dusty streets.

Umarrah looked out the window, already irritated at the prospect of travelling with this particular whitefella. You're out of the gaol, he reminded himself, though the pleasure in that was muted, remembering who he'd left behind. At least there would be three pairs of eyes on this journey he could trust, watching, learning and then plotting. They'd need it.

He spent the next few weeks wryly observing a fever of activity as preparations for their journey escalated. Robinson painstakingly explained to him the purpose of the different type of supplies they must take. Umarrah deemed the vast majority of little practical use, but kept his opinions to himself. He nearly laughed out loud when Robinson issued him with his clothing for their journey: a jacket, trousers, handkerchief and stockings.

In the dead of night he saw her eyes again, defiant, forsaken, loving.

He had no more sleep after that, and a few hours later they set off.

CHAPTER TWENTY-THREE

March 1830 – Norfolk Plains

"Hurry, Thomas! We need Mrs Gibson urgently."

Thomas sprinted to the stables, George's plea ringing in his ears, and moments later was galloping towards Pleasant Banks.

"It's alright, George," said Mary Ann. "Don't panic. It's the fourth time I've done this, remember."

"But the baby's coming early!" he blurted.

"I'm quite aware of that!" She grabbed the back of the chair and began to rock until another contraction eased.

"What can I get you?" he asked.

"A cold flannel for my face."

He dipped one into a nearby bucket, squeezed it and handed it to her.

"Remember, George," she added, dabbing her face and neck, "Eliza is ready, even with the baby coming early. Between us, we've got a lot of experience in these matters."

She took a sip of tea. "Perhaps Shauna could take the girls outside."

At that, Shauna, their new servant, came in with the girls. She must have been eavesdropping, thought George. Harriet, sensing drama, began to cry. Mary Ann slowly walked over to her, nuzzled her ear and murmured a few soothing words. Then she moved back to her position against the chair in readiness for the next wave as Shauna and the girls disappeared out the door.

As the next contraction's intensity rose, she closed her eyes and swayed from side to side. As it subsided, she held the flannel out.

"I don't think this is going to take long, George," she announced a short while later. George said a quick prayer for Eliza's arrival, and minutes later the door flew open and his sister burst in, tying back strands of hair made unruly by the mad dash from home.

"Eliza, thank God," cried George.

Eliza gave her brother a quick kiss. "I'm sure all will be well," she reassured him. "Why don't you leave it to me? I'll yell out if I need help."

She moved swiftly to Mary Ann's side. "How far apart are they, darling?" she crooned.

"Close. I think I'll need to push soon," Mary Ann replied.

George gave his wife a quick kiss, shut the door quietly behind him, and went to find Shauna and the girls. He found them down by the river and was immediately soothed by a gentle breeze blowing small ripples over its surface. He stared blankly at the Great Western Tiers in the distance while Shauna continued entertaining the girls with a game. Then he took off his shoes and gasping, plunged his feet into the river. Harriet heard him and began to giggle. Moments later all four of them had done the same, the girls squealing with laughter. Two pairs of eastern rosellas chattered overhead, then landed amongst the trees by the bank, and proceeded to supervise the scene. Occasionally, cries emanated from the house and George winced, but the little ones seemed not to notice. He was grateful for Shauna's skill in distraction and reminded himself to compliment her later.

"Mr Collins?" came a shout. "Down here!" he called back, hauling his feet out of the soft riverbed.

"A letter's come for you," panted Thomas, handing it over and noting his master's muddied feet. George snatched the letter and turned back to the riverbank, glad to have something else to occupy his mind.

He was surprised to see that William Pahle had written again.

March 3, 1830

Dear Mr Collins,

Thank you for your letter of December 6. I am writing to inform you that, since your visit of November last, there is more news. The Chief Umarrah is no longer with us.

George gasped.

*On Christmas Eve, he was taken from the gaol to
have an audience with Governor Arthur. He was then to
be moved into the Aboriginal Asylum next to the home of
Mr George Robinson. I can tell you that he was glad to
be taking the opportunity to leave the gaol, but remains
very concerned about his wife and the companions in
his group. The Chief's wife was brave at his departure
but has missed him sorely since. Mr Robinson has since
seen fit to inform us that a group of natives, including
Umarrah, were to accompany him on a boat to Port
Davey. I understand they were to be travelling up the
west coast to find, and conciliate, as Mr Robinson
informs us, any other blacks they meet.*

*That is all the information that I have of the Chief's
movements. I also have news of the Chief's wife. Last
month she was taken from here to Mr Robinson's
house, and was apparently going to be sent back to
Launceston, along with some other female natives. It
was hoped they would rejoin their tribes and urge their
people to surrender.*

> *Yours faithfully,*
> *William Pahle*

George put the letter down. They were all gone from the
gaol. And Umarrah saw Arthur again. He must have made an
impression on the governor. But who was this man Robinson?
Robinson or Robertson? Could Pahle mean the same man?
And what was this trip to the west coast?

He pondered the letter's contents. Then came another
shout from the house. He sprinted up the riverbank to hear the
unmistakeable cries of a newborn.

Eliza's face was triumphant. "Congratulations, brother. Go
in and see," she smiled.

He dropped the letter on the table and raced in to Mary
Ann.

"Come and meet your firstborn son," she beamed.

George's eyes filled with tears as he peeked at the tiny face swaddled in cloths. "A boy," he marvelled.

"How are you feeling?" he asked, seeing her grimace. "Just the afterpains – they're quite strong," she replied.

"You were right – it didn't take long," he observed. "Compared to the previous times. But still long enough, I know."

He kissed her forehead, and then his son's.

Annie and Harriet burst in, the younger immediately climbing to the bed. "Come and meet your baby brother," said George. "A boy!" Annie giggled as she took her first peek. Harriet, more concerned with climbing onto her mother, was swiftly placed on the opposite side to her brother, and promptly nuzzled into Mary Ann. "I hope there might be room for me in that bed!" he laughed.

Eliza came in with tea and bread. "George, how about we send Thomas back over to Pleasant Banks to collect some dinner?"

"That would be good, Eliza, thanks."

A few hours later, Thomas returned with an enormous stew and David's message that they would send for Elizabeth in the morning. George and Eliza, with Mary Ann cradling baby George, sat quietly around the table eating dinner, before Eliza returned home.

The next afternoon, David arrived with George's mother, plus more meals. George helped Elizabeth down from the cart. She gave him a big hug then rushed inside.

"Have you decided on a name?" asked David. "George," came the reply. "My name is the name of the father I never knew. I hope my son will have many years to know the man whose name he carries."

"Nicely said," replied David. "Sometimes I forget that Joseph was your stepfather."

Thomas began to unpack the provisions.

"Your sister has a confession," said David, over a cup of tea.

"Good God, what would she have to confess?"

"She read the letter that you had left open on the table yesterday. Curiosity got the better of her. She feels badly about it and wanted me to say she was sorry."

"I assume you know the contents?"

"Yes, I do."

Elizabeth came into the room, carefully shutting the door. "Please talk quietly. Mary Ann and the baby are sleeping."

She paused, sensing the tense atmosphere.

"You might as well read this too," grumbled George, handing his mother the letter. "It seems everyone else has." Elizabeth sat down, poured herself some tea, and began to read.

She looked up at him. "So they've gone from the gaol."

"So it seems."

"You knew about this too?" asked David.

"I did," she replied evenly.

"What on earth possessed you to visit him, George?" demanded David.

"Out of Christian charity, and to see if he was alright."

"I didn't think you would be that stupid."

"Keep your voices down," hissed Elizabeth.

"Why do you have to keep involving yourself with the Aborigines like this?" David persisted.

"I went to see Margaret, as you well know. Then Thomas said he was going to Hobart, so I used the opportunity to make a personal appeal for my one hundred acres. But they said they have to investigate the reason for the delay and would just write when that's done. So after being dismissed without any consideration, I wanted to do something useful. I imagined how awful it would be for Umarrah and his companions to be gaoled, and just wanted to bring some comfort."

"They actually let you in to see him," said David. "I can hardly believe it."

"There was correspondence, and whisky, involved."

David ignored the last comment. "What did Umarrah tell you?"

"That he was shot by Robertson when he was captured. Just a minor injury. Strangely they've become quite good friends. Umarrah spoke well of him. I think he feels Robertson is one of the few people who actually considers there's a war going on. Umarrah doesn't think Arthur looks at it like that, and he doesn't trust him."

"Well that feeling would be mutual," muttered David.

"As you now know, he's out of the gaol, and been sent off with this man called Robinson. Have you heard of him?"

"No. The name doesn't mean anything."

"I don't know what 'conciliate' the Blacks in that area means."

"Something more peaceful than I suspect will eventuate."

George nodded.

"Your visit to the gaol would have put you under suspicion from the authorities," David argued. "You haven't heard anything about your second grant, despite appealing personally?"

George said nothing.

"Their investigation wouldn't have taken this long. I'd say your chances of ever getting those one hundred acres are now zero."

"You think I don't know that?" George snapped.

"I think that's enough of this discussion," demanded Elizabeth. She looked at her son. "Darling, this is a day of happiness. Your first son is safely delivered. Focus on that for now."

George squeezed her arm.

"You're right Mother, of course," he smiled.

"Wise words," agreed David.

Elizabeth and George said nothing but David was in no doubt that his last comment was not appreciated.

CHAPTER TWENTY-FOUR

May 1830 – Laydewyreek

T he three of them huddled together as sheets of lightning lit the night sky in an eerie electric blue.

"We'll have to wait," trembled Parwareter. Trepanner's reply was drowned out by a large crack of thunder. Umarrah hoped the next sheet of lightning would illuminate the river level, but knew he was wasting his time.

"We'll have to wait for it to go down," he said.

They reinforced their shelter, and hunkered down.

The storm eased as the first streaks of dawn appeared and they crept eastward along the southern bank of the river. Ears and eyes were constantly alert but there were no signs they were being followed. As the sky cleared to a pale winter blue, the bush opened out into the open plains they sought and they made good ground on easier terrain.

But other days were the opposite. During the short and bitterly cold days they also negotiated the sides of snow-capped mountains and valleys snaked with turbulent icy rivers. But with more distance between them and those they had fled, it was eventually safe enough to make a fire, and carry a firestick.

Freedom, and antipathy, spurred them on. At night they buoyed each other's spirits with scathing critiques of Robinson. Umarrah laughed recalling how Robinson had sent him and Woorrady to the whitefella settlement for supplies, wearing their costume of red coats and trousers. They had pranced around, pretending they were noble whitefellas before they left.

At the same time, Umarrah was forced to admit a grudging admiration for the man. Their large group had made slow progress on their journey of 'conciliation', often through thick forest that spilled down to the rocky coastline. There were many streams and rivers to cross, some fast moving and dangerous, and the weather was often wet and bitterly cold. Yet Robinson rarely complained.

On dry nights, Umarrah acknowledged that he had actually enjoyed himself, indulging his favourite pastime of telling stories. The romantic ones were the most popular. The whitefellas, though not able to understand, seemed to find them amusing as well. Robinson had even complimented him on his storytelling skill.

But the last straw was the man's refusal to capture their enemy, the Toogee. Having made contact with them, Robinson had made it clear that they were welcome to leave at any time. The Toogee must have laughed at this, and at the blackfellas with whom he travelled. The prevarication was humiliating. Robinson refused to listen to him. It was clear they were there on this journey to suit his motivations. He did not want to see what the Toogee, or Robinson, might do next. They had to leave, and work their way back home.

On the coldest nights since their escape, Umarrah dreamt of the turquoise ocean of the east, the winter landscape he had always known. And of Laoninneloonner's body, warming his.

Gradually the days lengthened, and it was heartening to feel some glimmers of warmth from the sun. The familiar east-west road at the base of the mountains of Koorparoona Niara was a welcome sight, and from there they made faster progress. But the reach of whitefella settlement had expanded even further in the two years since his capture. Having arrived back in familiar Country, they were confronted with almost impossible detours. Trepanner and Parwareter's joy at being close to Country – like his own – had turned to fear, anger and exhaustion.

There was only one choice. Despite the risks involved, they would seek shelter once again at George's farm.

He wouldn't have considered it if George hadn't come to the gaol. He knew from that visit that George had reason to hate the authorities and might still offer assistance. And yet, after the angry words exchanged when he was last at the farm, he felt he would never go back. One other hope lingered. Perhaps, having had contact with Speed and Pahle, George might have news of Laoninneloonner. Of Planobeena he had no expectations, having almost given up hope.

Despite, or perhaps because of, his exhaustion, tears filled his eyes when Moorronnoe twinkled at him as they approached the riverbank under cover of dusk.

They slept under the trees before the morning dawned crisp and clear. "I'll go first," he said. "Wait, then follow." As the rising sun glinted on the farm buildings, he walked out of cover across the frosty ground towards the house.

He didn't see the gun levelled at him. There was no shout, no warning. He heard the thud of the bullet lodging in the tree trunk and dropped to the ground. Heart pumping, he peered through the low sunlight to see a young man and a barrel far too close for a second mistake. Then there was a hiss and an agonising cry as a second bullet found its mark. Wheeling round, he saw Trepanner on his knees, shrieking in pain and clutching his forearm.

"No, Patrick!" George cried as he and Thomas raced towards him.

"I have them, master!" shouted Patrick. "I can finish them off."

"If you do, I will shoot you myself!" shouted George as he reached him. Stunned by his master's command, Patrick lowered the barrel and handed it to George.

"But they are enemies on your land."

"Shut up, Patrick. Get the mistress. And bring towels," growled Thomas.

Trepanner groaned, rocking himself back and forth. His right lower arm was shattered. Shreds of skin and muscle were covered in blood. No pumping blood, though, noted Umarrah, relieved.

Mary Ann, laden with towels came running up to them, Patrick dragging his heels behind her. Umarrah watched her shock as she took in Trepanner's injury. Their eyes met, but she said nothing. So he decided he would.

"Hello Mary Ann," he said.

"You know him?" Patrick gasped.

Mary Ann ignored Patrick. "Umarrah," she acknowledged, kneeling down.

"Do you think the bullet's still in there?" asked George, to no-one in particular. Umarrah spoke quietly but firmly to Trepanner, who stopped rocking. Umarrah forced himself to examine the shattered arm from the front.

"No," he replied. "We'll have to look at the back." He lifted his arm gently, holding it between the elbow and fingers. George and Mary Ann peeked underneath.

"It's gone straight through," she said. Umarrah lowered the arm.

"We'll have to clean this … mess before we take him inside," said George. "Thomas, get a large pitcher of warm water, and a full bottle of whisky," he ordered.

They waited in an awkward silence.

"Is there anyone else with you?" George asked, looking beyond Umarrah to the riverbank trees.

"No," he replied.

"I thought you were with Robinson."

"We were."

The whisky appeared in front of them. "Give him some," said George. "We have to try and patch this up, and it'll hurt."

Umarrah spoke gently to Trepanner, then poured a small amount into his mouth. He waited for the coughing to subside, then repeated the process several times, and hoped it would work quickly.

The wound was washed clean and the bleeding singed with a red-hot poker from the fire. The straps of muscle that were not blasted off by the gunshot were re-laid and covered with sheets of cloth. Trepanner's cries became more muted as the minutes passed. Finally they shifted him onto a makeshift stretcher.

"We can't do anything about his bones," Mary Ann said to Umarrah as they headed inside. She hesitated. "I thought he was very brave."

"Thank you for your help," he replied.

The stretcher was laid by the fire. Shauna walked into the room and froze. Umarrah saw her glance at Patrick, whose face remained thunderous. "It's alright, Shauna," said George. "This man needs our help. Why don't you take the children for a walk?" Umarrah watched her nod and head to the bedroom, colliding with a chair on the way.

Mary Ann put the billy on the stove.

"So where were you?" George repeated.

Umarrah ignored the question. "How did you know about Robinson?" he asked.

"Pahle wrote to me to say you'd left the gaol."

"We were with Robinson. He made us walk towards our enemies. We asked him many times to capture them. But he did not listen to us. So we left."

George's face was incredulous. "So you've walked all the way from the west coast to here? In winter?"

He looked from Umarrah to Parwareter, as Mary Ann handed out eggs and bread and watched it disappear in seconds.

"How on earth did you know where you were going?" he added.

Umarrah shrugged.

"Pahle had news about Laoninneloonner," said George.

Umarrah's eyes widened. "What news?"

"She was released from Robinson's house some weeks back. Pahle said the plan was that she, and some other women, would be taken to Launceston, set free, and encouraged to persuade their people to surrender."

"Do you know more?" Umarrah asked.

"No, I'm sorry. That's all," concluded George.

Where would she go? thought Umarrah. She'd want to head back to the remnants of her clans, after being in that gaol. But nowhere was safe, she knew that. The whitefellas' tentacles were everywhere. So where would she go?

He felt a desperate urge to go, now, and search for her. He glanced towards the door, and saw it open. Patrick entered, and shut it quietly behind him. He stood against the wall.

Umarrah scrutinised him. That whitefella'd kill them if he had another chance, or inform on them at least.

"Tell me about him," he commanded George, pointing at Patrick.

George sighed. "Patrick has not been with us for very long. I don't think he has really appreciated the particular nature of our ... acquaintance."

Patrick said nothing. His mouth had closed but his eyes were mutinous.

George turned to him. "Patrick, there has been violence committed by both sides, Black and white, these last years, despite what the papers say. You may not realise this, but it wasn't always like that, certainly not when I first came here as a boy. We lived alongside one another, to some extent, and sometimes helped each other." Patrick looked unconvinced. "Our farm has never been raided. Why do you think that is?" persisted George.

Umarrah watched intently as understanding slowly dawned on Patrick's face.

"But we live under martial law now," Patrick muttered.

"Yes, well, some things were already in place before that came along. If you want to keep your assignment here, and not go back to the chain gang, you will appreciate that this is something we do not discuss. Don't even think of talking about it to anyone. I will know where it came from," threatened George.

Patrick nodded, his face now a mixture of fear and puzzled amazement. He looked around the room then put his head down.

After a few moments of awkward silence, George dismissed him, but had a quiet word with Thomas to watch him carefully.

Umarrah watched Patrick leave.

"What are you going to do?" asked George.

"I want to find Laoninneloonner."

George sighed. "There's something you need to know."

Umarrah's eyes narrowed.

"The Government is planning to round up all the Aborigines on the island."

"What?" cried Umarrah in disbelief. Parwareter looked at him in panic.

"All available settlers and their servants have to report on the seventh of next month to the police magistrates. We are going to be part of a 'volunteer force' that will move with the police and the military across the island."

"You not going to do this, are you George?" demanded Umarrah.

"I don't have any choice. I think I'm already under suspicion. If I don't join this operation, I'll be accused openly of being a traitor."

Despite thinking only moments ago that coming here was a bad mistake, Umarrah had changed his mind. This was news with potentially catastrophic implications, and it was far better to be warned than not.

"Even if I could think of some excuse, there's no point after today. I'll have to join up or Patrick will inform on us."

But Umarrah had stopped listening to George's hand-wringing angst. Despite his exhaustion, he felt galvanised to find as many people as possible and warn them, Laoninneloonner first and foremost. There was no time to lose. Soon the settled areas would be crawling with soldiers, police, settlers and convicts.

"So when will this start?" he asked.

"In three weeks."

Umarrah stood up. Parwareter did the same but glanced anxiously at Trepanner.

"Please sit down," insisted George. "You're exhausted, which is no surprise given how far you've come. You can't leave until Trepanner is at least somewhat recovered. We'll keep Patrick under close watch. He mustn't know I've told you about this ... government operation. The other servants can be trusted."

"Not Shauna," interrupted Mary Ann from across the room. "She fancies Patrick."

"So she won't want him sent back to the chain gang then," calculated George.

"True," she replied.

"It's not in the interest of anyone in this household to talk about you being here," concluded George.

Umarrah and Parwareter sat down again.

"We won't stay long," he replied, thinking George was being overly optimistic.

A few days later, more information about the operation arrived. George and Umarrah were both shocked at the scale of the government's plans, the military and civilian involvement, the extent to which the island would be swept in a large line to capture Aborigines.

"You must get away before I have to leave," said George. "I can't guarantee your safety after that." He paused. "I hope you find Laoninneloonner before … before we do."

The three of them left before sunrise the next morning, Trepanner's arm well wrapped. He shouldn't have been moving but they had no choice. "My legs are good," he insisted, though Umarrah saw the ongoing pain etched across his face.

Once again, he thought, George has proven useful.

If we had not left Robinson, we would never have known this was coming.

Arthur's words and picture boards had been an outright lie.

CHAPTER TWENTY-FIVE

October 1830 – The central plateau

I t was a terrible start. Here they were, halfway up the steeply sided slope and nearly freezing. George was grateful for the temporary respite provided by the mountain's saddle. They would need to pass their first night here. The southerly gale roared over their heads, and when the gusts eased, snow drifted down to cover all they carried.

What a contrast to the fanfare of earlier in the day, George grumbled. Captain Donaldson had stood in front of the three hundred or so assembled men and reminded them that their task was to act as the western section of the government line. They were to drive the Aborigines in a south-easterly direction as well as prevent them heading up to the central plateau from the east. Donaldson's enthusiasm was palpable, but George sensed it wasn't shared by all those who stood before him. Some of the assembled cheered loudly, but looking around him, George saw many other faces, resigned, even cynical. Like him.

Donaldson then gave the command and they began their southward bound march from the Norfolk Plains. George, in charge of a party of ten men, began to trudge towards the Great Western Tiers, over which they must climb to reach the rendezvous point on the central plateau.

As the light faded, George checked that his group's supplies, and the men, were relatively sheltered. The last visible snow drifts passed overhead in another gust before darkness finally descended.

As the sky lightened the next morning, the winds had eased a little. The patchy sleep George got was disturbed by images of Umarrah laughing sardonically while George read to him Arthur's orders about the operation.

"Mr Collins?" came a voice in the dawn light.

"Over here," he replied.

Patrick scrambled over to him. "Shall we make a start, sir?"

George rubbed his eyes and saw other bodies stir. "Let's just make sure we've got enough light before we keep heading up. Don't want anyone losing their footing."

Patrick nodded and carefully moved back amongst the moving bodies. George crawled over to check the supplies. He was relieved to see that they weren't soaked, but made a mental note that they eat any damp rations first.

He heard movement as other groups of men began trudging up the slope. As another group passed nearby, George thought what a sorry sight they all made. Once their footsteps faded, he turned to his huddled group.

"Come on then. Don't want to be the last ones to the top."

There were some murmurs, whether agreement or complaint George couldn't tell. With him leading, they set off. This isn't a march, he observed soon after, more of a clutching scramble over large boulders. He was thankful when, a few hours later, the hard climb had levelled out. They rewarded themselves with a stop for rest and food. While water boiled for tea, George looked around and saw a succession of small camp fires dotted over the boulder strewn landscape. Occasional gusts of wind drew men closer to the warmth as they blew on their hands and willed their water to heat quickly.

George met with some of the other party leaders as they tried to implement the instructions they'd been given, and form a continuous line. To ensure this, each party had to signal their position.

"For those of us who don't have a bugle or a musket," said George, "I'd suggest calling out their assigned number."

"You mean shout it out, Collins, especially in this wind," replied the section leader.

"Of course," George agreed.

The section leader looked up from his map. "I think we need to head in this direction," he pointed.

"If you don't mind me saying, sir, it's actually this way," contradicted George. He indicated the south-east. "Then we'll skirt the eastern side of the Great Lake."

"How do you know that?"

George was remembering teenage hunting expeditions with Umarrah.

"Oh, I've been hunting up here a few times," he replied.

The man's crooked smiled assumed an unwanted comradeship. "Hunting. I know exactly what you mean Mr Collins. Well, I will be guided by you. Let's get our groups lined up, and progress with shouts, bugles or muskets along the line."

Fuelled by meat, damper, and sugared tea, they set off. But they were still nowhere near the Great Lake when progress was abandoned for the day in a sudden heavy fall of snow. The line of men could hardly be glimpsed and it completely dissolved in a scramble for shelter once the command was given.

Their second night began in only slightly better conditions than the first, and the flat landscape matched morale.

Trying to rest, George fretted, thinking of home. Of Mary Ann, waving him off with a brave face as he and Patrick departed to join up with other men in Perth. His mother, stoic as she stood by her daughter-in-law. The children, too young to understand but sensing his reluctance. Before they disappeared from view, George turned round to see his wife's face dissolve against her mother-in-law's shoulder, setting young Harriet to tears, while Annie held baby George.

Five days after they left Norfolk Plains, their bodies stood wearily together as part of the human line between Lakes Sorell and Echo. There was general consensus that it had been a challenge – some of the men, George conceded, expressing their thoughts rather more vigorously than that. Patrick and two other men had fallen sick from contaminated meat during the week, and the group's progress was slowed considerably as a result. The leader of another party had allowed kangaroos to be shot for food, despite them all being told this was not allowed. George was reluctant to disobey orders.

To top it off, their shoes were falling to pieces. Patrick's shoes had been reduced to shreds and several of George's men were having similar problems. As soon as they reached the meeting point, he reported to Captain Donaldson, and made sure to mention the state of the men's footwear. Donaldson replied irritably that they were obviously not the only ones with this problem, and that replacement shoes were on their way. He had no idea when the supplies would arrive.

His men were relieved that there was no expectation to continue, and that for now, they could stay where they were.

They camped in a long line, took turns on sentry duty, and otherwise rested. Donaldson had changed his mind and gunshots rang out as wallabies and kangaroos were shot for food. Their rations were becoming more rancid by the day.

One morning dawned with clear skies and gentle wind. George turned his face to the sun, enjoying its warmth. He wheeled round as Harry Rogers, the head of another small party, came running up.

"Mr Collins, we've sighted some natives!"

George held his breath as the rest of his group circled the two of them.

"Where?" shouted Patrick excitedly.

"They've just crossed the Shannon and are heading north, we're guessing to the Great Lake," reported Harry.

"How many?" asked George.

"Not sure exactly, but it's a big group. Our party is going to follow them."

"You can't just leave," countered George, trying to be the voice of reason. "You'll have to get permission from Donaldson. He's already had to send some men further south, and if Arthur asks for more, he won't be able to keep the line secure. And, Harry, if your estimate of the Aborigines' numbers is right, you'd be outnumbered. What would you be able to do exactly?"

But no one was listening. Their eyes were gleaming.

Harry hesitated. He knew George was right. But he and his men were thirsty for the chase. He shook his head.

"We can't wait, Collins. You'll have to tell Donaldson what we're doing."

"We have to go with them, sir," cried Patrick, so close that George could feel his breath.

Relieved that he could hide behind orders, George lashed out.

"You're crazy Harry, you're disobeying orders and the natives will outrun you, if they don't turn and attack you first. You don't even know where to find extra supplies if you get lost, which you will," he shouted.

"Just tell Donaldson, Collins. That's all I ask. If you want to stay here doing nothing, that's your lookout," Harry retorted, before going back to gather his men.

George stood there, watching him go. Dissenting murmurs from his men started to fill his ears. They were bored and wanted action. He knew that what he told them now would determine their ongoing cooperation as well as Patrick's silence. He levelled his gaze to each of them in turn.

"If a large group of natives has managed to break through this line, then we don't have a line. What Harry's doing, going off half-cocked without even informing Donaldson, is only making things worse. If we want to do our bit to make this operation successful, if we really want to capture the natives, then this line must be intact. No gaps. If some Blacks have got through, then we must redouble our efforts and close those gaps. There'll be others who will want to follow them. And we'll round them up."

He cast a quick look at Patrick, whose face was a picture of thwarted enthusiasm, and sighed inwardly. Some people would never be convinced, he knew. But the dissent turned to nods and a few lame cheers. Enough of his men were agreeing and they would sway the others.

He'd convinced them. He only hoped his prediction would turn out to be untrue.

CHAPTER TWENTY-SIX

October 1830 – Leterremairrener country

Mannalargenna was coming for him – Umarrah was convinced of it. The vengeful breath of the chief – the only blackfella he truly feared – he could almost feel it on his neck.

After leaving George's, and despite ever more circuitous detours around the whitefellas' hawthorn hedges, they managed to track down a small number of people from remnant friendly clans. Every person found increased his motivation to keep going. But Trepanner's death was a bitter blow. He had been in constant pain but rarely complained or slowed them down. Then fever wracked his body for several days. During his lucid moments, Umarrah was stunned not to see hurt in his friend's eyes, even when he knew his own face betrayed both grief and frustration. They found Trepanner's body at the bottom of the cliff one morning. As he touched his friend's ravaged face, he wearily grieved for the length and depth of their friendship. They dragged Trepanner's body to a nearby tree hollow, hid him there, and moved on.

The shock was palpable when some days later they stumbled across Mannalargenna and his warriors. They were not where he expected them to be. He had not sought them out, and could only guess that this government operation to round up blackfellas had forced them from their usual routes and safe places. In the ensuing confusion of fighting, people on both sides were wounded or killed, including Parwareter, who was felled by multiple spears. Afterwards, Umarrah wondered how they found the energy to inflict damage and death on each other when they faced a common enemy. But old hatreds persisted. His own anger was fuelled by increasing despair at not being able to find Laoninneloonner. As the fighting petered out, he managed to round up a few people and flee, but knew it would only be a matter of time before Mannalargenna tracked him down.

After a few days hard travel, they found themselves hiding in the hills above Kunermurlukeker, far enough away from the settlement of Launceston to feel safe. He watched the river's ebb and flow while calculating the risks, to himself and the others, then made his decision. He would use the whitefella as a shield against Mannalargenna. He would volunteer himself to them, and use the opportunity to find out as much as he could about this operation that George had described. Then he would flee, just as he had fled Robinson.

He had to go alone. To the government he was a prize worth keeping alive, but the others were not. No one questioned his decision, though some respectfully said it was too risky. He smiled wryly at their lack of disappointment at being excluded.

The next morning he pulled his fur closer against a cold and blustery wind, and headed towards the town. Stepping along the bridge, he reluctantly acknowledged its sturdiness and practicality in addition to its symbol of permanence, before heading towards the barracks near the town centre. A few people stepped back in horror, but no one accosted him. He could handle their fear. It was hatred he was watchful for. His heart was pounding as he approached the barracks. He had to get close enough to whoever was in charge, for some semblance of protection. He didn't want some rogue whitefella shooting him and thinking himself a hero.

After the shock had left the soldiers' faces, he could see that they didn't know what to do with him. So they kept him out of the way for a few days, locked and under guard. Then the order came in. The Governor wanted him down south, and they were glad to be rid of him. The soldier who had been assigned to watch him looked relieved when they took him away.

They made slow progress southward, the whitefella roads boggy with spring rain. He noticed how their attitude towards him changed, knowing that the Governor wanted him. As his personal assistant, the order said. They assumed he knew nothing about their operation. But he did, thanks to George.

The day after arriving in Hobart, he was taken to the Chief Police Magistrate. "My instructions are to arrange for your transfer to Orielton to act as the Governor's personal assistant," Mulgrave announced without introductions. So useful, thought Umarrah, this pretending to not understand, admitting to himself at the same time that he didn't catch every word just said. Mulgrave was clearly unsure about his grasp of English. In the confused silence, they locked eyes. Mulgrave broke off first. Then he reworded things.

"The Governor is your friend. He wants you to go to him," Mulgrave persisted.

Deliberately, slowly, Umarrah allowed a dawning recognition to cross his face. "Yes, I go," he replied.

Mulgrave's eyes widened. He nodded curtly. "Good. You will ... help the Governor, and through him, your people." Umarrah watched Mulgrave spit the last words like too many pepperberries.

As they travelled east from Hobart Town the next morning, he began to doubt his decision. Security was very tight. Soldiers, horses, and bullock drays groaning with supplies were on the move everywhere. Sucked into the centre of a military vortex, he started to fear there might be no possibility of escape.

Arriving in Orielton, he was marched to the Governor's tent, clearly the largest among many. Before entering he held out his hands for his chains to be removed. The flap was pulled aside and he was motioned to enter. Inside the tent was a table and a small portable writing desk perched unevenly on the covered ground. On the table was a series of maps, above which were scattered some wooden pointers. At the desk lay several heaps of paper and writing materials. Wooden chairs were dotted around the table.

After a moment, Arthur put down his pen and walked towards him. They regarded each other for a moment. Arthur held out his hand. Umarrah shook it. "Your presence here as my personal assistant is most welcome, Umarrah," Arthur announced. "Thank you for coming," he added, before dismissing the soldiers.

Arthur pulled two chairs over, sat, and motioned for Umarrah to join him.

"I hope you will help us to find your countrymen," he began.

I have nothing to say to that, thought Umarrah. He watched Arthur wait for several seconds before continuing.

"I was surprised to be told that you had volunteered your services in Launceston. You had been travelling with Mr Robinson, then left him during his journey. Why was that?"

"He not listen to us. He not capture the Toogee."

Umarrah watched a frown cross Arthur's face.

"I was sorry to hear that you had left. Mr Robinson is working hard to conciliate your countrymen. But you are here now."

That word 'conciliate' again, thought Umarrah, deciding not to comment.

"Please tell me if I am speaking too quickly for you," added Arthur.

"I understand."

Arthur walked over to his desk, and pulled out one of the picture-boards that Frankland had shown the last time they met. He held it out to him. Umarrah took it and looked at the pictures once more – the black women with the white baby, the white woman with the black baby, the white man hung for shooting a blackfella, the blackfella hung for spearing a white man. He put it down.

"You remember these?" asked Arthur.

"Yes," Umarrah nodded.

"I still believe in peace. But there has been much violence on both sides." He pointed to the images. "We need to find all the natives we can, so they cannot be harmed, and in turn cannot harm the settlers and their families."

Smooth words, noted Umarrah angrily, watching Arthur observe him for a reaction. Be very careful what you say, he told himself. As he tried to formulate a reply, a crawling feeling of enclosure spread through him. I'm back in the south, where we were gaoled, he panicked, and now there are more soldiers than I've ever seen.

Fighting to keep his face impassive, he focussed on an answer.

Arthur waited.

"What happens after you find them?" he asked.

"We will discuss this at the time. But first things first. Will you help?"

Who is this 'we'? he asked himself, noting Arthur dodging his question. Acknowledging that at this point he had little choice, he simply nodded.

Arthur smiled. "Excellent. Then I would like you to join Mr Gilbert Robertson out in the field as soon as possible."

Robertson! The man who had made his year of imprisonment far more tolerable, despite their violent introduction.

"Robertson a good man," he smiled, and saw a flicker of suspicion cross Arthur's face.

"Yes, well, I know he will be pleased to be reacquainted with you. I hope you will have more success with him than you had with Mr Robinson." He took some blank paper from his desk and scratched instructions with his pen.

"I am the only blackfella to help you?" Umarrah asked.

Arthur's pen paused. "Yes, you are, at the moment."

"But you would use other blackfellas if you can?"

"I will ask any of your people to help me find and remove your countrymen from harm," Arthur replied.

So if Mannalargenna was captured, we could be forced together, thought Umarrah, appalled at the prospect.

The flap opened, and a soldier announced Gilbert Robertson. Umarrah stood up, smiling, as Robertson strode towards him. They shook hands.

"I can see, Mr Robertson, that you will not be reluctant to take Chief Umarrah with you," Arthur commented sardonically from his desk.

"I am happy to do your Excellency's bidding," came the reply. "And I apologise for my poor manners," he added, hastily moving to Arthur and offering his hand.

Arthur rose. "I have been explaining to the Chief my desire to find as many of his countrymen as possible so that they may be protected from harm," he said smoothly. He glanced at Umarrah then turned his back and drew Robertson to the other side of the tent. "My orders," he whispered rapidly, "are for your party, and others, to move ahead of the line of men and drive the natives south, towards and through the small neck of land here," he pointed, "which leads to the two peninsulas. They will not be able to escape from there. We will remain here, keep the line intact and prevent any escape northward."

Umarrah had heard and understood enough. The word 'escape'. Twice. He stared at their backs while Roberston murmured a tactful reply. "We are all working towards a good solution, Sir," he said. They turned to look at Umarrah cautiously, but his face betrayed nothing. He felt deception chill the air around him, and the panic he had pushed down earlier start to rise again. Then a red hot fury smothered it.

CHAPTER TWENTY-SEVEN

October 1830 – The central plateau

S tanding together in the Captain's tent on the lakeside, George saw in Donaldson's face a man frustrated both by poor planning, and the effort of trying to command soldiers, settlers and convicts simultaneously.

"When did Harry Rogers tell you this?" he spat.

"A short while ago."

"Well he's a damn fool. And why didn't you stop him?"

"Forgive me Captain Donaldson," George snapped, "but I had a hard enough time keeping my men from going off with him! They only didn't go because I reminded them, strenuously, that your orders were to be obeyed. I had no control over Harry or his men."

He dropped his voice. "My apologies. It's not just the shoes that are fraying."

Expecting a reprimand, he was surprised to see Donaldson's shoulders slump.

"You've done your best, Collins. I'm well aware there are already gaps in the line, but your section has remained relatively well intact, probably thanks to your actions."

George stunned, was momentarily lost for words. "Thank you," he mumbled.

Donaldson smiled briefly. "While we wait for instructions about our next movements, we have to keep the line between the two lakes intact. If we do, we might be able to stop any natives from further south reaching their meeting places up here on the plateau."

His men's complaints about lack of food, firewood and shoes were still ringing in George's ears. He'd tried to placate them by promising he would ask at the first opportunity. It looked like this was it.

"Sir, do you have any idea when the new supplies will arrive?"

"No, I don't," replied Donaldson irritably. "They should be here by now, along with our orders."

"If no supplies accompany the orders, my men will refuse to move, being virtually barefoot."

Donaldson was about to interject.

"However, while we wait, some of us could head for one of the other supply depots. There are a few men in my party whose shoes are reasonably intact and would come with me."

"Thank you, Collins," Donaldson replied. "I've been thinking the same, and you've saved me the trouble of deciding who to ask. Come back in the morning and we'll discuss this further."

"Of course, sir." George nodded, before turning to leave.

"Collins?"

He looked back at Donaldson's face, suddenly grim.

"If you do come across any Blacks, at any time, you are not to spare man, woman or child. You are not to parley with them."

George was aghast. "I thought the plan was to round them up, not kill them!" he blurted.

"The Blacks killed two of my men. That's all the reason I need."

They looked at each other for a long moment.

"I understand your position, sir," replied George, stumbling through a deliberately ambiguous response.

"Good," said Donaldson.

George opened the tent flap and walked out into the cold air.

Sitting on a rock that evening, he examined the dry bread and piece of salted beef in his hand, but had lost his appetite. He prayed that they wouldn't come across anyone, and hoped there were many and large holes in the line. On the other side of the fire, Patrick scowled at him, furious at being unable to join the journey to the supply depot, by virtue of his dilapidated shoes. Patrick was the last person George wanted in the group, especially if they came across any Aborigines. Who else, apart from Patrick, he wondered, shared Donaldson's views? Was this whole exercise a front for sanctioned murder?

The wind had dropped and the stars were out. He looked up at the night sky, relieved that it was dry. He took off what was left of his shoes, propped them against a rock then dragged his tired body into his makeshift tent. Outside, sentries shouted their position on the line, voices closer and then fainter, and inside he railed in solitary angst against this organised madness, before finally lapsing into a fitful sleep.

On return from their search three days later, they found out how well they'd done. Having discovered the depot, more by accident than design, they'd brought back rations that were reasonably intact and dry. He'd also used his musket to shoot and kill a kangaroo, which he dropped from around his shoulders.

"Thank God," Donaldson said when they reported to him. "I sent out groups to other depots but everything was soaked and the meat was rotten. And Harry Roger's party has not yet returned. I fear they are lost, too weak to get back, or worse."

"You fear the natives might have attacked them?"

"It's a possibility we have to consider," replied Donaldson.

George was unsurprised at the news or Donaldson's response. Momentarily guilty for not being more concerned, he was also grateful that he'd managed to convince his men not to join Harry when the temptation was greatest.

"Will we send out a search party?"

"I'm pondering that now. If we do, your men won't be included. You've done enough for now."

George stood his men down, then left as Donaldson took charge of distributing the rations.

As darkness fell, and the line's sentries perused their surroundings, George was surprised to see Donaldson approach him.

"Orders have arrived. We'll head south to Bothwell in the morning."

"How many days march will that be?" George asked.

"About a week, I expect," he replied.

"What about Harry and his men?"

"They disobeyed orders, Collins. We can't wait for them. Anyway, they've probably stumbled on a farmhouse somewhere."

"Have more supplies come?"

"Limited shoes and food. We'll pick up more in Bothwell."

Donaldson walked off to notify the other party leaders.

Revived somewhat by the supplies, they managed to reach Bothwell a day ahead of schedule. Seeing settler cottages, a few wide streets and even a church spreading out below them lifted the men's morale. In contrast, George noticed Donaldson's mood darken.

"Aren't you pleased with our progress?" he asked him.

"Yes, but I've had bad news. Rogers was right about seeing some natives," he said to George. "Two groups of them have broken through our part of the line. It could be as many as sixty people," he conceded.

George concealed his relief. I wonder if Umarrah and I passed each other in the bush? he thought.

"And I have new orders. Tomorrow, we head to Richmond. Let's hope a night here in town will be enough for the men, because there's a lot of walking still to go."

George opened his mouth to protest, but instantly thought better of it. He looked across the street as a group of men, drunk and singing, burst out of the hotel and stumbled down the wide unsealed road. George waited for Donaldson to unleash a furious reprimand, but he said nothing.

"What time would you like us mustered in the morning?" he asked.

"Nine o'clock will do," Donaldson muttered. "Some of them will have drink to sleep off."

After a chaotic muster the next morning, it was ten o'clock before they left the town. George could only describe the journey to Richmond as a shambles. The line of men disintegrated. There was no attempt to even keep it. Despite, or perhaps because of the contact with some semblance of town life, motivation died. While it was heartening to be able to sometimes walk along roads, rather than through bush, some of the men visited inns along the way, and drunken groups were seen staggering at their own pace.

George tried to keep his men together with some semblance of authority, but there was open talk of desertion. Two days before they reached Richmond, four of his men snuck away. He knew they had spring crops to tend, and families anxious for their return. He had the same. There had been no captures of Aborigines, poor supplies and poorer morale. Perhaps that's why they didn't see Harry and his men again, thought George. They'd given up and gone home too.

He spent more and more time with Donaldson as they headed south. The Captain seemed to desire his company. George lost nothing by obliging him, and at least had the benefit of finding out what was going on.

He hoped Umarrah was well away from all this, but wondered whether his navigation and avoidance skills would stand up to the military and civilian might being wielded against them.

A motley bunch of men staggered up to the designated point outside Richmond four days later, and were marshalled into order. The presence of the governor galvanised them into a reasonably presenting group, they were inspected, and then informed that they would soon be moving forward for the final stages of the operation.

George's heart sank. After two weeks that felt like an eternity, he watched more people melt away. Like them, he was desperate to get home, worrying now if Aborigines who might have dodged the line would discover and attack farms stripped of men able to defend them.

The next day, he walked with Donaldson towards a local inn, where civilian party leaders were meeting to discuss how to boost morale. The late afternoon sunlight illuminated a large group further along the main road heading in their direction.

"That's Gilbert Robertson," indicated Donaldson as the groups drew closer. "He must have come in from the bush to replenish supplies. Oh yes, and the Chief Umarrah. Appointed by Arthur no less, as his personal assistant."

George's eyes widened in disbelief. There was Umarrah, walking beside Robertson's horse. As the two groups passed each other, Donaldson called out to Robertson, asking how he had fared. "No luck yet," replied Robertson, slowing down briefly. Hearing the exchange, Umarrah scanned the strangers before his eyes locked on George. Neither gave any sign of recognition, then moments later the groups separated.

As they arrived at the inn, George turned and watched Umarrah in the distance, talking to Robertson. Donaldson noticed. "There'll be more of those parties going out, now that we are here," he said.

"What do they do?" asked George.

"Move ahead of the line, and force any natives in the area southward into the peninsula, where they'll be trapped," came the reply.

How on earth did Umarrah end up here, so far from home? wondered George. Did they capture him? What about Laoninneloonner, Parwareter and Trepanner? Were they killed and he capitulated? I'll bet he understands what Arthur's using him for, and must reason that there is something in it for him. Would he be able to escape, assuming he still wanted to?

Inside the inn, drinks in hand, they began their deliberations. But it was a pointless exercise. Over the following days, morale and discipline among the men declined even further. While they waited for the last push to start, Arthur commanded that the line be rigorously maintained between Sorell and Orford, to stop Aborigines from breaking through and heading north. They walked through the bush, scouring fruitlessly for any sightings.

George envied, rather than resented, those who'd given up and gone home. But by now he'd become Donaldson's confidante, boosting his Captain's morale at the cost of his own. If he left now, as the operation neared its peak, it would be held against him. He had to stay.

CHAPTER TWENTY-EIGHT

November 1830 – Pydairrerme country

U marrah slumped against a boulder outside the camp and watched blankly as the sun dipped below the western sky. No one followed him, having long given up restraining him on the Governor's insistence. He found it exhausting trying to follow the whitefella discussions. The intense concentration of listening and piecing together their plans, when some of the words were indecipherable, while at the same time appearing ignorant, took its toll. But the ruse appeared to have worked. Arthur did not hesitate to share information. He'd learnt much more than they suspected. They asked for his opinion at times and he gave vaguely helpful answers. They would nod, he would nod back.

A big push was coming. Soon the whitefellas would focus all their resources into driving, and trapping, blackfellas into the southernmost peninsula. They hadn't actually seen anyone but reassured themselves this was because their mere presence was enough to corral the Aborigines towards the area. But they were wrong. Blackfellas were slipping through their fingers, not many, but enough to give him heart. One morning he saw three people peering at them from behind eucalypts up on a ridge line. He made sure not to spend too much time looking, so as not to draw attention to them. No one else noticed anyway. A few minutes later, when the horses had moved on, he looked back. They'd gone.

He needed to be well away before the operation was over and they realised how badly they'd failed. If he stayed, the blaming would start and he might be accused of not trying hard enough, or worse, sabotage. The question burning in his mind was, where was Laoninneloonner, where was Mannalargenna, and who might he still find to cobble together a war party?

Robertson had told him that Mannalargenna was at Batman's farm until recently, but had fled one night, raided some huts along the South Esk, then disappeared. He half hoped that Mannalargenna wouldn't have been able to evade the whitefella line. But it appeared he had.

Of Laoninneloonner, he knew nothing more than what George had told him.

There was one more factor to consider. The rumours were that whitefellas were leaving, in droves. Going back to their farms, giving up on this obsession of the Governor's. And that changed things. What had been undefended, would now be so again. A window that had been open for raiding, was closing.

So why hadn't George left? He seemed friendly with that soldier on the street at Richmond. Robertson's face was grim when he asked him about it. A cruel man, Donaldson, he said. George was probably just close to him to deflect suspicion. We are both doing what it takes, thought Umarrah – saying one thing and intending another.

And yet he'd had a nagging feeling ever since the day they saw each other. What if they promised George he'd finally get that land, and more, if he shared everything he knew. Would he do that? Had he done it already?

Eventually he stood up, stretched his arms to the sky then out as wide as his muscles would stretch. He raised his head and sniffed the eucalypt-scented air, fresh after rain. He rubbed the muscles of his legs. They itched to run. His arms itched to throw. He itched to stand high above Kunermurlukeker and sweep his gaze from the south, where the two rivers that joined to make it, met, all the way north to the sea. To breathe it in, and out again. He shut his eyes and saw it in his mind.

He shivered. It was nearly dark. He looked at the last streaks of pale pink above the hills, and decided to head back to camp. Having gained Arthur's trust, his days were easier than he anticipated. They even allowed him to hunt sometimes – supervised, of course. That meant two men, who often lagged behind while he chased kangaroo or wallaby. He could even disappear from view in the thick, hilly scrub. He'd always pop back into view so they wouldn't get alarmed. They even helped him make a spear one time, an easy exchange of labour since he was hunting for dinner. The soldiers were tired, bored, and hungry. And he enjoyed the manipulation.

He turned around as footsteps approached.

"Here you are," said Robertson.

Something about his voice was different. Umarrah looked at him, and his face betrayed it too. An unusual awkwardness.

"I have news." He hesitated. "It's bad, I'm sorry."

Umarrah waited.

"We've had a report from Robinson. He's at Ansons Bay. Some Aborigines have joined him there, having come back from a dispute with the Big River people. They claim to have killed three of them – your wife being one."

"Laoninneloonner? Are you sure?"

"We've no reason to doubt Robinson's account."

"Who are the blackfellas who say this?" he growled.

"We're not sure," he replied.

He watched Robertson's face, trying to determine the truth. Did Robertson, or Arthur, have something to gain by lying to him about Laoninneloonner? But he couldn't think of a reason, and he trusted Robertson enough by now to think he would not stoop to this sort of deception.

"Thank you for telling me," he said, and looked away.

"I am truly sorry, Umarrah. She seemed a fine woman" he added.

"You knew her. That is something," Umarrah replied.

Robertson nodded. "I'll leave you," he said. He hesitated momentarily, then walked away.

Umarrah stared into the sky's darkness then put his hands on his head while his chest rose and fell with ragged breaths. Then his legs gave way and his knees thudded onto the ground. I left her there in that gaol, he accused himself. Why couldn't I find her after her release? She must have been desperately trying to find me, too. And then to be betrayed by blackfellas.

And then what did I do? Hand myself over to the whitefellas and end up back down here.

Eventually his breath stilled. The jarring sounds of camp life intruded again. Squaring his shoulders he stood up, and forced himself to go back.

But not for long. He allowed himself a small smile, imagining Arthur's fury after he escaped. The Governor would take it personally, and there would be no third chance. Which meant nothing now.

The next two days seemed never-ending. Arthur expressed his condolences, whatever that meant. Umarrah said little, his throat tight and his mind elsewhere.

Out hunting early the next day, he could hardly believe it when an opportunity came. It was surprising how long it took for the shouting to begin. He watched them from a good distance away then focussed on picking up the familiar road tracking north. After several hours, he found a safe spot on top of a hill overlooking a couple of small farms. He had found some trynueler when his hunger couldn't be ignored, and chewed most of a large handful of the salty leaves, waiting for cover of darkness. When it came, he crept to the closest farm, raided a chicken roost and found two eggs. He drank his fill from a water trough, listened for any movement, and hearing none, retreated to the hill. He found a stick and cracked a small hole at the end of each egg, sucking out the insides. His hunger quieted, he managed to snatch a few hours of disrupted sleep, one ear alert to any sounds of pursuit.

The next morning, as the eastern sky began to lighten, the mildness in the air warned of the heat to come. He set off in the early dawn, eating the remaining trynueler on the way. He covered as much ground as he could, but by late morning, and with little sustenance, had to stop. He managed to find a shaded rock ledge high enough to offer some protection and rested while the sun began its descent. As dusk fell, he set off again, and soon after heard it: the welcome sound of running water. Rounding a hill with galvanised legs, he saw the river below him. He could hardly restrain himself but watched and waited till it was almost dark before nearly falling in the water in his relief. You've never been so keen to see a river, he thought ruefully. And the bonus was that this one was shallow. He could feel the reassurance of the river bed against the soles of his feet. He drank his fill. He cooled his body. Relieved, he trudged to a safe spot above the northern river bank and lay down, his back pressed against a wide tree trunk.

A stroke of luck. A possum was scratching around not far above him. He saw their eyes, and aimed his only spear with deadly accuracy. The possum fell to the ground with a thud, and he finished him off swiftly with a rock. The question then was whether to risk lighting a fire. If I can get back up to that rock ledge, I can risk it, he calculated. He slung the possum round his aching shoulders, grabbed his spear and trudged back up the hill. But the effort was worth it and the warmth and a full belly a relief.

As the second night wore on, grief again washed over him. During fitful sleep, she came to him in a dream, and stood there, silent but penetrating with her gaze – the fierce woman he loved, not the one whose despair at incarceration would sometimes overtake her. He woke with a start and stared into the blackness. As the tears streaked his cheeks, questions and self recrimination resurfaced. How much did she suffer? What if she thought I hadn't tried to find her? He could feel himself almost revelling in the pain and refused to allow himself any relief from it. Finally, there was nothing left. His eyes and cheeks were dry.

There was one question he had no answer for. Where and to whom was he heading now? How could he keep going, without her?

Before dawn he slipped back into a dreamless sleep. Waking later than planned, he listened carefully, heard no sounds to give him pause, and crept down to the river to drink. It was a landmark he could use. The markenner, a road he knew well, was just north west of here, and would take him back home. Once there, he would search for some, any, allies, share what he'd learnt from his time with Arthur, try and determine Mannalargenna's whereabouts, and keep away from him. Then fight back. Raid whitefella properties for anything of use, kill if necessary.

His grip tightened on the spear.

Were there any whitefellas left he could trust for shelter, or food? George might still be down here, and his motives were now questionable. Hugh Murray? No. David Gibson? Of course not.

How long had he risked going to anyone other than George?

Get moving, he urged himself. Get home before all the whitefellas are back on their farms.

He started to walk, then broke into a trot. Soon his legs were flying.

CHAPTER TWENTY-NINE

November 1830 – Forestier peninsula

T he final push was a complete failure, thought George. The doubters were right.

Those men who hadn't absconded, and who still trudged dutifully onwards, achieved nothing for nine extra days of effort. They reached East Bay Neck, the little isthmus at the beginning of the Forestier Peninsula, and just stopped. They were supposed to have overtaken the advance scouring parties who roamed ahead of them, but none had been seen. This could only mean that the gaps in the line must have been huge.

It was beyond embarrassing.

Instead of feeling pride that his duty was done, George felt only stupidity at not leaving earlier.

Then he heard that Umarrah had absconded.

"Not the first time he's run off," Donaldson proclaimed when he shared the news, as George struggled to comprehend it.

"Unbelievably ungrateful," he added. "Arthur's furious apparently. Robertson said he'd never seen him like it."

"I wonder why he left?" asked George innocently.

"Well normally George, I would have said 'who knows?'" Donaldson quipped. "Because no one knows how their uncivilised minds work. But in this case, there appears to be a reason."

"And what's that?"

"Apparently some of the black tribes have been fighting amongst themselves. That can only be to our advantage, of course. Umarrah's wife was apparently killed during this inter-tribal dispute, and that seems to be why he left."

"I see," replied George, keeping his voice even. Donaldson, who seemed to have expected more interest in the news, shrugged at George's response, and walked off. George was relieved to see him go. He found some dappled shade under a tall eucalypt and leant back against the trunk. What would it be like if he'd been given news that Mary Ann had died? He'd just want to go home. Immediately. At least he knew where Mary Ann was.

George could only guess at Umarrah's state of mind, but he imagined that retribution was top of the list. Against his own enemies as well as the settlers, and the government. Him, and any other compatriots still at large that he could find, against the world.

I've got to get back home, George fumed.

After one more night camped at the neck of the bay, they were suddenly discharged to go home. Relief flooded through the bedraggled remnants of men. A few stripped off and ran into the sea, gasping as they plunged into the beautiful but cold turquoise water. They picked up three days of rations to help them on their way, and it was astounding to see how men could pick up speed when the direction was homeward.

In Sorell, the newspapers reported that attacks from Aborigines had continued to occur even while the operation proceeded. George didn't bother to get details. He was furious that not only had there been no reward for his loyalty, but that in his absence his family could have been put at risk. To make matters worse, no punishment had been meted out to the absconders, some of whom would be home by now.

He debated whether to visit Margaret on his way home. It would slow his progress, but he was keen to see family, and desperate for a bath and some clean clothes.

He managed to get a seat on a coach leaving Hobart a week later. As he headed north, grateful for the transport, he wondered how long it would take Umarrah to get home on foot.

His spirits rose as the coach pulled into Bagdad. Remembering the right track to take to reach the house, before long he was on the veranda, brushing his clothes and trying to smooth his hair. He knocked on the door. His niece

Charlotte opened it, looked at George without recognition, and disappeared back inside. Moments later Margaret was at the door, threw her arms around him and dissolved into tears.

"Well this is a fine greeting, sister," he began. "I know I must look dreadful, but I'm glad you can recognise me, even if your children might not," he added, laughing.

Something about the way Charlotte stood still and silent in the middle of the hallway, watching her mother's tears, stopped him. He pulled away from Margaret and scanned her face.

"What on earth is it, Meg?"

"Oh George, it's been a nightmare," she blurted.

She dragged him into the front room, not even commenting on his appearance. After calling out for Charlotte to bring refreshments, she took a few deep breaths, grabbed her handkerchief from her pocket, and began.

"Louisa's younger sisters came to visit a few weeks ago. We hadn't seen them for a while – we'd had some bad weather. After it improved, they took the chance to visit Louisa and John before Christmas. You haven't met them, of course," she stumbled. "And now ..." her face crumpled and she blew her nose before struggling to speak.

George didn't want to hear what was coming next.

"Some natives attacked their place. They speared Anne. To death. She was sixteen years old."

He froze.

"And young Sophia, she's only seven," Margaret choked.

He was almost too scared to ask.

"Is she alive?"

"Yes, just. They speared her, but the doctor says she'll survive."

Margaret blew her nose.

"John and Thomas were away, like you, on this government operation. For all the good it did."

Charlotte returned, put tea on the table, glanced at their faces and left the room.

George, stunned, waited silently for Margaret to pour a cup. A creeping sense of nausea filled him, knowing that the violence across the island had arrived on his extended family's doorstep.

"How are Louisa and John?" he asked.

"Terrible, as you can imagine. They managed to get word to both Thomas and John, and the authorities let them leave, but it was too late by then." She sniffed. "Louisa won't leave Sophia's bedside. The poor young thing's not in her right mind."

"What do you mean?" asked George.

"Oh she says very little, but wakes up most nights, screaming."

George could see Margaret bracing herself for the sharing of more pain. He took her hand and held it as she haltingly described Anne's funeral.

As he lay in the bath an hour later, he allowed himself a few moments to luxuriate in the warm water and the pleasure of becoming clean again. He was glad that he had come. For while he had soothed his big sister in her grief, she had also put his mind at ease. As Margaret had shared the awful news, his fears about his farm's vulnerability to attack intensified. She read his face and revealed that Mary Ann had recently written to say that she, the children and all the servants had decamped to Pleasant Banks at David and Eliza's insistence. All were all safe and well.

Dinner that night was very quiet. Louisa and John gave their apologies. The children's boisterous chattiness was notably absent and they were excused early from the table. As they departed, George realised that their eldest was not amongst them.

"Where's Beth?" he asked.

"Oh you haven't heard!" said Margaret, brightening a little. "She is married. To a young man by the name of Henry Glover. Their wedding was in September. He's a lovely young man. Her in-laws seem nice too – her father-in-law, John, is an established painter in England. Apparently, he is joining his sons here next year."

"Congratulations," said George. "You must be proud."

"We are. We miss her, but we're glad she's not here."

Margaret's eyes filled with tears again.

Thomas, sitting beside her, squeezed her hand.

"Understandably," said George.

Meg sniffed, then stood up. "I'll clear this up. Why don't you both sit out on the verandah?"

They nodded and pushed back their chairs.

"What did you think of the operation?" George asked Thomas, as they sat with their whisky.

"I was convinced it was the right thing to do, but the reality was a disorganised bloody mess. We catch one or two Blacks, and behind our backs they attack our home ..."

His face was bleak.

"I'm thinking of resigning, and moving the family back into Hobart. John's seriously considering doing the same. It's just that we've put all our efforts into the farms and ..." He stopped and rubbed his hand across his mouth.

"I'd be thinking the same, Thomas, for what it's worth. It'd be an upheaval, certainly, but perhaps moving to town would help in the recovery."

Thomas nodded. "Perhaps."

"Can you tell me what happened?"

"There were three of them. Looking for food, we think. Sophia and Anne were coming out of the barn when they saw them peering round the side of the house. The girls ran for the back door of the house but ... Anne didn't reach it. Sophia was lucky. She managed to get inside before a second spear hit her."

"God, how awful. Is there anything I can do?"

"Well, yes. I'm sorry to ask, but you'd be doing us a favour by telling the rest of the family in person, and saving Meg the pain of having to write all this in a letter. She's been dreading doing it."

"No need to apologise. It's the least I can do, and Meg will be able to share the news of Beth's wedding. That will give her, and the rest of the family, some joy."

Before he boarded the coach a few days later, Margaret kissed the envelope addressed to their mother, a wad of sheets inside, and handed it to him. He hugged her tightly and shook Thomas's hand.

The next day, rattled from lack of sleep, and as the dread of being the bearer of fearful news bore down on him, George could not push aside something else he did not want to contemplate. Could Umarrah have been involved in the attack? It had happened not long after he escaped. Could he have met up with other Aborigines so soon, and found himself near Bagdad? It seemed an unlikely westerly diversion on a northward route home. George thought he would have stuck to the eastern side of the island until he reached Great Oyster Bay and then headed inland. It was unlikely he'd get lost – his navigation skills were excellent. But who knew what detours he would've needed to make in a part of the island he did not know well, and this part the most heavily colonised, and with disbanded groups of men heading home themselves? Worse still, perhaps losing his wife was the last straw and Umarrah was assuaging his grief in indiscriminately violent rage. Horrifying images filled George's head of Umarrah attacking his sister's nieces, of them pleading with him.

He shoved open the carriage window and took gulps of fresh air.

Eventually he slumped back, ignored the perplexed looks of his fellow passengers, and the inexorable movement of the carriage finally lulled him to sleep.

By the time the coach neared home, he craved his family's faces and the distraction of domesticity. He spent the last part of the journey considering Donaldson's recent overtures of ongoing acquaintance. He didn't like him, but considered whether such an acquaintance would be of help in the future and therefore worth the effort.

He smiled at the one undiluted pleasure to come. It would be his son's first Christmas.

The end of his journey came with a gentle shove awake, from the passenger next to him. The driver had kindly paused on the Hobart road before they reached the usual stop at the Perth punt.

He stumbled out of the carriage into the sunshine, picked up his bag, waved the driver goodbye and began to walk stiffly along the track towards Pleasant Banks. By the time he was nearly there, his legs, warmed up, were running.

Thomas spied him first. "Master!" he shouted from the yard, and that was all it took. Seconds later the door flew open and Mary Ann stood in the doorway, shrieking with joy, then running across the yard to greet him, Eliza behind her.

CHAPTER THIRTY

March 1831 – Leterremairrener country

The freshness of the morning air filled Umarrah's nostrils. The long summer days were shortening, but there was still little rain. Kunermurlukeker's waters meandered lazily towards the northern coast, its vivid blue mirroring the sky above.

Umarrah and his companions gazed down on the little farm bordering the wide east arm of the river. "We've watched them for long enough," he declared. "There's only the two of them, and a child. No one else has come. I say we do it tomorrow."

He looked at each of them in turn and they nodded. It had been days since their bellies were full. Thirst stalked them. Desperation had begun to bite.

Relieved that the decision was agreed, he walked over to the shallow creek and drank. They would be loath to leave their sheltered position beside a supply of water, even though its level was low and starting to stagnate in murky pools. There were still risks in the attack. Although they'd not seen it during their reconnaissance, the farmer was almost guaranteed to have a gun, and he wouldn't hesitate to use it. Umarrah wondered if he'd been part of the whitefellas' recent operation, and imagined a scenario where, at the point of a spear, the man would describe his involvement in the operation, while Umarrah teased him that all this work culminated not in his and his family's safety, as Arthur had promised, but in this last living moment. Where is your Governor now? he would sneer.

He walked over to the edge of the ridge, and looked down again on the farm, its neat fences extending to the river's edge. Their quarry emerged from the shed with some tools and went to work tilling his garden. Some time later, the woman called to him from the doorway of the house. He put his tools down, and walked over to her. The door thudded to a close behind them.

They waited for nightfall.

He sat slightly apart and observed them, this unlikely group. He'd searched through all the customary meeting places on Leterremairrener and Panninher country, and eventually found just the four warriors. They were all relieved to have found each other and simultaneously appalled there were no others, at least not yet.

Finding Kubmanner was particularly surprising. She and Laoninneloonner had been among the group of women released from incarceration in Hobart and sent back to Launceston. Told to spread a "message of peace", she spat, describing how some whitefellas had molested them after their release. Laoninneloonner had fled towards Yinginner and that was the last time Kubmanner said she saw her. But she confirmed the news that Robertson had given him. There had been fighting, The Big River people had killed three people, and Laoninneloonner was one.

Kubmanner's broken jaw, sustained during the assault at the time of their release, was a daily reminder for Umarrah of what the women had endured. At least Laoninneloonner's suffering is over, he told himself, though it gave him no comfort. There felt like no other option than to track and visit retribution upon whitefellas in general, and her killers in particular.

Kubmanner's priorities were different. She demanded revenge on "the whitefellas who abused us," sure that Umarrah would agree.

"Where are they?" he'd asked.

"In the town," she replied.

"It's too dangerous to go into Launceston," he snapped, knowing he'd done the very same himself not that long ago.

"Don't you want to kill the men who violated us?" she retorted.

"And be killed ourselves?" he shouted. The look of disgust on her face when he said this told him she didn't care.

As for the Big River people's whereabouts, she only frustrated him. They're heading north east, she said. But that was Mannalargenna's Country. He had no desire to come across his traditional enemy. Retribution would be found elsewhere.

Such as the farm below.

Let's hope we all keep our nerve tomorrow, he muttered. Glancing back at Kubmanner, he saw her grim determination. Her courage was not in the slightest doubt. He'd have more of a problem stopping her from killing them all single handed.

When darkness fell, they headed across and partly down the next ridge, judging it safe enough to start a fire from that distance. Kubmanner spied an unlucky possum clambering down a small tree. She grabbed its tail before it got away. A large stone finished it off efficiently and their morale improved with the smell of roasting meat for dinner. They took their time to eat, making each mouthful last, and enjoying the fire's comfort. Eventually they headed back, to sleep near the creek and take shifts to keep watch.

After going through their plan for tomorrow one final time, Umarrah lay down, but sleep was elusive. He looked up at the tiny sliver of moon and the thick white river of stars twisting through the night sky. Another possum hissed and clicked above him, melding with the faint snores around the campfire. There has to be more than just these four, he railed. We have to keep searching, cover every piece of ground. But with enemies in the towns, on farms, and blackfella enemies as well, who would likely be hiding like they were, what were their options? I've learnt much at the side of Arthur, he railed, and I don't want this to go to waste! We all need to know what we're up against. Would you share what you know with Mannalargenna? a voice inside asked. He had no answer for that.

His thoughts turned to George. He was still surprised to have seen him in Richmond, but in the months since his doubts as to where George's loyalties now lay had grown. He'd even watched the farm from a distance for a while after his return. But he'd not revealed himself even after George had arrived back home, unsure of the reception he'd get.

After some fitful dozing, he woke them at dawn. Kubmanner was furious when he ordered her to remain on the hill as a lookout for any strangers. The remaining four of them crept silently down to the farm. They took up hidden positions around the boundary, with a clear view of the front and back doors of the house. A short while after sunrise, the front door opened. The man emerged and walked to the stable. He led his horse out, mounted and paused at the front of the cottage where the woman, holding the young child, waved him goodbye from the verandah, watched him disappear from view and then returned inside.

The five of them watched the man trot to the farm boundary, then urge his horse to a canter and disappear over the hill.

Frustrated at the man's unanticipated escape, Umarrah considered abandoning the raid. Then a sudden movement made him glance up the hill. Kubmanner had emerged from hiding in the bush and stood in clear view of the farmhouse.

While he fumed, debating whether to drag her down to join them so he could keep her close, the door opened and the woman and her child emerged again. She was carrying a gun. The two of them pottered across to the vegetable garden. The child wandered off and the woman put the gun down and began perusing the vegetables. A moment later she stopped, looked up very slowly, scanned the hill and her eyes landed on Kubmanner. Immobilised by shock, her face registered disbelief, then terror. "You! Whitefella woman, your man not here," Kubmanner shouted, then laughed.

Her words jolted the woman into action. "Oh God," she cried, grabbing the gun and running towards the little boy.

Umarrah cursed, ran into the yard, extended his arm back at full stretch and released a spear. It flew levelly through the air and thudded into the woman's back before she could reach him. She pitched forward, dropping the gun onto the ground beside her. She was still for several seconds and then slowly began to haul herself up onto her elbows and drag herself towards the boy. Umarrah's second spear landed above the first one. The woman collapsed, her elbows folded beneath her, and was still. Only feet away, the child stared, uncomprehending, at the spears still quivering in his mother's back. Umarrah approached and stood beside them. Blood gurgled in the woman's mouth as she tried to speak. He ignored her and turned instead to the child's dirt-streaked face. Their eyes met. The child began to cry. Ignoring the sound, Umarrah walked to the front door, followed by the others, including Kubmanner, who had run up to join them.

"Get back up there and stay lookout," Umarrah hissed.

"I want the dog," she shouted.

He saw it tied up and cowering against the barn wall, and shrugged.

"Be quick," he ordered.

Inside the house, they moved fast. After some searching, they found bullets but no other weapons. There was plenty of flour, tea, sugar, even some beef, and bags for carrying. They worked quickly, calculating how much they could take without the weight slowing them down. Kubmanner yelled no warnings, though Umarrah cursed that the dog was probably distracting her.

They emerged from the house, looked up and Kubmanner signalled the 'all clear'.

The woman did not move as they walked past. The child lay down on the ground beside her, one hand touching her face, crying and saying the same sound over and over.

At the base of the hill they adjusted their loads and began to climb. Time was critical. There would be a pursuit and distance would need to be covered.

As the nearby bush swallowed them, the child's cries faded.

"You wanted her dead," Umarrah accused Kubmanner.

"And you didn't?" she retorted.

"Don't force my hand," he snapped.

But Kubmanner was smiling for the first time in a long while, the dog trotting along beside her.

CHAPTER THIRTY-ONE

April 1831 – Norfolk Plains

Pen poised, George sat in front of the fire. He read his application one last time, his eyes lingering over the words of support it contained:

> *We, the undersigned, do hereby certify that Mr George Collins, is of respectable Character, and we have every reason to believe the Statement, in his letter to the Surveyor General, of his Stock and Effects, the Value of the Improvements made on the Lands he holds, and the Quantity of Fencing completed thereon, is true and correct.*

The signatures were scratched beneath – James Cox, James Hill and Captain Donaldson. Donaldson had added:

> *I hereby certify that George Collins was leader of a party of volunteers under my orders in pursuit of the hostile Aborigines and that he conducted himself very much to my satisfaction and I believe him to be a man of most excellent character.*

His offer of ongoing acquaintance had indeed proved useful, thought George, pushing away the guilt by association he always felt when reading the captain's name.

Those feelings he didn't want to share with the family. In their eyes, he was a hero. For leading his party of men up and over the Western Tiers and right across the central plateau, all the way to the peninsulas of the south east. For enduring hardship in appalling conditions and not deserting. For staying to the bitter end, unlike so many others.

The question was, would the authorities, when assessing this new land application, feel the same way, grant him the land he asked for, and ensure he received it this time?

He picked up the pen and quickly scratched his signature at the bottom. Putting the pen down, he watched the ink's shine fade and his shoulders dropped.

Mary Ann, arms full with little George, came up to him, saw his signature and smiled.

"Well done," she said.

"Here's hoping," he replied. "If nothing else, it's been useful to see in writing what we've achieved in the ten years since those first sixty acres."

"Read that bit out to me again" she asked.

"120 acres are cleared and under tillage, we have 120 cattle, 800 sheep, 6 horses, a large weatherboard dwelling house and outkitchen, granary, stable with 4 stalls, and a large barn. I have also in the last year maintained six convict servants."

"It's very impressive George," she said. "Fingers crossed."

Two weeks later a request came from the Land Board Office to attend an interview in town. After seven years of silence from the authorities, it could only be an encouraging sign. Mary Ann threw her arms around him in delight. "I knew it!" she whooped.

"It's only a request for an interview – not a grant. We're not there yet," he cautioned.

"To hear back so quickly though. It must be a good sign," she insisted.

"Perhaps," he countered. "After all this time, I don't know what to think." He looked at the interview date. "At least I won't have long to wait."

Four days later, he prepared himself to set off for town. Mary Ann pressed and re-pressed his trousers and jacket. The servants sensed the tension and suddenly had a lot of outside chores to do.

Mary Ann planted a good luck kiss on his cheek before he swung himself up into the saddle. Her shout of "good luck" reached him before he broke into a trot and headed towards the Hobart–Launceston road.

The journey time was long enough for doubts and worries to trickle into his consciousness and undermine his confidence.

Mary Ann was the first. She wanted this to be a success so badly, to bring some longed-for good fortune. Since his return home from the government operation, he'd seen anxiety harden her, especially in the aftermath of the awful attack on the Peters girls. But then came a peaceful summer, one without attacks from the Aborigines. Everyone had started to relax, assuming that the operation must have been a success. It was devastating when violence returned in the autumn and properties in and around Launceston were raided. The worst report came in March with the awful death of Mrs Cunningham at their farm on the Tamar River. Her husband had gone to town and left her and their little boy alone. She had died defending their farm. The only consolation was that the little boy was unhurt.

It was clear to all now that the operation had been an abject failure. Morale in the community plummeted. George felt a crushing responsibility for delivering good news.

Umarrah was the other problem. George tried repeatedly to force thoughts of him from his mind, but questions remained. Could he have carried out any or all of these autumn attacks? They were in familiar territory, thought George, unlike the attack on the Peters girls down south. He'd kept his fears to himself, but he had a sinking feeling that his suspicions might be correct.

This application has nothing to do with Umarrah, he told himself. Focus your thoughts on the interview. But he couldn't help wondering if knowledge of his history with Umarrah would come out, today of all days.

Five hours later, he felt there was only one word to describe what he'd just experienced: intimidating. He shuddered at the memory of the lonely wooden chair on which he sweated, while the three men determining the outcome of his application sat opposite him behind a long table. They interrogated him without pause for what felt like an eternity. At the end, he staggered out with his confidence severely shaken, the only consolation knowing that he would receive their decision within the week.

He had planned to visit his mother afterwards at her cottage in Wellington Street, but now had no desire whatsoever, knowing she too would pepper him with questions. Dejected, he hauled himself up in the saddle and headed at a slow trot out of town. The countryside passed unseen until the sweat and slowed pace of his horse returned him to the present. He turned for the ford by the South Esk and on reaching it, dismounted on the riverbank and let his horse step into the river to drink. Suddenly aware of his own thirst, he crouched down and began to scoop up handfuls of water.

Stones behind him crunched. He froze, drops of water escaping between his cupped fingers.

He stood up slowly, took a deep breath, but before he could turn around a whirring sound sped towards him. Fire exploded in his lower leg and he fell onto his knees into the shallow water. He screamed in agony, grasping fruitlessly for the back of his leg. Then reality dawned. The next spear would come, the final spear in his back, or the waddy to splinter his skull. He shut his eyes and fumbled a prayer.

Over his frantic pleas for salvation came shouts. Anger. A familiar voice.

"Don't move, George."

There came another jolt of pain as the spear was pulled out, then his sleeve ripped off. He was dragged out of the water and dumped on the riverbank.

Umarrah wrapped the torn sleeve around George's calf. As blood darkened the makeshift bandage, he ripped off the other sleeve and tied it on top of the first.

George moaned with pain, then squinted into the long shadows of the retreating sun, straining to read for danger in the face, the voice.

"Was that you?" he croaked.

"No," came the curt reply. "But to the others you are just another whitefella, stupid to be out on his own."

George sat up, grimacing. He looked hastily around.

"How did you know I was here?"

Umarrah ignored the question. He bent down and checked the bandage, then fired volleys of words into the trees. Angry replies shouted back.

"I send them away," he shrugged. "I understand why they're angry."

George felt a flicker of relief through the pain. Part of him wanted to crawl to his horse and flee; the other knew he had no choice but to stay.

For distraction and for answers, he had many questions to ask. But Umarrah beat him to it.

"Why did you really join the whitefella war, George?" asked Umarrah.

"I had no choice," George groaned. "I told you all the settlers had to join up. How did you end up with Robertson?" he countered.

"Arthur wanted my help. They sent me down to him. He asked me to work with Robertson. That's when you saw me. I learned many things," came the cryptic reply.

"What did you learn?"

"Just how much whitefellas want us dead."

George winced. He looked at the face in front of him, thinner, grimmer, illuminated by fiercely burning eyes. His blunt, pain-filled reply tore away pretence.

"Yes, many do," he replied. "So what will Arthur think of you leaving?"

Umarrah shrugged. "Many times he say one thing, and do something different. Now, I want to find who is left of our people, our allies. My wife is dead – I want to find her killers."

"I heard those killers are your own people," countered George.

"There are enemies everywhere, George."

"You're not the only one with enemies amongst your own kind."

"You were not with enemies when I see you in Richmond that day."

"Donaldson? Yes, you'd want to keep away from him," George whispered.

Somewhere through the fog of pain came the question he knew he had to ask.

"My sister's nieces in Bagdad were attacked. It was around the same time that you escaped."

"You think it was me?"

"Was it?"

"Where is Bagdad?"

"On the Hobart to Launceston road, a day's ride north of Hobart."

Umarrah shrugged.

"I walked *our* roads back to here, George. I made sure not to cross any whitefella roads, or people. Not unless I wanted to," he added with a hint of menace.

George felt a twinge of relief.

"What about the recent killings? The ones along the Tamar?"

"You read the papers too much," sneered Umarrah.

"Did you have anything to do with them?" persisted George.

Umarrah's eyes locked with his. He waited for the denial to emerge from his lips.

The silence seemed to stretch an eternity.

"Did you kill that Mrs Cunningham?"

"Who?"

"The woman on the farm on the Tamar. Without her husband."

There was no hesitation. "Yes, we did, but not her child."

"So you admit to killing an innocent woman."

"We needed food, and weapons. And haven't whitefellas killed blackfella women, and taken our children?"

It was George's turn to be silent.

"You're a wanted man," he eventually spluttered.

"Are you going to capture me, George?" Umarrah laughed.

Humiliation, then anger, blocked out George's pain. He grunted, then clicked his tongue and his horse, hooves still in the swirling river shallows, plodded over.

He forced himself to stand up, determined to face Umarrah directly.

"I'd like to, sometimes I ..." he muttered. But he had no strength for words, just enough left to stagger over to lean against the warm flank.

"Are you going to stop me?" he asked.

"No."

On his third attempt, George managed to climb into the saddle. He lifted the reins slowly, concentrating on staying upright.

"I'm sorry about your wife," he muttered, swinging the horse away. Umarrah made no reply. The horse moved away from the riverbank and trotted towards the track.

George didn't care about the Land Board now. He just wanted the pain to stop.

Umarrah wondered whether, if the bleeding had slowed enough and George did make it home, he would raise the alarm.

He turned and ran to catch up with the others.

CHAPTER THIRTY-TWO

May 1831 – Norfolk Plains

He made it home. There was no avoiding telling the truth of what had happened. Mary Ann was shocked and frightened, and demanded that the police magistrate for Norfolk Plains be informed. George refused to allow it. Without Umarrah's intervention, he would be dead, he insisted. No one else needed to know.

In grim silence, Mary Ann turned her focus over the next days to treating his leg wound. They talked about the interview with the Land Board but George did not reveal the timeframe for the notification of their decision, just so expectations weren't raised needlessly. Days passed slowly in frustration that he couldn't work and escape the strained atmosphere inside the house. He was reduced to limping around the farmyard and issuing instructions. Thomas was asked to keep an eye out for the mail and bring anything directly to him.

He was brought the letter ten days later. Slipping it into his coat pocket, he told Mary Ann he had something to do. Before she could protest, or ask where he was going, he set off. Relieved to be by himself, he rode for the hotel, dismounted cautiously, and limped to the door.

The barman greeted him with an enquiring glance. "Whisky," he grunted. He grabbed the quickly filled glass and eyeballed a table near the window. Sitting down, he pulled out the letter and ripped it open. He scanned the first page, then hastily turned it over. Reading as quickly as he dared, on the second page he found the words he had waited so long to receive:

The Board recommend in consideration of Mr George
Collins' excellent character, of his improvements and of

The adrenalin coursing through his body gave way to a surge of relief. He dropped the letter in his lap. Tears prickled his eyes. He wiped his nose and glanced at the lone drinker on the other side of the room before turning to look out the window.

Eleven years since he'd read words like that.

He grabbed the letter again, seeking reassurance that it was not a mistake.

Five hundred acres. It was beyond his wildest hopes. He looked across at the bar. "Another?" the barman asked.

"Thank you," nodded George. "And one for yourself." The barman brought the second glass over and thanked him. As the whisky's warmth started to permeate his senses, George began to luxuriate in the dawning possibilities.

The door flew open and the cold wind blew in a new customer, who slammed the door behind him and headed towards the bar.

"What can I get you, Mr Batman?" asked the barman. George's heart sank. Batman ordered, scanned the room, collected his drink and headed in George's direction.

"George Collins, isn't it?"

"Yes, that's right. John Batman, I remember," acknowledged George.

Batman sat down, noting the official correspondence in George's lap.

"Good news?" he asked.

George hesitated. "Yes, it is. The governor has kindly favoured me with a second grant of land."

Batman chuckled. "If I remember correctly, your first grant was only small."

George folded the letter and put it away.

"How much did you get?"

"Five hundred acres."

Batman's eyebrows shot up momentarily.

"Not bad," he conceded. "Most of the good land has gone, so you've done well."

"Thank you," replied George.

"Did anyone vouch for you?"

"Yes, James Cox, Captain Donaldson and James Hill."

"Good referees," Batman nodded. He sipped his drink. "Where will this five hundred acres be?"

"I don't know yet, but hope to hear soon."

"I expect you will," replied Batman.

They sat in silence. George was in no hurry to break it.

"Did you hear what happened to Roderic O'Connor?" asked Batman.

"No," mumbled George.

"He's had five of his properties attacked by Aborigines on the one day. It's probably a record, but not one you'd want," Batman grimaced.

"Where was this?" asked George.

"Over on the Lake River. O'Connor apparently exploded with rage, and that would be something to see, coming from an Irishman!" Batman chuckled.

George shook his head in disbelief.

"He's quite a man. Apparently told the Aborigines Committee a few months back that stockmen used to hunt Aborigines on horseback and shoot them from the saddle."

George took a gulp from his glass. "Good God, that's terrible."

Batman looked at him quizzically but said nothing.

More silence.

"How did you meet Donaldson?"

"During the government operation. I was with him to the bitter end."

"You must have impressed him if he's been a referee for you."

"It was kind of him to help."

"Well Collins, getting back to what I was saying about O'Connor, and the Aborigines, there's clearly more work to be done. Umarrah for one is still out there. Who knows which of these attacks and atrocities he's been responsible for. It's a real embarrassment for Arthur. And now that women and children are being attacked and killed, he must be stopped."

"Do you have any idea of his whereabouts?"

"Umarrah? Impossible to know. How he and his compatriots evade capture, I almost admire. Some natives have actually come to my property and placed themselves under my protection. It's as if they know they can't survive on their own anymore."

"Which natives?"

"Mannalargenna and some others."

"Are they still with you?"

Batman screwed up his face.

"They left again before I could hand them over," he admitted, "but I'm keen to track as many of them down as I can. They can only be surviving by staying far from the Settled Districts."

"So what are you planning to do?"

"Why don't you get us another drink George, and we can chew the fat on that."

George started to feel trapped. The whisky's warm glow had dissipated and his leg was throbbing. He stood up and walked slowly to the bar, ordered two more, engaged in a moment of half hearted banter with the barman, then reluctantly returned to their table.

Batman grunted his thanks. "We have to track the remainder of the natives down. It's much harder when they are far away from the Settled Districts but morale is bad and people are frightened."

George nodded, which was all the encouragement Batman needed.

"I heard Umarrah even killed a black woman."

"What?" said George.

"He killed the wife of Black Bill Ponsonby, one of my servants. Ponsonby had hit her, Kathleen that is. Kathleen Kennedy – such a white-sounding name, but she was a full lubra, for sure. Anyway she left him, went off up bush, and ended up living with two sawyers around Stringy Bark Tier. Maybe she prefers white men, I don't know. A group of Blacks attacked their place, and carried her off. She couldn't even speak their language. Amazing isn't it. You think they all speak the same tongue – but they don't."

"What makes you think Umarrah was there?"

"The sawyers described him. And he spoke English. I'd seen him once with Arthur, down at Sorell. So I knew from their description it was him."

"I've seen him too."

Batman eyed George with interest. "You have? When?"

"In Richmond, after our troops finally got there from Bothwell. I was with a group of other volunteer leaders. We were walking down the street, and Robertson was coming in with his party. Umarrah was amongst them."

Batman leaned forward. "How did you know that was Umarrah? There were Blacks with a number of parties."

George's heart started racing under Batman's gaze. He hesitated only slightly. "I didn't at the time. After we saw them, we went on to a meeting. We described what we'd seen and the others said who he was."

Batman sat back and nodded. He continued to look at George with speculation.

"You know, you could be of use to us."

The statement hung in the air.

"You've eyeballed Umarrah. You've been on Arthur's big push, and Donaldson's impressed enough with your efforts to vouch for you. I've applied to Arthur to get a roving party going in search of Umarrah. There's some newly captured Aborigines in Campbell Town gaol who I could take with me. We need to get Umarrah and end this embarrassment for the authorities."

George felt a prickle of sweat. He'd heard enough about Batman's activities since meeting him to know he was as bad as Donaldson. The rumour was that he, and his man Ponsonby, had tracked down an Aboriginal camp and killed several people, more than a dozen, some said. Batman would have no hesitation in taking Umarrah's freedom, if not his life. He'd only restrain himself if explicitly ordered to keep him alive. And as for motivation, ending the authorities' embarrassment might be his stated aim, but Batman would be after a hefty bounty payment.

George played for time, trying to think of a way to decline the invitation that would not arouse suspicion.

"I am only too aware that many of us, my family included, are anxious for the violence to end. However, I have an extra stipulation as part of my new grant. I've also been ordered to surrender my original one, which doubles the work we have to do. I'm not sure I could be away from the farm while we move everything from one place to the other, in the time the Colonial Secretary has stipulated."

Batman looked unimpressed.

"When do you expect to hear back from the Governor, John?"

"Soon. I sympathise with your situation, George, but this is a priority. I'm sure the Colonial Secretary would give you more time if you wrote and asked."

He paused, allowing time for the suggestion to sink in.

"Shall I send a messenger over when I have news? I hope I can count on your support."

It was his presumption that flicked a switch in George's head. He focussed a steady gaze on Batman. "I'm sorry John, but after enduring weeks of hardship and deprivation on the governor's 'big push', I have paid my dues and now been rewarded with land I desperately need. You speak as if you're the Governor, but have no right to pressure me. *If* Arthur gives you permission, and *if* I am able to assist, I will, but I make no promises."

He smacked his glass on the table and stood up.

"Good day to you."

Batman stared at him as he grabbed his coat, the barman winking at him as he passed. He mounted his horse with anger-fuelled ease, and rode into a westerly wind whose chill he did not register.

How dare Batman spoil the moment for me, and order me around, he raged. Who does he think he is? He let the anger course through him, hoping it would dissipate and he could reclaim his earlier elation. But it didn't work. As the farm approached, the fear that lay underneath began to surface. Even though he had the letter, would the actual grant materialise this time? And would Batman be knocking on his door, trying to pressure him to join his search?

He trotted into the yard, and Mary Ann came out to meet him. She looked wary.

For her sake, he smiled.

"Good news my love," he announced after dismounting, and pulled out the letter. Mary Ann grabbed it and scanned the contents.

"Oh George, well done!" she gasped, and threw her arms around him.

The next few days they celebrated their good fortune with David and Eliza, and George's mother. Everyone reassured him that with his good references, the land was sure to come this time. Comforted by this, he tried to push Batman to the back of his mind.

Five days later, Batman's message came. The Governor had said No.

Soon after that, follow-up correspondence came from the authorities, revealing that his new land would be on the south side of the village of Evandale.

"Not too close to the river to get flooded," he told Mary Ann. She picked up little George and danced around the room.

He luxuriated in plans for the future.

And forgot about Umarrah for now.

CHAPTER THIRTY-THREE

August 1831 – Peeberrangner country

The change of season had swapped one problem for another. Last summer's struggle for water was well and truly over. Now winter rains seeped through their thin kangaroo skins. Cold and damp, the seven of them and their fourteen dogs moved cautiously through the landscape, heading deeper into the north east, wedged between whitefella towns and farms on one side, and Umarrah's oldest enemy on the other.

It was an ongoing desperate search for food, warmth and safe shelter. As they moved from place to place, Umarrah often thought of Kubmanner, who'd left the group's protection. Her unending though understandable bitterness consumed her, piling on top of their own bleakness. He suspected she wouldn't last long on her own, and had told her so, admitting to himself that his attempts to dissuade her were half hearted. She didn't seem to care about his warning. She didn't even want to take her dog.

He didn't like this Country. It was flat and featureless, without the majesty of the great rivers and mountains of his home. It was also Mannalargenna's Country. Reason enough to avoid this corner of the island. Only a few weeks earlier they'd fought the Chief's sons in an unplanned, unwanted and scrappy encounter. One had been killed, another injured. Their small group of seven had fled without serious injury but the fight had taken its toll.

In its wake, their pace had slowed. Umarrah's dread of Mannalargenna's reaction when he heard the news about his sons intensified when they realised they were being stalked. Campfire smoke to the east suddenly appeared and was visible most days. Their group criss-crossed the land in an attempt to evade their pursuers, even going without a fire some nights, which only decreased their morale.

Looking at the smoke in the distance one evening, it dawned on him. This could be a group led by George Robinson. The cautious though dogged pursuit was exactly his method. If so, those with him would be a mixture of whitefellas and Aborigines, like the west coast expedition. And from experience, Umarrah knew that contact with this group could bring both opportunities and risks.

They debated their options. Some did not want to risk getting too close to a group that could contain whitefellas. But two can play this tracking game, he argued. If we can find out who they are without them knowing, then we control when and if we make contact. It does have risks but it's worth it.

He convinced them.

The cat-and-mouse game started off well, until one day they got too close to the other group's camp, and heard voices approaching. They fled their position and made for higher ground. Umarrah thought he recognised a woman's voice, but though he went over and over it in his mind, it was too fleeting and he couldn't place it.

Two days later he heard it again. This time they had warning. Five people were approaching their camp from the plains below. Umarrah's muscles tensed as he saw Mannalargenna walking at the front, followed by Kickerterpoller and three women whose faces he did not recognise. So, the Chief is coming, he thought. He observed the cautious approach Mannalargenna took, scanning his surrounds for any surprise attack. He's not sure about the reception he'll get, noted Umarrah, watching for a few more moments before returning to their camp.

In anxious anticipation, his group built up the fire and gathered their spears and waddies, laying them to one side.

Mannalargenna appeared first and paused at the edge of the clearing. He looked at them across the campfire, and they returned his silent gaze. A few of the dogs began to growl at the intrusion and were silenced with a sharp command. The Chief walked with measured steps around the campfire and, rather unnecessarily, thought Umarrah, passed in front of the group, staring at them one by one. He then collected their spears and handed them over to Kickerterpoller, who walked a few paces behind.

The three women entered the clearing, fanned out and looked around. One of the women suddenly screamed, broke away from the others and raced towards Umarrah, crying his name. He gaped in shock as she barrelled into him and hugged him fiercely.

"It's me!" she shouted.

He peeled her away from his body to scrutinize her. "Planobeena?" he cried.

He stared at the grown woman in front of him, arms and legs strongly muscled, trunk solid, then gazed into her molten brown eyes, before pulling her back into his arms.

Laughter and whoops of delight burst from the other two women, mingling the strained atmosphere with threads of happiness.

She squeezed him tight, and began to sob. "I never thought I'd see you again," he murmured, tears running down his face.

Eventually he glanced over the top of her head, noting the many smiles. Mannalargenna's reaction, by contrast, he couldn't read.

The Chief waited, then announced that they had much to discuss, and his group would spend the night there.

"Plenty of time for us to talk later," Planobeena whispered, wiping her damp face on his arm. He nearly wept at the gesture of old, such a spontaneous confirmation that it was truly her.

Kickerterpoller and a few others went hunting and returned before dark with dinner. Umarrah noted with wry amusement that Kickerterpoller stayed at a distance from both the Chief and himself. Everyone soon sat down to eat and in the initial quiet, Umarrah could feel the Chief's eyes upon him.

"Why is Robinson not here?" he asked cautiously, after Mannalargenna had confirmed they had been travelling with him.

"He wanted us to come here alone. He thinks we will bring you back with us. But there is no rush. We have things to say that are not for his ears."

Umarrah paused, listening, then resumed eating.

"You were with Robinson before. Why did you leave?" asked Mannalargenna.

"What did Robinson tell you?" replied Umarrah, cagily.

"Nothing much."

Umarrah shrugged. "He would not listen to me, and refused to capture the Toogee."

Mannalargenna nodded.

"What do you want to discuss?" asked Umarrah, keen to get to the point.

"Do you trust him?" demanded Mannalargenna, ignoring his question.

"Robinson? No."

Mannalargenna scrutinised Umarrah's face for several seconds, but said nothing.

"Has he made you promises?" Umarrah asked.

"He says if we help him find all the blackfellas, then we will stay on Country and have a whitefella to protect us."

"Where would this Country be? Those of us left are from different parts of the island."

"He says we can each be on our Country."

"Do you believe him?"

"Perhaps."

"Is this an offer sent from Arthur?"

"Robinson says yes."

"Look at how much land they have taken. Do you think they would give back many places?"

"I am telling you what he has told us, what Arthur promises. But you must join us."

"We have to think about it."

"Alright. We talk in the morning. Go and be with your sister." He hesitated. "I have never seen her so happy."

Umarrah threw the bones of his meal in the fire. As the flames sizzled and the fat spat back at him, he stood up.

"How long have you been travelling with Robinson?"

"Long enough."

"You don't want to go back to him, do you? You're stalling for time."

Mannalargenna shrugged. But his nonchalance was unconvincing.

Umarrah stepped away and headed over to another campfire. Planobeena's eyes shone as he sat down beside her. She ran her hand up and down his arm, reassuring herself he was real. He took her hand and squeezed it.

As the stars blazed above, they watched the last logs burn down. There was grim news to share – the death of their father, and the slow decline of their mother. The attack as they walked into Launceston all those years ago, the early raids and killings he led. His life with Laoninneloonner, their capture by Robertson, having to leave her and join Robinson, escaping him, joining and then escaping Arthur. The news of Laoninneloonner's death. And finally the desperate raids of the last months.

Planobeena's eyes, deep brown wells of grief, never left his face. She flinched several times, and when it was all disclosed, the tears came again. He held her until she was spent.

"I searched for you, over and over," he said. "Some whitefellas I used to work for, they had news a couple of times, but then, nothing."

He glanced at her cautiously. "What was it like?"

"With the Hardwickes?" she smirked. "At first, they weren't sure what to do with me. When they decided, they worked me hard – cleaning, making beds, helping in the kitchen. But they fed me and I felt safe, mostly. They even did a painting of me! Then John, John Baker, took me. Grabbed me one day while we were up on the coast. Threatened the Hardwickes with a gun. They just let me go."

She paused and he watched the memories pass over her face. "He was a blackfella from America, John. Could be nasty. I made sure not to anger him. But sometimes it wasn't a bad life, better than the Hardwickes'. I learnt how to steer a schooner! Later, Parish took me and brought me here."

She paused. "But there's danger here too."

Umarrah glanced back at Mannalargenna. "Has he said anything about his sons?" he whispered.

"What do you mean?" she replied.

"You haven't heard then." His shoulders slumped in relief. "Two of his sons, part of a bigger group, found us a few weeks back. We weren't looking for trouble but there was a fight. One of them is dead. The other was speared but he got away. If Mannalargenna finds out that it was us, he'll kill me." He paused. "I would if I was him."

Planobeena poked the dying embers. "He would have tried harder to find you if he did. He and Robinson would have been arguing over it."

"But this could change," she continued. "Whitefellas come to Robinson with messages, and he sometimes changes what he does afterwards. He likes to know everything that happens, especially anything to do with Arthur – what he does, and thinks."

Umarrah contemplated this news as she stifled a yawn.

"Mannalargenna may not realise just how much time I've spent with Arthur." His eyes narrowed. "He may not know him as well as I do. That could be an advantage for us."

"Kanneherlargenna, my clever big brother. Sleep next to me," she demanded, yawning again. Despite his exhaustion, he almost laughed. They lay down, and he pulled a skin over her. Soon after, she rolled onto her side and her breathing slowed.

That name – it pierced his heart. He could hear the echoes of their mother's voice, saying it, calling him. Unwanted memories flooded back. The smell of those first whitefellas on the Koorparoona Niara track, and then the unravelling of all they'd known and loved as they were felled by weapons and disease from one side of the island to the other.

Those old stories that he used to hear up at Yinginner, about the big canoes that would appear along the coast, sometimes stopping and discharging what blackfellas first thought were white ghosts. Who didn't stay.

Until they did.

He turned his thoughts to his conversation with Mannalargenna. What were his own group's options?

Very few.

The Chief would have been trying to influence Robinson to his own ends as they travelled.

And none of it will be to my advantage, realised Umarrah.

The next thing he knew the sunlight was grazing his eyelids.

Their group huddled together once they had all woken. It was not a long conversation. Robinson had authority amongst the whitefellas and he could protect them, argued Umarrah. We might even be able to hunt. Robinson let us when I was with him before.

He gave Mannalargenna their decision, and was initially surprised at his response.

"We go back to Robinson without you. You wait, and come in a few days."

Stunned, Umarrah agreed.

They all ate together, then their visitors departed. Planobeena's face betrayed her anxiety at being separated again so soon, but he reassured her.

"We will come soon," he promised.

As he watched them depart, he tried to think of why Mannalargenna was so relaxed at heading back without them. He could only surmise that the Chief wanted to shore up his position with Robinson before competition arrived.

His group remained where they were for another day, then moved closer to the coast.

That night they indulged themselves in a larger fire, knowing full well it would be easily seen. After a freezing night where the fire's warmth was a comfort, Umarrah scanned the northern coast. The late winter sun glinted on two rivers closely wending their way to the sea, and a thin line of smoke filtered upward between them.

Just as Umarrah thought that they should start to move towards Robinson, their recent visitors were seen approaching again.

Planobeena's face lit up as she saw him, and the Chief's expression was one of satisfaction. He announced that the two groups should stay together for one more night. Umarrah had no objection. Clearly the Chief was wanting to string things out.

After another freezing winter night, they ate and gathered their things. It was time to go. They proceeded down the hill together, then paused and gathered fuel for a small fire to signal their intent to approach. Once they were sure their message had been received, Kickerterpoller shouted a loud cooee, with a response coming almost immediately. He followed up with a second as they reached the river.

Mannalargenna plunged in first. Umarrah watched with relief as the Chief's knees were still visible while he strode across. Planobeena remembered her brother's fear of water, nudged him and smiled.

Back on dry land, they headed into a swamp filled with tea trees.

Walking in single file, and surrounded by their dogs, they followed Mannalargenna into the camp. Umarrah saw Robinson waiting for their approach, and walked up to him purposefully, holding out his hand in the whitefella custom. Robinson grasped his hand with his own, shaking it heartily. Out of the corner of his eye, Umarrah saw Mannalargenna watching intently.

"It is good to see you, Umarrah," said Robinson. "You left us so unexpectedly".

"I am very glad to join you again," he replied smoothly, ignoring the implied criticism.

Robinson bestowed a benevolent smile upon him. Umarrah turned his gaze to his oldest enemy, with a faint smile that was not returned.

There was much work to be done, and influence with Robinson to gain.

CHAPTER THIRTY-FOUR

October 1831 – Norfolk Plains

"I think that's nearly everything, Sir," concluded Thomas. George cast his eye over the old farmhouse kitchen, stripped bare, and nodded. He rubbed his calf, healed but aching now after a hard day of moving, and ignored the painful reminder of his last contact with Umarrah.

"It's been a lot of work, for sure, but it's exciting, isn't it, Thomas?" he replied. "Constraint and limitation being replaced by growth and opportunity?"

"There'll be more room to move, that's for sure, " Thomas agreed.

They moved out into the cool spring air. "You go ahead, I'll double-check the barn," said George. He ducked inside for one more quick look at the high walls, bare of tools and the floor, empty of grain, which was now loaded up on the carts. In the yard, the bullocks' tails swished lazily as they waited the command to head off. Down the road, across the ford, and on to their new home.

"Master, there's a large party on the road, heading our way," shouted Thomas.

George froze, his heart pounding. *Why would an attacking party of Aborigines walk along a whitefella road? They'd be more secretive than that. Or maybe they've got nothing to lose. In which case we are dead men.*

He ran outside. "Where?" he cried.

"Not far," pointed Thomas, hurrying to the boundary. "Actually, Sir, it looks like a mixed group, Blacks and whites. They're all on foot, except one person's riding. And I think I can recognise Umarrah."

"What?" gasped George, running to catch up.

Thomas' keen eyes were right. Approaching on foot from Perth was a group of at least a dozen people. He could make out the unmistakeable figure of Umarrah amongst them as they moved along the Launceston-to-Hobart road. In a few minutes they would be walking right past. George remembered the accounts in the newspapers of George Robinson, the Conciliator, continuing his mission to locate the remaining Aborigines. Could this be them? If so, how did Umarrah come to be with Robinson again? He couldn't imagine him doing it willingly, after the way he described so witheringly the expedition to the west coast.

Curiosity trumped caution.

"I'm going to approach them."

"Are you sure that's wise, sir?"

"Possibly not, but I want to know what's going on."

He would have to give them a reason to stop. But they had little to offer by way of hospitality. Just a billy for tea, and some damper, a bit of beef, not quite enough to share. And fresh water. Would it be enough? Perhaps the gesture of goodwill from a settler would sway things.

"Top up the billy, Thomas."

"Alright Sir."

George waited by the fence and moments later the group drew alongside. He took a deep breath, and approached the white man on horseback.

"Good morning, sir. My name is George Collins. May I offer you some hospitality on your journey?"

The man look surprised, scrutinized George and then looked beyond to the farm. George flicked his gaze to Umarrah and they locked eyes, their faces betraying no recognition. Umarrah walked over to Robinson and spoke quietly to him. Robinson's eyebrows rose, and he turned quickly to appraise George for a second time.

"That is kind of you Mr Collins," responded Robinson, "if not somewhat unexpected. I have been anticipating, at best, silent gawking from those at work in their fields while we travel through the Settled Districts."

Thomas walked up and stood slightly behind and to the side of George.

"My name is George Augustus Robinson," the man added, rather grandly, thought George.

"I have heard of your work, Sir," George answered. "My servant Thomas and I are at your service."

Robinson glanced at Thomas then turned back to George.

"I am travelling with the Great Chief Mannalargenna here," he nodded, "as well as Umarrah, and others, in a party of conciliation. I understand that you are already acquainted with Umarrah?"

"That's correct, yes. I am long since acquainted with Umarrah, but none else of your party."

There was a murmur amongst the group, then silence. Umarrah stepped forward and George was struck by his sunken eyes. Umarrah stretched out his hand. George shook it. "Hello George," he said evenly. George returned the greeting then Umarrah reached out his hand to the woman he had been walking with, and drew her up to George. This is Woolaytopinneyer," he announced. "It is her people we looking for."

George looked at her and nodded in acknowledgement. Woolaytopinneyer met his gaze coolly. I'm not sure why Umarrah's introducing her, thought George, feeling awkward. She turned her gaze away from him and back to Umarrah, and in that lingering gaze was George's answer. The attraction between them was palpable, and mutual, and there was something else he could detect. Power. She's important to this mission, guessed George, and on Umarrah's side. He's enjoying this, and for more than just the attraction.

George stepped back. "Please, this way," he announced.

Robinson moved quickly to be at the front of the group. Thomas held open the gate as they passed through towards the empty cottage.

George watched for when Umarrah would notice how much barer the farm looked, and know that something was up.

Thomas strode ahead, checked the billy and added logs to the outside firepit. "I have to apologise," announced George, "I don't have a lot to offer. There's a bit of beef, some tea and damper, and water."

"In my work around this island with my Aboriginal friends," announced Robinson, "I have spent much time without comforts."

George wasn't sure how to reply to this, so said nothing.

They positioned themselves around the fire, George and Thomas sharing what they had, though not all offers were accepted.

George then deliberately sat beside Umarrah, who had Woolaytopinneyer on his other side.

"How far have you come?" he enquired cautiously, noting Mannalargenna's eyes upon him.

"From the town today. We are going to Wawlatter."

"When do you expect to reach Campbell Town?" asked George.

"Tomorrow."

"Well the rivers are running high with all the rain we've had, but I'm sure you'll take care crossing them."

Umarrah smiled faintly at the comment. The lines on his face softened.

"I found my sister," Umarrah announced.

"Planobeena?" asked George, incredulous. "Really? After all this time! How did that happen?"

"She was with Robinson when our group joined them."

"That is good news indeed. I am delighted for you. Is she here with you?"

"No," Umarrah replied, his mouth a thin line. "She is on one of the islands. With some of the others."

"I'm sorry that she couldn't join you," replied George, struggling for tact. "I hope you see her again before too long."

Would that be Robinson's doing? wondered George. It would be cruel keeping his sister away from him after they'd been reunited.

"You heard about our visit with the Governor in Launceston?" continued Umarrah, changing the topic, and slightly raising his voice.

"No, I haven't seen the papers the last few days. We have been so busy," George bluffed, before realising that he was not the only audience for whom this comment was intended.

Umarrah nodded at the Chief. "The Governor is going to give us a home in Wawlatter. He going to build houses for us and our families. We can hunt. It is good and we are all pleased."

George could hardly believe his ears, but was careful not to react. Who amongst the Campbell Town settlers would agree to give up some or all of their grant of land so the Aborigines could have a home of their own?

"Is that why you are going to Campbell Town?" asked George.

"No. Now we are helping Robinson find more blackfellas. At Yinginner, the lakes. We will start from Campbell Town."

"I see," replied George.

"Robinson has promised us that our troubles will be over once we do this," continued Umarrah.

George suspected Umarrah was trying to draw out some sort of public confirmation of private discussions. He glanced over at Robinson, who suddenly appeared uneasy at the turn in the conversation. Something felt very wrong. A snippet of information struggled to reach the forefront of George's brain. Then he remembered. It was the news of the recent murders of Captain Thomas and James Parker. And the huge outcry against the Aborigines that followed. For Thomas's brother was no other than Jocelyn Thomas, the Colonial Secretary. The violence perpetrated by Aborigines had reached the heart of government, and it was personal.

A permanent home on Country was never going to happen. Not after that. And the Governor must have known this when he met with them in Launceston.

"How long have you known Umarrah, Mr Collins?" asked Robinson, inserting himself in the conversation and changing the topic.

"Since my first year here, sir, in 1813," replied George. "My family, and my wife's too, were settled here from Norfolk Island."

"And how did you two meet exactly?" persisted Robinson.

Umarrah glared at George, who hesitated, reluctant to reveal details of their first meeting.

George decided to evade the question. "It was a struggle when we first started here. My stepfather was a boatman, not a farmer. Umarrah's family used to pass through a couple of times a year, and we got to know each other. I used to go hunting with some of the young men."

Umarrah seemed pleased with this answer, and Robinson appeared somewhat mollified.

"Were your parents convicts?"

"Yes sir, they were, but not by the time we arrived here," George replied.

"And how long have you been on this land here?"

"Since 1820. I was fortunate to receive a grant from Governor Macquarie when I was eighteen."

Robinson's eyebrows shot up. "You did well to obtain a grant at such a young age." He gazed around. "So why does it look like you are leaving?"

George swallowed. "Governor Arthur recently granted me five hundred acres a few miles upstream. We are in the process of moving there now."

Robinson nodded. He got to his feet. George flicked a glance at Umarrah, whose face had set hard.

"Thank you for your hospitality, Mr Collins, but it is time we continued our journey. We have a way to go before we reach Campbell Town. I am meeting Mr Cottrell and Mr Batman there to prepare for our next conciliatory journey. There is much to be done."

George wondered what role Batman and Cottrell would be playing in this mission.

"I wish you well for your journey, Mr Robinson," replied George.

The visitors followed Robinson's lead, gathered themselves, and headed towards for the road. George walked behind with Umarrah.

"You hoped I not find out about your five hundred acres," Umarrah whispered.

The accusation hung in the air.

"I'm sorry," George stuttered, "but it's much less land than most other people's."

"You know more than other whitefellas what stealing our land means. Maybe I make a mistake, George, letting you go last time."

"We can't survive on the sixty acres here. I told you that long ago."

"Many blackfellas die so you whitefellas can survive," said Umarrah, ignoring George's defence and brushing past him.

George stopped and watched his departing back. He was not surprised by the threat, but suddenly very weary and sad.

Then he remembered the recent murders, and knew he had to share his suspicions.

"Wait!" he shouted. "There's something else." Umarrah hesitated and George caught up with him. He dropped his voice. "Have you heard about the murder of Captain Thomas?"

Umarrah's eyes narrowed.

George plunged on. "Captain Thomas is the brother of the Colonial Treasurer."

Umarrah froze. "Robinson did not tell us this."

"The outcry has been huge. Don't believe any promises they make to you. There'll be no homeland in Wawlatter after this."

George watched the betrayal register on his face.

"Thank you, George," he whispered, his eyes glowing.

And walked on.

CHAPTER THIRTY-FIVE

October 1831 – Tyerrernotepanner country

Umarrah scratched at the trousers chafing his legs and gazed at the hills rising to the east. Having walked from Launceston, they had now come to a complete stop. How many letters is Robinson going to read, and write, how much talking with other whitefellas is he going to do before we can leave Campbell Town? he fumed. He paced back and forth once again, trying to remind himself of the benefits the delay had brought – thinking time.

His own plan for this 'expedition' was to lead Robinson on a merry dance around Country, to enjoy time hunting, take it slowly and delay meeting the Larmairremener for as long as possible. He had no desire at all to encounter these traditional enemies, who could be anywhere, but most likely up on the central plateau, their traditional home. Mannalargenna, Kickerterpoller, even Woolaytopinneyer were all in agreement. Woolaytopinneyer had family she longed to see amongst the Larmairremener, but finding them achieved Robinson's aim, and even she was conflicted. And what happened for them after this, was unknown. Would the government fulfil their promise? Could this trip be their last?

He had shared with the others, George's recent warning that Arthur would not, despite his promise, give them a homeland in Wawlatter. George appeared adamant that the murder of the Colonial Treasurer's brother had meant any promise of a homeland was a lie. Woolaytopinneyer had told him that Robinson asked her about the murders while she was in Launceston gaol, because he knew she had been there when they happened. So both Robinson and Arthur knew about the murders before they made the promise. He could still see the Governor's face as he said the words to them in Launceston.

Robinson had given them similar undertakings after his group surrendered to him a few months earlier. Did they have no intention of keeping their promise?

They debated this issue almost daily, with no resolution.

Umarrah had detected a recent change in Robinson, who appeared frustrated in needing their cooperation but also wanting to display his authority. Planobeena was a case in point. Robinson had refused to allow her to join them on this journey. It was as if he had seen how much the two of them meant to each other and then deliberately separated them as a power play. Planobeena had been sent away to Swan Island and Umarrah had no idea when he would see her next. At least she was alive, he consoled himself.

And yet, Umarrah frowned, without Robinson, he would not have met Woolaytopinneyer. Her knowledge of the Larmairremener was vital to this expedition, so Robinson had released her from the Launceston gaol, brought her to join the group, and introduced them. Umarrah felt his grief for Laoninneloonner soothed by her presence. The delay here in the town had given them more time to get to know each other. He felt increasingly attracted to her. She seemed to reciprocate. Out on Country they would have more time, and privacy, to explore their feelings. He yearned for it.

The next day, with Robinson's preparations finally complete, their group of nineteen blackfellas and whitefellas, two horses and several dogs left the town and headed east. Relieved, Umarrah opened himself to the embrace of the gentle rolling hills as they began to walk along roads and pass landmarks he had known all his life. He smirked at Robinson's disapproval as they discarded their whitefella clothing not long after setting out.

The days continued to lengthen and the sun's warmth shimmered above the land. Compared to traversing unfamiliar west coast forests dripping with icy rain or the featureless plain of north-east enemy Country, this travel was a joy. There was plenty of whitefella food, and time for hunting. The presence of Robinson and the other whitefellas afforded a level of protection, although, alarmingly, they saw two armed whitefellas on their first day. He intended to keep them well away from settler farms.

Mannalargenna's presence, though, was a blight on his contentment. He was always trying to assert his authority and influence Robinson to his way of thinking. He would stride ahead of the group and declare the route they would take, a galling thing to watch day after day. Worst of all was the worry that the Chief would learn the fate of his sons. Letters for Robinson bringing news arrived regularly via his servants. Umarrah's stomach chilled each time they turned up.

They walked, hunted, considered their enemies both inside and outside the camp, and spent evenings with ceremony and dancing around the campfire. He loved entertaining the others with his stories of adventure and amorous exploits. Woolaytopinneyer's beautiful face would crease with knowing smiles as she listened.

Gradually, despite their agreed pretence to be making progress in their search for her countrymen, Robinson became suspicious of their stalling tactics. He was convinced the Larmairremener were on their own Country, and they would have to go up to the highlands to find them. He was right, but none of them said so. Mannalargenna said he was old, and couldn't walk that far to their Country. Umarrah chuckled ruefully. Let's hope that's true, he thought. The battle of wills continued until finally Robinson insisted on the change of direction. They turned and headed in a more north-westerly direction, towards the homeland of their enemy.

Robinson became frustrated with their lack of enthusiasm and Umarrah was not alone in knowing he needed appeasing. Woolaytopinneyer came up with a solution. A few days later, she guided Robinson to a haul of weapons, spears, waddies, guns and ammunition. He was mightily pleased with the find, and Umarrah noted soon after how his tone changed from barely concealed anger to encouragement.

"He's pleased with us," Woolaytopinneyer smiled the next morning, as she lay beside him.

Umarrah squeezed her hand and looked up at the sky. The rain had cleared and the sun's rays were starting to filter through. The sounds of people stirring, as they rose and prepared for the day's walking, filtered through the camp.

Suddenly they could hear Mannalargenna shouting in anger. They jumped up to see the Chief thundering in their direction. Two others hurried behind, a whitefella messenger bringing up the rear.

"Stay away, all of you!" thundered Mannalargenna.

"Stop! What is this?" burst in Robinson, racing to overtake the Chief and straddling the closing gap between them.

"Keep away, white man. This our business," growled the Chief.

"No, I will not!" thundered Robinson. "There is to be no fighting. What is going on?"

"Ask your man," replied Mannalargenna, nodding at the whitefella messenger.

"Explain yourself, Tyrrell," commanded Robinson.

Umarrah tried to back away. Woolaytopinneyer pulled her eyes from the Chief's face and scanned quickly for their best escape route.

Looking decidedly uneasy, Tyrrell confessed that he had approached Mannalargenna on arriving at the camp, and broken the news about the attack on his sons, and who was, allegedly, responsible.

"How dare you not speak to me first!" Robinson thundered. "I shall be the one who acquaints the natives with any news."

Umarrah froze. It was getting the news second-hand that bothered Robinson, not the news itself. That could only mean one thing. He already knows about Mannalargenna's sons.

Suddenly Robinson's eyes were on him.

"Tell us what happened, Umarrah," he ordered.

Umarrah's mouth felt very dry.

"I didn't kill your son," he stammered, looking at Mannalargenna, whose eyes narrowed with rage. "I was there, but it was someone else. Perhaps I would have but they did it first."

"So you confirm that the Chief's son was killed?" replied Robinson.

"Yes. His brother was speared in the arm, but he escaped. We took their dogs."

Umarrah flinched as Mannalargenna's groan of grief reverberated around them. A hollow silence followed. Umarrah heard Woolaytopinneyer's anxious breathing beside him.

"This whitefella say it was you," accused Mannalargenna. "You lie plenty – we know from all your stories."

Umarrah said nothing.

"It *was* you," he repeated ominously.

Woolaytopinneyer's trembling hand clutched Umarrah's arm.

"Enough of this!" interrupted Robinson. "We are here to find the Big River people. Not to fight amongst ourselves. The Lord will not guide us to the Larmairremener if we are killing each other."

They ignored him.

He glared at each of them in turn. "I will have no killing! Do you understand me?"

They each mumbled an unconvincing platitude.

"We move on," commanded Robinson. He turned to Umarrah and Woolaytopinneyer. "You two are to walk with me."

"I will deal with you later, Tyrrell," he snapped at the messenger.

They set off. Mannalargenna changed tactics and refused to walk in front. As they wound their way through the bush Umarrah could feel the Chief's eyes boring into his back. Woolaytopinneyer's usual firm stride faltered.

A few hours later, to Umarrah's relief, the Chief went ahead and hunted kangaroo. During the afternoon, several of them thought they saw smoke and wondered if they were near to the Larmairremener, but as they moved toward it, the smoke disappeared. Mannalargenna came back from hunting and said he had not seen it. They climbed the nearest high point and seeing nothing, decided to stop for the night.

With Umarrah's worst fear realised, and the threat of the Chief's wrath hanging over him, the dragging of the days changed from being a delicate dance to one of dogged dread. The change began to take its toll. His pleasure in the journey leached away. Woolaytopinneyer's eyes were always wary. The two of them often left the group, telling Robinson they were following new clues or smoke that hinted at the Larmairremener presence. At night they sought comfort in each other and afterwards debated escape. But they could not decide where the greater danger lay: in fleeing, or in staying.

As the group continued to zigzag across Larmairremener territory, a strange lethargy started to pervade them all. They could not delay the inevitable. Even the great Chief's thirst for retribution appeared to wane. The gap between the two groups, the hunter and the invisible hunted, lessened. They were not far now from Woolaytopinneyer's people, and as they got closer, her longing to see her brother intensified and complicated their emotions. Umarrah remembered when, only a few months ago, his small group was the hunted one. He felt in his bones the weariness as the pursuit continued, the capitulation as you allow your smoke to be seen and your pursuers to close in.

Supplies arrived, along with another letter for Robinson. He read out its contents to them. A group of whitefellas, sent out into the bush by the Governor, had captured four blackfellas and shot and killed another four. The men involved had not been punished for these murders but instead rewarded with more of the same work.

Reading this to them had a chilling effect. It was an appalling tactic by Robinson, but it worked.

"Our only safety is with him," Woolaytopinneyer cried that night. "We have to do what he wants."

A few days later, Umarrah and Woolaytopinneyer led a small group and closed in on the Larmairremener. He felt increasingly anxious with each step, as Woolaytopinneyer studied the ground for signs of her brother's movements. They returned to camp and reported that his tracks had been seen. Now so close, Robinson was frustrated with yet another delay.

"Not a moment now is to be lost!" he pressed. "The Governor only wants me to get to the tribe and then our troubles will be over. We will not have to go after any more and you will be able to hunt." Umarrah and Woolaytopinneyer glanced at each other. He saw her eyes daring to hope.

The next day, the tactic of advancing with a small group was deployed again, and the two groups met. Woolaytopinneyer recognised her brother and ran ahead to greet him. Umarrah hung back and watched her, remembering his reunion with Planobeena. Moments later they were introduced to the Chief Montpelliater, and after a flurry of negotiation, more Larmairremener emerged from the bush. Umarrah was astonished to see the large number of people, twenty-six in total, including a child. The group gathered itself together, then with Montpelliater at its head, Umarrah led them through the scrub.

As they approached Robinson, Montpelliater ordered his people to shout their war cry and rattle their spears. This isn't over yet, thought Umarrah. But the whitefella stood his ground and greeted Montpelliater in his own language. The words completely disarmed the Chief. Umarrah looked around to gauge Mannalargenna's reaction, but was told the Chief had fled at the sound of the war cries. Umarrah felt a moment of triumph hearing this, but it was short lived when he later returned.

The next day Robinson ordered them to walk to Hobart Town. "I promise you a conference with the Lieutenant Governor," he announced. "He will be sure to address all your grievances."

It was barely enough time for the two groups to coalesce.

They began their journey south, lured by Robinson's repetition of the previously uttered promise. The summer breeze warmed them as they walked. The trees whispered – the Larmairremener have been found, your bargaining power has vanished. Umarrah's apprehension grew. It crossed his mind that Mannalargenna might seize the opportunity to take his revenge before they reached their destination. Part of him almost welcomed it, but he was also relieved to see the signs of white settlement approaching.

The promise made burned in his mind with every step – meet with Arthur, make a homeland in Wawlatter.

"Do you really believe he will keep it?" asked Woolay-topinneyer.

But George's warning burned just as fiercely.

CHAPTER THIRTY-SIX

January 1832 – Mouheneenner country

Growing crowds lined the road to gawk at their progress through Hobart Town. Umarrah watched their faces as they whispered in the ears of those beside them or pointed at the large number of their dogs. He saw curiosity, fear, and hatred, none of it surprising. As the streets and buildings swallowed them up, the numbers of onlookers increased. He felt a prickle of suspicion that their arrival had been anticipated.

On the faces of a few he saw sadness, even sympathy. That worried him even more.

Being Umarrah's third time in Hobart Town, he was keen to get Mannalargenna's first impression, and moved forward to stride beside him. The Chief's head was swivelling left and right, taking in the size of the whitefella settlement. He made no comment, and as they progressed, Umarrah watched his shoulders gradually sag forward and his pace slow. He glanced at his face and saw on it the realisation of the invader's grip on the island. He's in shock, Umarrah realised. But there's no time for this. We're going to be there soon. And when we arrive, Mannalargenna has to fight for us, make the government honour their promise. If he can't regain his composure, if we can't present a united front, we could lose this chance.

A hot wind from the north was pushing them relentlessly onward, towards Arthur. That name reverberated in Umarrah's head. He wiped the sweat from his forehead and stole another quick glance at Mannalargenna, whose face revealed nothing. A flicker of sweet fury ignited within Umarrah and began to course through his body. I want to see Arthur's face, he raged to himself, to shout at him, to force him to give what he promised, to kill him if he doesn't. Then Woolaytopinneyer cried out and he wheeled around to see a white man leering at her from the roadside. She clutched her fur defensively and turned her face away. Umarrah raced back and lunged at the man, shouting a whitefella curse. Startled to hear words he recognised, the man's mouth fell open, and he quickly backed away. Umarrah restrained an urge to pound him to the ground, put his arm around Woolaytopinneyer and steered her forward.

Despite all the energy they had expended during their weeks of meandering, he wanted to charge down the last hill to confront Arthur. But he matched his pace to the others until finally they arrived at Government House. Crowds encircled them in the adjacent open field near the harbour's edge. Robinson, with great ceremony, presented them to the Governor. Arthur replied by making a speech. I'll go along with all of this, Umarrah snarled quietly, as long as the promised meeting comes next. Finally, Arthur's voice fell silent. Now's our chance, he thought. Then the clashing sounds of a military band rang out. He slammed his hands over his ears at the dreadful cacophony of noise. When the last sounds finally died away, he turned to see Robinson approach Mannalargenna. The Chief listened with increasing anger, and despite Umarrah's relief at witnessing his fury, moments later they were steamrolled into the farce of a spear-throwing competition.

Then the festivities were over. The crowd began to disperse and Umarrah, along with Mannalargenna, marched up to Robinson, their faces a picture of twisted rage. "When is Arthur going to 'address our grievances' as you told us?" demanded Mannalargenna. "The Governor cannot see your party today," Robinson fudged. "He has other business to attend to. We are going to take you to your lodgings now." The dogs were rounded up and taken away, although several of their group tried unsuccessfully to intervene. Then they were told, politely but firmly, to 'accompany' the soldiers to the harbour. Umarrah swivelled around to see they were virtually encircled. He watched a moment of fleeting guilt cross Robinson's face, before he turned and walked away.

After no audience with Arthur, and no confirmation of when it would happen, they were marched away from Government

House. When they reached the wharf, Umarrah's puzzlement as to where their lodgings would be turned to horror as they were bundled on to a ship.

Once embarked, they gazed in disbelief at their surroundings and then began to slowly spread out and sit down.

They languished there day after day. Umarrah's fury dissipated as he struggled in a nightmare worse than Richmond Gaol. At least there, he remembered, the floor didn't move under your feet. In the afternoons, he clung to the railing as the ship rocked in the summer sea breeze that blew up the river.

No meeting with Arthur had materialised.

"Robinson lied to us," he spat. "He said we would have an 'audience' with the governor, and he would address our grievances. If the 'audience' we had with Arthur was just him talking, and not listening to us, then he hasn't addressed anything!"

"Arthur has betrayed us," agreed Mannalargenna.

"Maybe the meeting will come later," suggested Truganini, one of their group's longest guides.

"Possibly," he acknowledged, knowing how long she had worked with Robinson, "but I have my doubts."

After ten days they were notified of the governor's orders. Their group, those who had been working with Robinson, were being sent to Launceston, to await his arrival. He was planning another expedition, this time to the north-west of the island. The recently captured Larmairremener, however, were instead being taken to Flinders Island.

"Truganini was right," said Woolaytopinneyer. "I think Arthur will meet with us before we leave."

"I don't think he will," argued Umarrah.

"Robinson promised us!" snarled Mannalargenna.

"Do you think Arthur is going to do that now?" Umarrah snapped. "He might if we refused to do another journey with Robinson. That's the only leverage we have. Did any of us actually refuse? No."

"Because if we're honest, we're just relieved not to be going to Flinders Island with the others," said Truganini.

The silence that followed was filled with collective guilt.

"So we'll just keep helping Robinson gather up all the blackfellas he can find, and then what?" Umarrah argued.

"Arthur promised us himself that we would get a homeland on Wawlatter" argued Mannalargenna. "They still need us."

Umarrah wished he could believe him.

Robinson came onboard before their departure. Mannalargenna argued that they should go back to Launceston by land. Umarrah watched the Chief employ every tactic he could, determined that their request would be heeded. But Robinson refused to listen.

After the meeting was over, he watched Robinson walk away. Mannalargenna's eyes met his. Umarrah saw the Chief's mind calculating what to do next despite limited options. We have to work together to have any chance of success, he told himself. But the despairing part of his brain cried out "How did I get here, sitting on a small ship, surrounded by enemies white and black, and waiting to go on a sea voyage?"

The dreaded day of departure arrived. Amongst tears and hugs, the two groups were split up and put on different vessels. Both ships proceeded down the harbour towards the open sea. Umarrah turned his back on the water and propped himself between packs of stores, trying to ignore what was happening around him. Not long after they set off, the cries of the Larmairremener, grief-stricken with the knowledge they were being taken from their island home, travelled across the water. Woolaytopinneyer, on hearing the distress of her countrymen, covered her ears with her hands and began to sob. He drew her to him and they huddled together. He forced himself to focus, as Mannalargenna had been doing, on their options.

Calm clear conditions made for slow progress southward to the harbour mouth. Once they had rounded the south east coast and were heading north, the ship made fast progress, with a southerly wind pushing them at speed up the east coast.

The swell persisted until evening but by the time the captain moored for the night in a sheltered bay, the water was like dark blue glass all around them. Umarrah managed to stand on the deck holding the rail, grateful for the darkness around him rather than the unending sea.

Over the next few days the same conditions prevailed, afternoon southerly winds propelling them northward, and calm returning as the sun descended.

Mannalargenna joined Umarrah one evening at sunset as they were moored off Larapuna on the island's north east tip. They gazed across at the Chief's homeland.

"You do not like it when the winds come, do you?" he taunted.

"I don't like any of it," Umarrah grunted.

Mannalargenna smiled for a moment, then his face turned serious.

"You don't believe we will get a place on Wawlatter."

"I don't believe we will get a place anywhere. Do you, really? Robinson and Arthur have both lied to us, betrayed us."

"And yet we are still important to them."

"They need us, yes."

"If we refuse to walk with Robinson, what will happen?"

"I don't know. Probably take us to where they have taken the Larmairremener."

"Exactly. We must take our chances with Robinson, stay on Country as long as we can. Use the time to bend him to our thinking, work to make him keep his promises."

"Haven't we tried that already?" asked Umarrah sceptically.

"We try harder. The more we help them, the more they must feel obliged to reward us."

Umarrah sighed inwardly.

Mannalargenna turned his gaze north towards Flinders Island.

"I do not want to spend the rest of my life like the Larmairremener, looking across the water at my homeland."

Umarrah thought he was going to say more, but couldn't.

"I know," he mumbled in reply.

A few days later, the ship finally docked at the mouth of Kunermurlukeker on the north coast. As his feet touched the earth again, Umarrah sighed with relief at being back on familiar Country. Not in any hurry, and revelling in the bush fragrant after summer rain, they journeyed on foot towards Launceston, stretching out and reviving their cramped legs. On arriving in town at their destination, the home of Robinson's friends, the Whitcombs, they were genuinely welcomed, which surprised him. Here they waited for Robinson to arrive, and when he did, Umarrah's relief at the end of the recent sea voyage was short lived. Robinson said he was taking them to Flinders Island.

"It will be a short visit," he reassured. "We will come back to Launceston to prepare for our journey to the north west."

"If it is only a short visit, we should stay here," argued Umarrah.

"I know you dislike travel over water, Umarrah, but this is a much shorter journey than the one you have just been on."

Umarrah's stomach was turning over at the very thought of another voyage.

"I am sure Planobeena will be delighted to see her brother again," added Robinson.

So that's where she had been. His resistance melted in relief and joy at hearing her name, knowing he would see her face. He tried to hold on to it, but rage at the power Robinson exerted over them, persisted underneath.

Umarrah had to confess that Robinson was true to his word about the sea journey. The crossing from the mainland to the small island to its north-east, was mercifully short. He still sat with his back to the sea whilst aboard and focused on seeing Planobeena's face.

They disembarked, and there she was. Woolaytopinneyer looked on, smiling, as brother and sister flung their arms around each other. Planobeena began to cry, and when Umarrah finally pulled back to look at her, he saw tears not of joy, but of harrowing grief.

CHAPTER THIRTY-SEVEN

January 1832 – Norfolk Plains

"Wait, George," chuckled Mary Ann. "I have to do them both." She flung open the front door, ran to the back and did the same, and then returned. "Got to let in the new year and see the old one out."

"Naturally," he laughed.

"How close are we?" she asked, as she picked up a candle and followed him outside the front door.

He waited for the candlelight to illuminate his watch. "Two minutes to go," he said.

She threaded her hand through his arm and they waited.

"Happy New Year," they chorused as the watch's hands joined, before kissing in the New Year.

"Here's to a good 1832!" she proclaimed.

George smiled. "This time last year, who'd have thought we'd be where we are now?"

"I thought it might never happen," she whispered. "And then it did – five hundred acres."

"It's going to take a while," he cautioned.

"I know," she replied, "but we're here, and with so much more room to move."

They stood in the warm and inviting summer night air. George looked up and watched the Milky Way meandering its diamond-strewn path through the velvety blackness. He felt her quiet contentment beside him and tried to be the same. But the stargazing reminded him of the night many years ago when he and Umarrah had looked up into the same sky. He had pointed out some of the stars and constellations he knew. Umarrah had responded with his names for them. George had laughed at that, different names for the same thing.

"If men can have more than one name, the stars could too," Umarrah countered.

"Why would people have more than one name?" George asked, staring at him.

"We can have many names. Why would you only have one?"

"How many names have you got?" George asked.

"Three."

"What are they?"

"Kanneherlargenna and Moulteherlargenna, and Umarrah."

George turned his gaze back to the stars. There was much in his new home that he had to learn.

"Did you not hear me, George?" Mary Ann asked.

"What? No, sorry," he admitted.

"What's your New Year's resolution?"

He leaned over and kissed her cheek. "I can't say, you know that, or it won't come true. But I can say what I hope for, and that's peace. Peace, and prosperity."

"Sounds good to me," she replied.

George squeezed her hand. There was a lot of work ahead but much to be grateful for. He couldn't deny his relief that attacks from Aborigines were now virtually impossible, at least in the Settled Districts. And yet the implied threat made during his last conversation with Umarrah hung over him. He'd been open with Mary Ann about the encounter with Robinson and the Aborigines at the old farm, but had presented a version intended to interest and reassure her, describing Robinson's appearance, his conversation with him, as well as describing the woman Umarrah introduced him to.

But he'd not shared the discussion of government promises made and likely broken, of threatening words uttered with steely anger.

It was only a few months back when one of David's servants out at the Western Marshes, a man by the name of Cubit, had been speared by Aborigines. After the violence perpetrated by both sides that had touched their family on more than one occasion, he hoped as much as Mary Ann that this was a new beginning for their family.

But he couldn't fully relax until he knew where Umarrah was. He wanted certainty, not the unknown. There'd been years of unknown.

And so he scrutinised the newspapers.

In mid-January he was rewarded with news. He called out to her and she came running in from the next room, carrying George.

"Robinson and the Aborigines have been in Hobart!" he exclaimed. He threw the papers on the table, and poured them both a drink. She sat down and took a sip.

"Read it out then," she said, as he picked up the *Hobart Town Courier.*

> *"On Saturday, Mr. Robinson, as we had previously announced, made his triumphant entry into town with his party of blacks, amounting in all to 40, including 14 of his former domesticated companions, with the 26 of which the Oyster Bay and Big River mobs were composed. They walked very leisurely along the road, followed by a large pack of dogs, and were received by the inhabitants on their entry into town with the most lively curiosity and delight. Soon after their arrival they walked up to the Government house, and were introduced to His Excellency, and the interview that took place was truly interesting. They are delighted at the idea of proceeding to Flinders Island, where they will enjoy peace and plenty uninterrupted."*

"Let's see what this one says," he added, picking up the *Colonial Times* and scanning the page.

> *"On Saturday last, the twenty-six Aborigines captured by Mr. Robinson, marched into town. A more grotesque appearance we have seldom witnessed, than the arrival of these natives. At an early hour the inhabitants were expecting them; but it was 10 o'clock, when we observed a crowd of persons descending the hill, and soon after we discovered our worthy Chairman of the Quarter*

*Sessions in his gig, followed by " the strange band." The
number of blacks, including the tame mob, amounted
to forty, all of whom, with the exception of trousers that
had been presented to them a short distance from town,
were arrayed in battle order, each male carrying three
spears of twelve to fifteen feet long in the left hand, and
only one in the right. As they continued advancing they
shrieked their war song, and if report says true, the
view with which they were induced to accompany Mr.
Robinson, was, that they should seek redress from the
Governor, whom, next to Mr. Robinson, they had been
made to consider the greatest man in the Island.*

*"These men, it is said, were bent upon spearing
His Excellency, provided he did not grant them the
redress they were seeking. The whole mob immediately
proceeded to Government House, when His Excellency
came out to meet them, and after consulting some time
with those of the tame mob that could speak English,
he gave to each of these savage looking warriors a loaf
of bread, after which they retired to the green sward,
at another part of the premises, when the band was
sent for; on the first sound of the musical instruments
the astonishment with which they listened was truly
wonderful; there was a degree of fear portrayed on
their countenances, but as the music continued they
became more calm, and at the conclusion of the air,
applauded the musicians with a most hideous yell, after
the first few minutes it became very evident that the
music was not lost upon them; we noticed one savage
chief's countenance, which appeared the very picture of
delight, while at the same time a sterner looking object
began to beat time with his head. The slow music was
evidently preferred by them. After the band had ceased
playing a shutter was placed against a tree, and the
warriors were requested to aim with their spears at a
mark chalked upon it; the immense force with which*

*these instruments of destruction were darted through
the shutter was truly astonishing, but the men did not
perform well, the crowd pressing too closely upon them,
and the wind being very strong at the time. After having
thus amused the company, unfortunately a spear broke
in the hand of one of the blacks as he was throwing
it, the consequence was that part of the instrument
took an oblique direction, and a foolish lad who was
standing within a few feet of the target received the
spear (after its having touched the ground), in his leg;
the wound was not very serious, but the natives finding
that they had hurt the lad, could not be persuaded
to throw any more. Soon after this the natives were
persuaded to go on board a vessel in the harbour: they
consented, understanding that they were to be sent to
a place where there is plenty of kangaroo and no work.
It is now some years since the inhabitants of Hobart
Town have witnessed a tribe of Aborigines in their
native state. The hair of the women was shaved closely,
and their covering a blanket; the hair of the men, on
the contrary, was clotted with a sort of red ochre and
grease, resembling very much little strings of bugles; the
upper part of their bodies was also well greased, and
reddened with, a portion of the same earth.*

*"On the whole the arrival of these natives in Hobart
Town cannot but be highly satisfactory to the Colonists,
and although some imagine that Mr. Robinson has been
too well paid, still on such meritorious undertakings we
are not of that party who would calculate about pounds,
shillings, and pence."*

Mary Ann had been jiggling baby George on her lap while he
read, and now put him down on the floor. "So, all the Aborigines
that have threatened the Settled Districts have been rounded
up. No wonder the papers sound pleased."

"They certainly do," he agreed absently, as something
amongst what he'd read prickled at the back of his mind.

He went back to the first article and found the line he was looking for. Fourteen 'domesticated' Aborigines. The same number that passed by the old farm.

That meant one thing.

Umarrah must still be with them. He had not absconded between here and Hobart.

Relief washed over him. He began to reread both articles for further confirmation, then a prickle of anxiety began to travel up his back.

"This is good news, George. People can finally relax," said Mary Ann.

He didn't reply.

"Including us," she added pointedly. "So why do you look worried?"

What was this in the papers about Flinders Island? Umarrah had never mentioned that. It sounded like the Aborigines were now effectively prisoners. The expedition with Robinson was over. The government didn't need their help and they would have no remaining bargaining power.

I told him not to believe Arthur, thought George, uselessly.

"George, say something, you're scaring me," demanded Mary Ann.

He grimaced. "Sorry, it's nothing. I just don't understand what the *Courier* is saying. They've captured the remaining Aborigines that were causing most of the trouble. But why are they sending them to Flinders Island?"

"George, stop it. This is nothing to do with you anymore. Let's just be pleased there'll be no more attacks, and think of our future."

He brightened his face. "I am pleased, Mary Ann, absolutely."

"I'm relieved to hear it." Little George grizzled. Mary Ann picked him up and strode out of the room.

George walked outside with his drink and sat on the verandah. She's right. This is about our future. That's where I must focus my thoughts. And Umarrah can't hurt us now.

But I know him. He would hate to be trapped on board some ship in Hobart harbour. The only thing worse would be actually travelling on the open sea, which could even be happening right at this moment. The complete opposite to the life he loved, trapped on a boat rather than the freedom of being out in the bush. Even when he was travelling with Robinson, it was still better than that.

He would also know that they'd been betrayed. That their homeland was a false hope, promised but not fulfilled.

What would happen once they got to Flinders Island? Were they going to be dumped there and left?

George slugged the last of his drink. The relief he'd felt only moments ago lingered with a bitter aftertaste.

February 1832 – Wybalenna

Very quickly he understood his sister's tears. The small island was a place full of sickness and death. Some of the blackfellas living there were calling it Wybalenna – 'blackfella houses.' But blackfellas didn't live in houses. And that was their point.

They had buried a proud warrior only the week before. The man had sickened quickly and was dead in a few days. He was one of many. The whitefellas used words like influenza or dysentery as the death toll mounted.

The warrior was a fine, stout man, pronounced Robinson, as his body was buried alongside other graves. Umarrah growled softly, watching Robinson wring his hands and complain how the doctor hadn't even bothered to try and help. Not softly enough, he realised, as Robinson glanced angrily in his direction. Mannalargenna stood next to his wife Tanleboneyer, his eyes fixed on his Country glistening in the distance across the water, achingly close. Umarrah watched Tanleboneyer's fingers slide to her neck, touching the baby's bones, her defence against the illness and death that had also taken their child. Despite their age-old enmity, Umarrah felt a stab of grief for what they had lost, and for what he had never had. For the Chief had other, older children, but so far he, Umarrah, had none.

They filed away from the graveyard in silence.

"That's the only good thing I've seen since we've been here," said Woolaytopinneyer, nodding at Planobeena and Pevay walking in front of them.

"She seems happy with him," Umarrah agreed, watching the young man beside her. "But no one is safe here. I dread saying goodbye to her when we leave."

"If we don't go soon, I'm frightened we will get sick too," she replied. "But I feel bad saying that."

In no rush to reach the settlement houses, they dawdled in silence. Then they saw Robinson approach Planobeena and Pevay. After a short discussion, he moved away. Planobeena turned and waited for Umarrah and Woolaytopinneyer to catch up. She was smiling.

"Robinson wants us to join the next journey!" she blurted.

Umarrah whooped with joy, grabbed Planobeena and hugged her tightly.

Pevay looked around them. Laughter was not often heard in this place, and they were getting puzzled looks.

"Our good luck will not be shared by everyone," he cautioned.

Umarrah and Planobeena withdrew their embrace and the four of them walked on.

"Did Robinson say when we are leaving?" asked Umarrah.

"Just 'very soon'," she replied.

Umarrah grimaced, remembering how long it took for Robinson to get ready before their last expedition began.

A few days later a ship was spotted heading towards the island. The news spread quickly and several of them watched its slow progress in unfavourable winds.

"It's large. It could be the one that is taking us," suggested Woolaytopinneyer.

After it docked, nine soldiers and a white woman disembarked. They walked towards the settlement, followed by more whitefellas steering a herd of sheep and four deer. Umarrah's eyes widened in disbelief and he turned to Mannalargenna. "Soldiers!" he snarled. "Is this a prison now?"

"We must have answers from Robinson," Mannalargenna growled.

Mannalargenna, Kickerterpoller and Umarrah headed straight for Robinson's cottage. As they burst in the door, Robinson looked up in surprise, his face quickly revealing both irritation and, thought Umarrah, a hint of fear. "You told us," Mannalargenna shouted, "that we stay on Country; have flour, tea and sugar, clothes; that a good whitefella take care of us, not let bad whitefellas shoot us. But then you make us come to this island, and now you bring soldiers!"

Robinson raised his hands in a gesture of appeasement. "Do not be alarmed, any of you," he replied, his face and voice now smooth. "They are merely here to improve the running of the island. Convicts and sealers are not proper people to do that, as is clearly evident by the state of things."

Mannalargenna's thunderous expression showed he was not placated.

"You made promises to us," Umarrah reminded him.

"And you will be looked after! The flock of sheep that has just arrived here is proof of that."

"We don't want sheep!" retorted Mannalargenna. "We want to be gone from this bad place."

"The deaths have been … unfortunate," agreed Robinson. "And the death of your child particularly so. I know how your wife grieves, and you both have my sincere sympathy. But I want to assure you that we will be leaving again soon on our next mission. As soon as everything is made ready, we will be returning to Launceston. The Governor needs your help again."

"We not forget what you promised us," the Chief declared. He turned his back to Robinson and walked out. Umarrah locked eyes with Robinson, and the gaze that met his was stubbornly blank.

Umarrah followed the others out into the sunshine. "Wait!" he shouted. Kickerterpoller and Mannalargenna turned and faced him. "He knows we're never getting a homeland, because," he hesitated, "he thinks there might not be anyone left to live in it."

The final solution had emerged from his mouth and hung in the air.

"Do you think you're the only one to think of this, Umarrah?" railed Mannalargenna. "I've thought of little else since they bring us here." Seconds ticked by in an appalled silence. "Once we are back on Trouwerner, we have a chance."

"So this is our plan, is it? Get off this island? A plan where we are totally dependent on Robinson."

"Have you got a better one?" demanded Kickerterpoller.

Mannalargenna looked at Umarrah witheringly, then walked away.

Their remaining days on the island dragged out in summer sunshine which did not brighten anyone's mood. They watched for every sign of imminent departure, and there were hints, but also frustrations. Umarrah fumed when Robinson organised a church service one day and insisted on their attendance. It was a comical sight, nearly a hundred blackfellas and all of the whitefellas too, sitting under a piece of cloth that flapped in the breeze, while Robinson droned on and on. The only consolation was that it passed a few hours of time.

Woolaytopinneyer watched helplessly as a combination of rage and anxiety threatened to consume him. He wanted to get off the island, yet he feared the journey. He wanted to kill Robinson but knew that if his anger overtook him, their ticket out of here would vanish in an instant. And it wasn't just Woolaytopinneyer and himself to think of, but Planobeena and Pevay as well.

Finally, their third sea journey in as many months was imminent. The sixteen of them walked up the *Tamar*'s gangplank and arranged themselves about the deck. He glanced across at Planobeena and she smiled back at him. But hours passed, and the wind strengthened while they waited for Robinson to join them. By nightfall they were being buffeted by a gale and Umarrah could hardly bear the prospect of them setting sail.

The next morning Robinson graced them with his presence and they set sail. Woolaytopinneyer huddled beside Umarrah. She gazed at the faint lines that ran back from his eyes and disappeared under his ringlets, and squeezed his hand.

What should have been completed in a day, took three. Umarrah's relief at seeing the approaching mainland of Trouwerner was overtaken by a fever. As their windblown ship finally entered Kunermurlukeker and glided in calmer waters, he began to cough, intermittently at first and then in paroxysms. He tried to stay calm but what alarmed him more was that Woolaytopinneyer was sickening in exactly the same way. But they weren't the only ones. Two others, Kickerterpoller and Robert, looked and sounded equally as bad.

When they reached the wharf at Launceston, the others disembarked hastily ahead of them. They'd seen the signs back on Flinders Island. Umarrah saw the look of pity on Mannalargenna's face and his stomach lurched with dread.

They struggled along the streets from the wharf to the Whitcombs' house, where they were welcomed cautiously, and separated from the others. Umarrah slumped with relief onto the straw in the stables.

The next few days he spent in a haze of delirium. He remembered food and water being brought to the stable door, untouched plates being taken away, Woolaytopinneyer coughing incessantly in the dark, the two of them clinging to each other for comfort.

Later, she clung to him as Robert was taken off to hospital. His fever had gone, but in its place was noisy, laboured breathing and sunken eyes.

Woolaytopinneyer began to recover. Umarrah smiled weakly as she ate hungrily. Mrs Whitcomb smiled too as she collected the empty plate.

"Does your husband still not want some?" she asked the next day, as his food remained untouched. Hearing her concern, he tried to get up, but his legs gave way and he crashed to the floor. Woolaytopinneyer screamed and scrambled over to him. "I'll get help," cried Mrs Whitcomb, and raced for the house.

Woolaytopinneyer ran her hands over his face, her tears glistening on his ringlets. Her lovely eyes filled his gaze then were replaced with Robinson's. "He'll have to go to the hospital too," he said. "I'll get the cart ready," said another voice.

As they lifted Umarrah onto the cart, Woolaytopinneyer insisted, through gasping sobs, on accompanying him. Umarrah glimpsed Whitcomb shaking his head at his wife, who put restraining arms around her. He heard Woolaytopinneyer wailing.

Then all went black.

Later, how much later he couldn't tell, he opened his eyes to see an unexpected face.

"Hello," stammered George, standing at the foot of the bed.

Umarrah blinked, trying to clear his head and take in his surroundings. There were just the two of them in the room.

He tried to haul himself up the bed. George shook his head. "Please don't exert yourself," he urged.

Ignoring him, Umarrah tried to speak, triggering a bout of coughing.

George waited for the coughing to subside then pulled over a stool and sat down beside the bed.

"I shouldn't get too close," he said.

Umarrah thought about that, and smiled faintly, but the irony was lost on George.

"Where am I?"

"In hospital."

"How did you know I am here?" he whispered.

"I saw in the paper that the *Tamar* had docked, and that Robinson had been on board. It was all over town when you stayed at the Whitcombs' in January, so I guessed you would probably be there again. I called at the house and they told me you were here."

Umarrah studied his face. George seemed aghast at his appearance and unable to hide it.

"Where is Woolaytopinneyer?" he croaked.

"Still at the Whitcombs. Mrs Whitcomb said she is much improved."

Umarrah closed his eyes and said nothing for a few moments. A tear escaped from his right eye, ran down the side of his face and pooled in his ear. He raised his hand slowly and tried to rub it.

George shifted uneasily in his chair. Umarrah coughed again and cleared his throat.

"I read about what happened after I saw you last," said George.

"Ahh, we led Robinson all over Country before we found them. Along our roads, over many mountains, up and down. My Country, Woolaytopinneyer's Country. We had plenty of time to hunt, to talk. She was very good – saw where her people were, but made sure we did not get too close for a long time."

George frowned. "How long did you think you could get away with that?"

Umarrah sighed. "Robinson started to suspect us. But he promised again that when we find the Larmairremener, our troubles would be over."

"What happened?"

"He betrayed us. He promised us a meeting with Arthur. But it never happened. Arthur talked and talked, but did not listen to us. We were put on a boat prison, and sent to Flinders Island."

George swallowed.

"There are plenty sick there, and plenty dying. And then Robinson brings soldiers to the island! Robinson says they are there to help. We do not believe him."

"So why have some of you come back to Launceston?"

"Because Robinson wants us to go with him on another journey, gathering more blackfellas from the west and north."

"I don't understand. Robinson said you don't have to do this anymore. And you left his trip to the west coast because you didn't want to encounter the north-west tribes. Why would you agree to do it now?"

"You remember that, George."

"Of course I do."

"Being back here is better than staying on that island. Here, I am closer to Country."

Despite Umarrah's hoarseness, George could hear the longing streaming through his voice. After several seconds, he forced a smile. "Are you feeling better?"

Umarrah looked around him. "This is not a place to make blackfellas better."

He concentrated on his breathing for a few seconds, then his eyes blazed.

"You must tell Robinson I *am* getting better," he demanded.

"Me? Can't you do that yourself? Robinson will visit, surely?"

Umarrah shook his head. "He prepares for the journey – might not come. But they must not leave without me. I will get better on Country. And Mannalargenna thinks after this journey, the governor *will* give us what he promised."

"Land of your own? Do you still think that will happen?"

"Perhaps," Umarrah whispered.

George wondered if he'd run out of breath, or conviction. He looked away.

"Why did you come, George?"

"I don't know really." He hesitated. "I wanted to say sorry."

"Sorry?"

"About, well, everything. I couldn't stop thinking how you said I'm greedy just like all the other whitefellas."

"You're all greedy, George."

George nodded. "I know I've, we've, prospered at your expense."

Umarrah watched him wring his hands.

"I'm ashamed that I didn't try harder to help you."

"You helped us a few times. More than any other whitefella I know."

"But it was not enough. I can't forget that."

"It was never going to be enough, George. You must remember, I fight for my Country."

George wiped his eyes. "I know you did what you thought you had to."

A nurse appeared, frowning, in the doorway. "One more minute, Sir," she ordered. George nodded curtly and blew his nose.

"I have to go," he said softly.

Umarrah grabbed his arm. "You will talk to Robinson?"

George nodded. "Yes, I'll call in at the Whitcombs on my way home."

Umarrah sank back in the bed. "Thank you."

George nodded and stood up. "Get better soon," he replied, and headed for the door.

Umarrah called out. "George?"

He turned around. "Yes?"

"You alright, " he rasped, "for a whitefella." Another bout of coughing overtook him, and he did not hear the gentle click of the closing door.

CHAPTER THIRTY-NINE

March 1832 – Launceston

George stood outside the door, his feet bolted to the floor. He tried to compare the shell of the man he'd just seen with the images gathered over the years – the young man afraid of the water, the confident hunter, the shrewd observer of the invaders, the angry warrior, the bitter foe, the estranged friend. The thread connecting them had become very thin, but the last few strands, tangled and threadbare, he hoped were still there.

Was I forgiven? he asked himself. Did I really think he would forgive me? Would I, if I'd been him? After all this time, I want forgiveness so I can live with myself. Look at him! Only a bit older than me, he might die in that bed. And for what? Nothing, except knowing he's done everything he can, even killed, in a fruitless attempt to hold back the invader tide.

How awful must it feel to have whitefella leaders promise you, to your face, a homeland in your own Country, and then string you along, and act without honour.

George felt clothed in shame. He tried to deflect it for a moment. It's not just my own shame, he thought, it's the shame of being part of the invader's relentless greed. But deflection was impossible. He was an invader like the rest of them. Forced expatriation from Norfolk Island compared to arriving as a free settler made no difference to those for whom invasion came at such a grim cost.

He stumbled unseeing down the corridor, then turned a corner as the doctor came into view. "Mr Collins!" he reprimanded. "You're still here. Visiting time is over."

He apologised and headed towards the exit. Out in the early autumn sunshine he tried to focus on where he'd tied up his horse, finally remembered, then headed across the yard.

He had to work out how to approach Robinson. I don't think he's someone easily dissuaded from his course, he thought. How on earth am I going to convince him to wait for Umarrah to recover if he finds out how sick he is?

"Mr Collins, is that you?" came a voice. George's head swivelled round to see Robinson walking towards him. He froze. "Yes, it is you," Robinson confirmed. "We met last spring, if you remember, outside your property."

"Mr Robinson, yes. How are you?" George stammered.

"I am well, thank you, and about to start my next mission to help our sable friends. Unfortunately a few have sickened since our departure from Flinders Island. I am here to see how Chief Umarrah fares." His eyes narrowed. "Is that why you are here?"

Despite his preoccupation, George couldn't help but note Robinson's proprietorial tone, as if denoting authority, if not ownership of his 'sable friends'. Bristling at it, he played for time.

"I regret I've been told that Umarrah must not have any more visitors today, and none tomorrow. I was obliged to leave but moments ago. Umarrah is very tired, but he is recovering, thanks to God. The doctors have said the pace of recovery will be delayed if he has any more visitors."

George paused. "Umarrah did say that he is very anxious to rejoin your mission."

He watched a succession of reactions cross the Conciliator's face. Annoyance at having his visit thwarted, then satisfaction in hearing of Umarrah's enthusiasm. He nodded. "That is good news. I am keen for him to recover as soon as possible. Governor Arthur is depending on us for the success of this mission."

George felt a burning desire to somehow be a buffer between this self-serving man and the man he thought he 'owned'. I need to give him a reason to delay his trip, and fast.

He ignored the distaste he felt as an idea began to form in his mind. Something that would appeal to Robinson's vanity – a desire for good social connections usually does, thought George.

"I noted in the newspaper that you collected Mr Cottrell in George Town on your way here," said George, carefully sowing the seeds.

Robinson nodded.

"Mr Cottrell is an acquaintance of mine, and soon to be a closer neighbour. I have known him for a number of years. We are of similar age. He's a good man, obviously fortunate to be contributing to your efforts."

Robinson inclined his head, acknowledging the public recognition of his work.

"Mr Cottrell, yes, he has provided consistent support of me in my work. He is indeed a loyal servant of the authorities."

George played his other card.

"I wondered whether, in your recent travels to Hobart Town, Mr Robinson, you have met Mr Glover, the painter, lately come from England?"

"No," was the somewhat puzzled reply. "I have not met him, but have heard he is very talented."

"That he is, sir. My niece is married to his son Henry. My wife Mary Ann and I are looking forward to meeting Mr Glover shortly. He has received a large grant of land on the Nile River, and he and his family are making their way there from Hobart at the moment."

George watched his value rising in the older man's eyes.

"I would be very happy to introduce you, sir. I'm sure he would be delighted to hear more about your work."

Robinson smiled. "I should be glad to make his acquaintance, Mr Collins. Perhaps when we have completed our final missions, there will be time."

"We are hoping to have a small gathering at my sister's home in the coming week, sir. She is Mrs David Gibson. She and her husband entertained Governor Macquarie back in the early days, when Macquarie visited the island on his second trip in 1821. You would be very welcome to join us and make Mr Glover's acquaintance. You may have heard of my sister's property – Pleasant Banks. It is not far from my own farm."

He's considering it, thought George, and pushed on. "Perhaps we could contribute some fresh meat and vegetables for your mission? I'm sure my brother-in law David would also like the opportunity to support your work, and it would make any delay, while Umarrah recovers, worth the wait."

There was only the slightest hesitation. "This is generous of you, Mr Collins," responded Robinson. "I accept your offer on both counts."

"Then I shall send an invitation to the Whitcombs," confirmed George.

"Thank you," Robinson replied. He paused. "Mr Collins, you are very attentive to my group of natives. Perhaps you could enlighten me as to why."

George's palms began to sweat. "As I believe I said when we first met, I became friendly with Umarrah and his friends as a young boy, when our paths crossed each summer and autumn."

Robinson pressed him. "But there must have been some particular reason for your friendship. Your behaviour is not typical of settlers, particularly those from convict families, who in my experience have often been most cruel to the natives."

There was no way around this. He took a deep breath. "I am a strong swimmer, sir. My stepfather Joseph was part of the Norfolk Island boat crew. He taught me to swim. One day, not long after our arrival, I rescued Umarrah when the South Esk was in flood. He'd gotten into difficulty."

Robinson's eyes shot up at this revelation.

"And he felt obliged to you?"

"Yes, he did," came the perfunctory reply.

Robinson was now quite intrigued.

"May I ask how he showed his gratitude?"

George hesitated, reluctant to go on.

"It's quite simple, really. He became a friend to a lonely boy in a new colony. He would include me when hunting, as I think I had mentioned before."

George felt vulnerable in the ensuing silence. Robinson,

having pressed for more, considered his answer, and then appeared cautiously satisfied.

"How long have you been in the colony?" asked George, keen to change the subject.

"Eight years," replied Robinson automatically.

"You may think my experience as not typical of settlers, but my family has been here longer than most – it will be twenty years next year. In the early years … things were better. We used to mix more, Aborigines and whites. Not everyone did, mind. Umarrah even worked for me, before he worked for others such as Hugh Murray. And then the pace of settlement increased, and things … changed."

George felt Robinson's stare, and then realised why. Robinson didn't like being at a historical disadvantage.

It was time to go. "Apologies Mr Robinson, I am detaining you," brightened George. "I look forward to you joining us soon and meeting Mr Glover and his family. I shall send the invitation as soon as the date is confirmed."

"Thank you, Collins. Good day to you." Robinson extended his hand. George shook it, then watched him stride away. As he mounted his own horse, George was stunned at how quickly he'd came up with his idea. It had been a close shave. With luck, I've bought Umarrah the time he needs, he thought.

He suddenly remembered that he didn't now have to go to the Whitcombs. Relief mingled with guilt, knowing he wouldn't come across Woolaytopinneyer and have to consider what he would say in reply to her questions.

He glanced back at the hospital entrance, then mounted his horse and trotted away.

CHAPTER FORTY

March 1832 – Norfolk Plains

"She's only twenty years old," said Elizabeth. "I'm worried about the journey and whether she'll have had enough time to rest."

"Who are you talking about?" asked George, who had come in, thirsty from a busy harvest.

"Beth," replied Elizabeth. "The trip up from Hobart would be hard for a pregnant woman."

"She'll be fine, Mother," said Mary Ann. "Margaret stressed last time she wrote that Henry's family were not going to rush the trip. They are well aware of how bad the roads are compared to England. And the fact that they were stopping for two days in Bagdad with Meg and Thomas is proof that they're taking their time."

"I'm sure they're keen to see their new land, though," added George. He cut off a hunk of cheese and then carefully wrapped it again in its protective muslin. The whole household was excited by the visit to Pleasant Banks tomorrow of Beth and her in-laws, the Glovers. George's decision to also invite Robinson was met with puzzled looks by the family, but Eliza and David accepted the unexpected addition with good grace. He was a government representative, of sorts, after all. George intended to keep his promise and introduce Robinson to John Glover, and hoped in return that Robinson would have news of Umarrah.

The next morning's mild, dry autumnal day promised pleasant travel. John Glover and his wife Sarah, along with Henry Glover and Beth, bumped and rattled in their cart behind David and Eliza's as they journeyed along the Nile Road towards Pleasant Banks. They stopped to pick up George en route. It was becoming clear to the Glovers how near to Beth's extended family their new land was. George thought Beth seemed especially pleased by this, having said goodbye to her parents, Meg and Thomas, in the south of the island.

Mary Ann, George's mother and all the Gibson and Collins children were waiting when they arrived at Pleasant Banks. The introductions took quite some time and then the children were sent off to the garden to play. George scanned the road for Robinson before they all went inside, but there was no sign. They moved into the dining room and George took a seat with a view of the window, earning a frown from Eliza for ruining her seating plan. Eliza took special care to attend to Mrs Glover and Mary Ann looked after Beth. He and Henry, and David and John Glover, being of similar ages, paired off spontaneously. Elizabeth appeared to be anticipating much enjoyment from her place at the head of the table, revelling in her role as matriarch of an expanding family.

"I'm sorry that you have not yet met my brother James and his wife," said Henry to George. "They are quite exhausted from travelling ahead of us, and making all the preparations for our arrival."

George smiled. "I look forward to meeting them another time. They must have worked very hard to prepare things for you."

"Father is fond of saying how fortunate he is to have so many sons. It does mean we can divide up the work."

"You have sisters still in England. Is that right?" asked George.

"Yes. My sister Mary we left behind. Fortunately she is happily married. My other sister Emma died last year. We only found out last month."

"I am sorry to hear that, Henry."

Henry nodded his appreciation. George glanced at Sarah Glover, who was now quietly talking with his mother. Mrs Glover seemed quite an elderly lady to undertake such an arduous journey across the oceans, and now this overland journey from Hobart Town to the north of the state. He couldn't help comparing her to his mother, looking very much fifteen years her junior. He was struck by the different ages and circumstances under which they both arrived in the colony.

They waited as long as possible before starting lunch, hoping that Robinson would arrive. George apologised for his absent guest, and started to worry what the delay meant.

He listened distractedly as they ate, while John described the final part of their epic sea voyage the previous year. Before heading down the east coast to Hobart, their ship had called in to Launceston. On departing again for the south, it had taken them sixteen days to reach the sea.

"We couldn't believe that we had come all this way, and then were so delayed in reaching our final destination. Such frustration! We had to stop to find water before we'd even reached the mouth of the Tamar. Some of the crew went ashore, but they found more than they bargained for, when they came across a group of natives."

The last word stalled the different conversations in the room. George waited to hear what the colony's newest artist would say next.

"What happened?" enquired David.

"Someone fired on them, and one of the Aboriginal men apparently dropped to the ground, injured or dead they could not say when they returned to the boat. From on board we had heard a gunshot and were understandably worried. No one from the boat was injured, and they did not say they had been attacked, so we were at a loss to know why the shot was fired."

"Well you have been here a year now, and must have read and heard much of the problems we have had with the natives," said David evenly.

"But your family has been here for many years," said Henry. "Arriving in 1813, I understand? There would be much you have seen and heard. Being the youngest, did you have any dealings with the Aborigines in those early years?" he asked, turning to George.

George was taken aback. He found himself staring at his mother while he struggled for a reply.

"George virtually grew up with some young Aboriginal men," Elizabeth said. "One time, he rescued a young man from drowning."

All the Glover heads swivelled instantly in George's direction.

"I should like to hear some of your tales one day, George," said John. "I'm sure they'd be fascinating."

George smiled but did not elaborate.

Dessert was served, and the noise of separate conversations once again filled the room. Then tea was brought in to conclude the meal. As George refilled his teacup, one of David's servants entered the room. He walked over to George.

"I'm sorry to interrupt sir, but there's a message for you."

George grabbed the note impatiently and muttered his thanks.

The other guests tactfully continued their conversations, but with watchful eyes on George.

He opened the envelope.

24 March 1832

Dear Mr Collins,

I send my apologies for not being able to attend your luncheon today. The Chief Umarrah passed away this morning. This is sad news to convey to you, as I know you were of long-standing acquaintance. Robert died two days ago, and his funeral will be conducted this afternoon at St John's, hence my not being able to take up your kind hospitality. We will have to adjust our plans for departure as Umarrah's funeral will need to be held, and this is planned for two days time. (I will send a separate note via the Whitcombs with the specifics.)

I hope that I may have the opportunity to make everyone's acquaintance on another occasion.

 With kind regards,
 George Augustus Robinson

George's chair scraped the floor as he stood up. The room was a sea of expectant faces. He dropped the note on the table, said "Excuse me," and walked out of the room.

His mother leaned over and took the note, scanning it quickly. "Umarrah has died," she revealed. Her words reverberated down the hall and struck him in the back.

He stumbled down to the sunlit blue river and watched it glide effortlessly between the paddocks. There were sounds of the children laughing, crying and shouting in the garden. A small flock of musk lorikeets darted overhead and landed in a large gum tree, chattering as they plundered for nectar amongst the remains of its bright red flowers.

He turned his gaze towards Umarrah's homeland, his eyes lingering over the plains.

Then he heard footsteps.

"Mr Collins, George, I hope you don't mind me disturbing you."

Angered by the intrusion, he wiped his eyes, surprised nonetheless to hear that the voice was John Glover's.

He smiled perfunctorily as the older man joined him, though standing at a respectful distance.

"I'm sorry for your bad news," he said.

"Thank you," replied George.

"I have heard of this leader, Umarrah," continued Glover. "They say he was a fearsome man."

"Some did say that, yes."

"Was he the person you rescued?"

George stared at Glover, trying to understand the reason for the question, the side of the fence this man was on. He turned his gaze back to the river, and shrugged.

"Yes, on this very river, a few miles downstream."

Glover nodded.

"So you have known him a long time then. And through ... much change."

"I have ... I mean, I did."

"Had you seen him in recent times?"

"Only a few days ago, in hospital."

Glovers eyebrows shot up.

George's legs suddenly felt very heavy. This man is a virtual stranger, he thought. I can't explain all this to him, not right now.

"Shall we go back inside?" George suggested.

"Yes of course, George," replied Glover. "I apologise again for intruding on your grief. I think it is time for us to take our leave. Thank you to you and David, and your wives, for inviting us to lunch. We are so pleased that Beth has family close by."

"You're very welcome," said George, gesturing for John to walk ahead of him back to the house.

Conversation was flowing again in their absence, though their return to the table soon ended it. Henry stood up.

"Mr Gibson, you have been very kind to have us all here today. Will you please excuse us now? I think Beth should not be late home."

David stood up. "Of course, Henry. It has been lovely that you could come and visit us so soon after your arrival in the north."

"You have been very generous," said Glover, turning his gaze from George to his host.

The goodbyes were warm but brief. David and Eliza, George, Mary Ann and Elizabeth waved them off in a line, and watched till they were out of sight. Mary Ann, without further word, went to round up young Annie, Harriet and George.

"What are you going to do?" said Eliza to her brother, as their mother joined them.

"Attend his funeral," said George, curtly. "I can't believe he's dead. A lot happened, I acknowledge it's complicated, but I knew him for a long time."

She nodded, but said nothing.

"Robinson is sending a separate note re the funeral, which is planned for two days time," he added.

"If it's alright, I'll go back to town with you then, George," Elizabeth said.

"That's fine, Mother. I'd appreciate the company, to be honest. I'll let you know," he replied.

Mary Ann quickly installed all the children in the cart, George perfunctorily kissed his sister and mother goodbye, shook David's hand and hauled himself up.

His mother looked at him with concern.

"I'll wait for your message, son."

He nodded, click-clicked the horses, and they pulled away.

The two women exchanged a knowing look, then went inside.

CHAPTER FORTY-ONE

March 1832 – Launceston

With a sinking feeling, George ripped open the note from the Whitcombs. Umarrah's funeral would be held in Launceston tomorrow at 5pm. He wanted to go, but dreaded it at the same time, unsure what to expect, how he should behave, or what he'd feel. But really none of those things matter, he told himself. I'll pay my respects. At least I can do that.

He sent a note to his mother, and then tried to get on with the jobs at hand. But he often found himself staring into space, memories intruding at every turn.

As he swung down from his cart at Pleasant Banks the next afternoon, his sister's unsmiling face greeted him. "Mother's just coming down," she said as she kissed his cheek. She hesitated. "George, are you sure you should be going?"

"To the funeral?" he asked.

"Yes. What if you are seen there?" she persisted.

"So what if I am?" he argued.

David strode out to join them. "George, there's no need to raise your voice," he said.

Eliza turned to her husband. "David, it's all right."

"No it's not alright," snapped George. "Who cares if I'm seen?"

"Think about it," demanded David. "You've only had your new land for less than a year. You know how long it took to get it. Are you really going to risk your chances of getting any more by being seen at the funeral of a mass murderer? Remember Mrs Cunningham!"

George fought to keep his tone even. "After everything that's happened, the things done by both sides, this is your sum total of Umarrah's life? I've known him since I was eleven. He was only a few years older than me. You don't know the half of it. There was good and bad."

David's face turned red. He opened his mouth. Here comes the tirade, thought George, but then Elizabeth emerged through the front door. Behind her came a servant, who placed her bags in the cart before scurrying back inside.

"I sense some disagreement between you all," she observed wryly, noting the tension.

"David and Eliza are trying to dissuade me from going to the funeral," replied George.

"I think it's a bad error of judgment" argued David.

Elizabeth turned to George. "It's your decision, son. You have known Umarrah longer and better than most whites on this island. We know he's done some terrible things. We also know some of the awful things done by whites," she added, turning to David, "including by your own men. So I don't think you're in a position to 'advise' George."

No one moved.

Finally, Eliza broke the silence.

"We're just concerned that George could risk his future prospects by attending. And that's only because we care. You understand that, don't you George?" Before George could reply, David muttered a wish for a safe journey, and stormed inside.

George smiled grimly at David's departing back then climbed onto the cart. "See you soon, Mother," said Eliza, kissing her and handing her up to George.

"I hope you are okay," she said to George. "Thanks," he replied, before taking the reins and clicking the horses into motion.

The golden autumn countryside was gradually replaced by the small brick cottages of Launceston town, topped by the few taller buildings that gazed down on them. "How are you feeling now?" asked Elizabeth as they drew closer. "I'm dreading it," he grimaced. "I'm not surprised," she replied. "You've known him almost twenty years. It's not exactly been an uncomplicated acquaintance."

"That's an understatement," he muttered.

"I won't lie to you, George. I'm relieved that attacks by Aborigines have plummeted. But we've utterly trampled on their rights and their homeland in our rush to take over this island. There's not many settlers who are troubled by this, although some handwringing may come after the fact."

"I won't be holding my breath for an outpouring of guilt."

"You may be right. But you know what I'll remember?"

He glanced at her.

"What it was like in those early days, where living side by side was a brief possibility. No one else will remember that, but we will."

He put both reins in one hand, and put an arm around her shoulder. "Yes, we will," he replied, and nudged her head with his.

As they pulled up to her cottage in Wellington Street, Elizabeth grabbed his hand.

"Don't be afraid, George, just put one step in front of the other. Listen, observe, allow the sadness, and be grateful."

"Grateful for what?" was all he could get out.

"Everything you have," she replied, and smiled.

He lifted her hand to his lips. She smiled at the kiss, climbed down and stepped back, watching as he set off again.

It was only a few miles to the church graveyard and he arrived a few minutes before 5 p.m. Shortly afterwards, Robinson and a group of Aborigines appeared, proceeding slowly behind a cloth covered wooden coffin. Some of the faces of the Aborigines were streaked with ochre.

George recognised a number of them from the group that had stopped at the old farm in the spring. He assumed they would head inside the burial ground itself, and so watched from a respectful distance away. But they turned and moved in procession towards an area just outside consecrated ground. And then he saw the large pit that had been dug in readiness.

He hadn't noticed that a small crowd of onlookers had by now gathered around the scene.

"What do you paint yourself for?" called out one of them. The procession stopped as they turned towards the voice. George saw Mannalargenna's face, twisted in anger. The Chief opened his mouth, but Lacklay got in first.

"What do you wear fine clothes for?" he shot back.

The heckler was stung by the perfect retort. In silence, the procession resumed. Woolaytopinneyer was visibly upset and walked slowly alongside Truganini.

The coffin reached the grave. There followed an awkward pause. Dr Browne, the clergyman, seemed uncomfortable standing outside consecrated ground. Finally he coughed and began to explain that, since Umarrah was not a baptized Christian, he could not be buried with Christian rites. He asked Robinson to say a few words. Robinson nodded and spent the next few minutes extolling what Umarrah had done to further the goal of bringing to safety many of the Aborigines. George watched the Aborigines' faces as he spoke but they were impassive, apart from Woolaytopinneyer, whose sobs occasionally drowned out his words. When Robinson finished, the clergyman asked if anyone else wanted to speak. George looked at Mannalargenna in expectation, but the Chief's face was a mask. He suspected the silence spoke of their disapproval of these whitefella rituals.

Dr Browne nodded and the pallbearers lowered the coffin to the ground, pulling away the ropes and covering it with earth. When this was done, Robinson began to walk away, and observing his cue, the Aborigines followed suit.

As they passed by George, Woolaytopinneyer paused. She looked at him as tears rolled down her cheeks.

"I'm so sorry," he stumbled. "I guess this," he gestured towards the burial mound, "is not what he would have wanted."

Kickerterpoller scowled. "None of this is what he wanted," he snapped.

Woolaytopinneyer's chin rose in defiance. "We bury him our way, we paint him," she said proudly.

George nodded.

"Good luck, er, on your journey with Mr Robinson," he muttered, casting his eyes over the group.

Mannalargenna glanced obliquely at George, nodded slightly then the group moved on.

The crowd had begun to disperse. George looked across at the mound of freshly dug earth, and wondered whether to walk over and say a private goodbye. But you already said your goodbye at the hospital, he told himself. It's time to go.

He walked slowly towards his cart. Out of the corner of his eye, he spied Robinson heading his way.

"A sad day, Mr Collins," announced Robinson.

"It is," he replied. "I'm grateful that I could pay my respects."

"Your grief does you credit, Mr Collins," the older man replied.

George, in turn, could not fathom how much grief Robinson himself felt.

"I hope we will meet again another time," Robinson continued. "There is still much to be done before our mission can depart, but perhaps I could call on you another day."

If I never see you again, I won't care, thought George. He nodded without offering anything, shook Robinson's hand, and walked away.

There was still daylight left. The horse had no desire for speed, and neither did he.

As he ambled out of town, images floated in front of him. The heckler and his comment. He was ashamed to be standing near them. People probably assumed he had the same opinion. Which would probably reassure David, he grimaced. Kickerterpoller's stinging and well-chosen words. Woolaytopinneyer's grief and defiance. Now he understood why he had dreaded it so much. He tried to remember his mother's advice. The only thing he could feel any gratitude for was being able to utter his apology to Umarrah before he died. Even if he wasn't forgiven, it was still a comfort.

He was hot by the time he reached the Perth punt. Instead of waiting to cross, he turned and headed upstream, tied up the horses, glanced around, stripped off, and waded in. The accumulated heat of the recent summer had made no difference to Van Diemen Land's longest river, and despite a more languorous flow, he gasped at its chill. He swam upstream for several minutes, then over to the opposite bank. Climbing out of the cold, he turned round and sat in the sun. To his left, the punt glided downstream between the eastern and western banks. He watched its progress, then turned his gaze upstream as the river came round the bend from the ford, flowing past him and the punt before again curving out of site. Beyond, to the west, the Western Tiers gazed down on all the rivers that made their way to empty into this one.

He could see it then, before they scarred it. No punt. His first farm, downstream beyond the punt, not there. David and Eliza's, not there, all the farms, on the river and beyond it, never built, never fenced, no sheep and cattle, and all the trees never struck down. And the old roads – the markenner Umarrah had called them – spreading out across the island, an intricate lacework still pulsing beneath the soil. The landscape that Umarrah had loved. He could see it, unspoiled, in that moment.

Faintly, at first, then gradually louder and more raucous, a dozen black cockatoos appeared, chattering and meandering laconically overhead as they moved towards the western sky. He looked up at them and wondered how many hundreds of years their sweetly mournful cries had echoed across these plains.

A shout intruded, the punt launched itself into the current, and his vision vanished. The punt progressed steadily towards the opposite bank, while George followed the path of the cockatoos until they disappeared into the late afternoon sun.

Author's Note

angelabakerwriter.com

T he vast majority of characters in *Umarrah & George* are based on real people. While I hope I have portrayed the characters fairly, this is a work of fiction. Umarrah and George were of similar age and living in the same area, and while it is quite possible that their paths crossed, there is no direct evidence that they actually met. The ideas that I began to tentatively put on the page, were anchored in a reference from James Boyce's book *Van Diemen's Land*[1] about Aboriginal and white children playing and boys hunting together in the early years of colonisation.

Many of the events described are also on the historical record. For example, the first return journey overland from Launceston to Hobart Town occurred in early 1807 and may have been witnessed by Aboriginal people. Planobeena's abduction and raising by a white family was an example of a practice which was sadly not uncommon. A painting of *Fanny Hardwicke: a native ... Van Diemen's Land* is attributed to Frederic Hardwicke.

Governor Macquarie did stay with the Gibsons at Pleasant Banks in May 1821. John Batman, Anthony Cottrell and Hugh and David Murray, like many other settlers, either ex-convict or free, were given significant grants of land, particularly along the corridor between Hobart and Launceston. John Batman later played a significant role in the founding of the city of Melbourne.

---

1   James Boyce, *Van Diemen's Land*, Black Inc., Melbourne, 2008.

George's family, like many others, were forcibly expatriated from Norfolk Island in 1813. Having spent his first eleven years there, and with his stepfather Joseph Lowe a member of the boat crew, George may have been able to swim, which gave me an idea.

Later, having outgrown his first land grant of sixty acres, he pleaded unsuccessfully for more. Eventually, after participating in the government operation to round up Aborigines in 1830, he was given further grants. Historical records reveal mere glimpses of his personality. A grainy image of him in his later years betrays little. His headstone in a cemetery in Evandale has the words "The Memory Of The Just Is Blessed: But The Name Of The Wicked Shall Rot."

Umarrah has been characterised as both charismatic and ruthless. The colonial authorities sought to use him for their purposes and he did the same to them, engaging with them, then leaving when it suited him. His two overland journeys, from the west coast with Parwareter and Trepanner in 1830, and then alone from the south east later that same year, both times back to his beloved north, are awe-inspiring treks through difficult terrain and enemy territory.

He has been described as having a particular fear of water. This suggested a way for him and George to meet, given that the Norfolk Islanders were eking out their existence on the banks of the South Esk River/Moorronnoe, the island's longest river, and one prone to flooding.

The name Umarrah is considered a colonial fabrication, a distortion of his one-time employer Hugh Murray's name. His other names were Kanneherlargenna and Moulteherlargenna but I have used Umarrah simply because it is the one by which he is most usually known. It is sometimes spelt as Eumarrah.

My research also uncovered some shocks and surprises, such as the attack on the Peters sisters, the violence committed by Baker, an employee of David Gibson, and George's niece Beth marrying Henry, the son of the artist John Glover.

George Robinson's mission to 'conciliate' Aboriginal people in the north-west of the island continued without Umarrah, and concluded in late 1832. Two more expeditions followed it, the last ending in August 1834. In 1839, Robinson was appointed Chief Protector of the Aborigines at Port Phillip (later Melbourne). Some of the Aborigines who had been part of his 'conciliation' missions in Van Diemen's Land went with him. This included Pevay and Planobeena. Pevay was later one of the first people to be executed in the new colony.

George's close family included three women named Elizabeth – his mother, eldest sister and niece. To avoid confusion, his mother is referred to throughout as Elizabeth, but his sister has become Eliza, and his niece, Margaret's daughter, is Beth.

The names of Umarrah's parents are unknown, so I invented these. I could not find records for convict servants in George and Mary Ann's household, so invented their names also. Some Aboriginal words are either generally recognised or, if not a word Umarrah would likely have used, from the language used by neighbouring clans. The names of minor characters, such as George and Mary Ann's children, and others who appear only briefly or who are not considered significant in the historical context, have not been included in the character list.

I have used terms from the colonial period. Referring to people as "Blacks" or "natives", would be insensitive in the modern era, but are the terms which would have been used at the time. I have used Aboriginal people's names, clan names and place names from historical records, although I acknowledge there can be different spellings for the same name or place, even within the same book.

Apart from the Aboriginal words described above, I have used English throughout. Umarrah's English is fluent when he is thinking or in conversation with other Aboriginal people, in order to enable the reader to follow the story. His English is limited, though developing over time, when he is in conversation with George. It remains more stilted when speaking with colonial authorities, a deliberate act to deceive them into inadvertently revealing more in his presence than they intend.

My gratitude and heartfelt thanks to the friends, acquaintances, colleagues, family members and fellow writers, in Tasmania or beyond its shores, who provided feedback, encouragement, and pots of tea. Special thanks and deep gratitude to Dr Aunty Patsy Cameron for her generosity with her time, and her guidance.

For readers who may wish to read more on the subject, I would recommend as a starting point the late historian Lyndall Ryan's book *Tasmanian Aborigines: A history since 1803.*[2]

2 Lyndall Ryan, *Tasmanian Aborigines: A history since 1803*, Allen & Unwin, Sydney, 2012.